THE GILDED NEST

CROW INVESTIGATIONS BOOK NINE

SARAH PAINTER

Siskin
Press

Published by Siskin Press Limited

Cover Design by Stuart Bache

ALSO BY SARAH PAINTER

The Language of Spells

The Secrets of Ghosts

The Garden of Magic

In The Light of What We See

Beneath The Water

The Lost Girls

The Crow Investigations Series

The Night Raven

The Silver Mark

The Fox's Curse

The Pearl King

The Copper Heart

The Shadow Wing

The Broken Cage

The Magpie Key

The Gilded Nest

The Unholy Island Series

The Ward Witch

The Book Keeper

The Island God

Blood will have blood

— MACBETH, WILLIAM
SHAKESPEARE

CHAPTER ONE

Aberdeen, Ten Years Ago

Lydia checked herself in the full-length mirror of the ladies' toilet. It was a faux-gold affair with scrolls and curlicues and, set against the dark red walls, the whole effect was downmarket cabaret club or upmarket brothel. Her black dress was short and very tight, revealing rather more cleavage and a lot more thigh than she usually allowed out in public. Her make up was immaculate and sultry. Smoky eyes, flicked eyeliner, and shiny red lips. She stretched these into a smile and then checked her teeth. She didn't have a large clump of spinach between them, and she had sniffed under her arms to confirm that she hadn't forgotten deodorant. There was no earthly reason why the mark wasn't approaching her. Unless...

Thirty seconds later, Lydia made her way to the bar and one of the tall, padded stools. She put a little too much into her hip sway and executed a very slight stagger before pulling herself up onto the perch. The mirror behind the bar revealed her handiwork. Eyeliner smudged under both eyes and a smear of red lipstick on her front teeth.

She let her eyes wander around the crowd reflected in the mirrored wall, the faces and bodies truncated by the row of booze bottles.

'Hello, little lady. You're too pretty to be drinking alone.'

And there he was. Brad Carter. An American oil exec and her target. She had clearly been too intimidating before, and she needed to present a less-perfect image. Or, and this was depressingly most likely, he was a predator and he liked his prey a little wounded. Coward.

She turned and smiled, making sure to keep her eyes soft. 'Is that so?'

His gaze was fixed on her cleavage as he replied. 'Let me refresh your drink.'

'I think I've had enough,' Lydia said, giving him a last chance to do the right thing. She turned to the bartender, who had materialised with professional speed. 'Can I get a tap water?'

'No, no, no,' Carter said, leaning against the bar and getting another eyeful down her top. 'That's no good. You're not a tap water girl, you're a champagne princess.'

Inside, Lydia mimed sticking her fingers down her throat. Outside, she blinked at him, feigning confusion.

'A martini for the lady and another of these,' he held up his tumbler and shook it slightly. He glanced at

Lydia, eyes skimming her lips before landing back at her neckline. 'Trust me. You'll love this. It's a classic.'

And a martini was about twice the strength of a glass of champagne. Lydia could practically see the man's plan flashing above his head in neon letters. She curbed the smile that threatened to spoil her drunken-prey act. She didn't love honey-trap work, but sometimes it felt like karmic retribution.

There was a lot of oil money sloshing around Aberdeen, and they were in one of the most expensive hotels in the city. The bartender was well trained and discreet, and he raised an eyebrow very slightly at Lydia as he placed the martini onto a black napkin and added a tall glass of water with ice cubes. Lydia wanted to smile and tell him she was all right, but she couldn't break character. She leaned an elbow onto the bar and cupped her chin, gazing up at her mark as he started telling her about his important job. He added a couple of corporate words to his job title, presumably to sound impressive, but Lydia was keen to move things along. The sooner she got him out of the bar, the sooner Stuart could get the pictures and she could go home.

That was the thing with honey-trap work. You couldn't just tell the client that their husband or wife had been chatting you up in a bar or gym or wherever, you had to get photographic evidence. Even when the client was convinced they already knew the truth, had evidence of their own from their partner's phone or a receipt from their pocket, they needed external verification. 'It's a delaying tactic,' Karen, her boss, had said, shrugging. 'If you always need one more piece of evidence, you never have to truly accept the truth.'

'I don't get it.' Lydia trusted her gut. If she thought something was rotten, then it usually was.

'If you never truly accept it, you never have to take action. Limbo is bad, but hell is worse.'

In the bar, Brad Carter was still talking to her cleavage about oil derivatives. He was wearing his wedding ring, which was unusual. Lydia had expected a thin band of untanned skin where one usually lived. He caught her glance and smiled ruefully. For a split second, she saw what Mrs Carter must have seen in him, back in the day. The smile transformed his pink shiny face into something more boyish and charming. 'I'm not going to lie to you,' he said. 'I'm married. I'm not in a position to offer anything serious. But,' he leaned in, breathing whisky fumes into her face, 'I can promise you lots of fun.' Another charming smile. 'What do you say? You like fun?'

Lydia imagined herself jumping off the stool and saying 'no, I hate fun' before kneeing him in the bollocks. Instead, she blinked slowly and drained the rest of her disgusting martini.

He paid his bar tab and Lydia slid from the stool, making sure to seem unsteady on her feet. As she expected, Brad Carter held out an arm for her to lean on. When she moved closer to do just that, he snaked it around her waist and pulled her tightly against his bulk. 'I know where we should go next,' he was saying as he led her from the bar. Her feet felt as if they were barely touching the ground. She ground her teeth, imagining other drunk and vulnerable women he had undoubtedly done this with. Not with, she corrected. To. He wasn't asking, he was taking.

They needed to leave by the front of the hotel. Stuart was across the road in a parked car, ready with his telephoto lens to capture the moment. A couple of clear shots of them leaving together would do it. Brad had his arm around her, and it was clear he wasn't just being friendly.

Carter didn't go for the front of the hotel, though, he steered her to the lifts. Before Lydia had realised quite what was happening, he had punched the button and the doors opened. The inside was mirrored and she could see the alarm on her face. She quickly smoothed it away and tried to think. This was not the plan. She did not want to be alone with this man. She had some training and was stronger than she appeared, but he had a foot of height on her, and a great deal more bulk. He also appeared very sure of himself, which suggested practice. A thrill of fear ran through her body. *Hell Hawk.*

Never deviate from the plan. Karen had drilled this into her. The plan will keep you safe. And she had let this middle-aged lothario steer her into an enclosed space.

Carter's arm was snug around her waist, his grip strong and unyielding. He was looking at himself in the mirror and Lydia wondered what he saw. Another conquest? Another triumph?

Her small handbag was still over her free arm. Inside, she had a mobile phone that Stuart was tracking.

He wouldn't know anything was wrong, though. Her location hadn't really altered.

The lift was smooth, but she feigned a stumble when it stopped. Important to keep Carter feeling superior. Oblivious.

'Woah there, little lady. I think you could do with a lie down.' He was towing her along the corridor. The hotel looked less plush up here, like it needed a refurb. There were scuffs on the walls and one of the light fittings was hanging loose.

He opened the door and pushed her inside first. She stumbled in and aimed a look that was meant to be drunk but also flirty. 'I'm going to freshen...' she trailed off, pointing at the door to the ensuite and moving to it at the same time.

'Don't be long,' Carter said, looking put out.

She turned the lock and started running the taps. Then she tapped an SOS message to Stuart with the room number.

Once it showed as delivered and she had received a thumbs up emoji in response, she felt a little better. She would have preferred a different emoji from him. Something more appropriate to the situation, like a bomb or fire or even a sad face, but Stuart had only recently discovered emojis and he was famously bad at them.

In addition to her phone, which she switched to record, Lydia had a voice recorder in the shape of a pen, which she switched on before putting back inside her handbag. Belt and braces.

Out of the bathroom, she discovered that Brad Carter had been busy. He had taken off his shoes and jacket and unbuttoned the top three buttons of his shirt. He was pouring a gin and tonic from a can into a glass.

It was a large room, decorated in what Lydia recognised as 'classy Scottish' with earth tones and subtle tartans. The furniture was dark wood and solid-looking. She stumbled toward the nearest surface and opened her bag, pawing through it as if looking for something. Then she let the contents spill out, gripping her phone tightly through the thin leather so that it would stay put. She didn't want Carter to realise it was on.

'What are you doing, honey?'

'Lipstick,' Lydia said, snatching it clumsily from the small pile. The pen rolled toward the edge, but didn't fall off.

'You don't need that.' Carter was suddenly very close. His head bent down to land a messy kiss, which Lydia avoided by moving toward the bed.

'You want to play? We can play.'

He caught her around the waist and pulled her tight to his body. His erection pressed against her lower back. She felt a wave of revulsion. And, annoyingly, fear.

Lydia struggled. 'I don't want to play.' She hated sounding weak. Hated every single thing about what was happening, but she needed the audio recording to make it clear what was happening. 'Let go of me. I want to go home.'

'Not until I've had some fun,' Carter said. He kissed her neck wetly and grabbed her chest with one hand, squeezing and kneading.

'Please stop touching me,' Lydia said, enunciating clearly in the direction of the recorder.

'That accent,' Carter growled in her ear. 'It's sending me wild. Like a naughty British school girl.'

At that moment, the door flew open.

'Thank feathers,' Lydia said, and stamped on Brad Carter's instep.

LATER, ONCE SHE AND STUART WERE SAFELY ACROSS the street and in the car, Stuart was lecturing her. 'Never let the mark control the location.'

Lydia thought about saying it had happened too fast and that she hadn't known how to stop it without breaking character, but she knew he was right, so she kept her mouth shut. She had messed up. It was her ninth month on the job and she should know better. One of the reasons she was on honey-trap work was because it was low-risk, but low-risk didn't mean no-risk. And the number one rule was to stay in public spaces. Letting a horny man get you alone was a recipe for disaster and she had just allowed exactly that to happen.

'You all right, though, hen?' There was a worried crease in the middle of Stuart's eyebrows.

'I'm fine,' Lydia said. 'Just embarrassed that I messed up.' She stopped herself from swearing just in time. Stuart wasn't a fan of bad language.

'No harm done,' the big man said, starting the car. 'Karen's going to go ballistic, though.'

KAREN DID, INDEED, GO BALLISTIC. SHE LECTURED Lydia for twenty minutes without seeming to take a breath. Lydia hadn't been spoken to like a wayward child since school and hadn't much liked it then, but she knew Karen was essentially right, so she took it on the chin. Besides, she liked her job. She wanted to keep her job. She knew she was learning things and, apart from the essential misery of honey-trap work, she liked feeling useful to people. Clients came into Karen's office, shoulders slumped and heads low, defeated and unhappy, and they left with their eyes up. Not happy, but with a sense of agency. Someone had listened and offered help. Help that was probably going to land them straight back in misery town, but they would be better off in the end. 'The truth will set you free,' Karen always said. 'But it will kick you in the balls first.'

CHAPTER TWO

London, Now

Lydia Crow spun in a slow circle. Her weight was on her heel and her foot squeaked slightly on the sprung wooden floor of the practice room. The full-length wall mirrors confirmed that her form was good and she could feel that her core was strong. She made experimental leaps forward and back, from side to side, varying her speed and rhythm, as if dodging an assailant.

It had been almost a year since anybody had attempted to come at her physically, but she wasn't taking any chances.

Complacency was the mother of dead.

And while she had begun to feel her Crow power returning, she still couldn't produce her coin, let alone reach into another person and control them. She needed more prosaic forms of self-defence.

The tattoos on her arms were tingling. It was almost painful and when she looked at the ink, stark against her pale skin, the sensation increased until it was burning. She willed the images to move, the way they had used to do. She knew it would relieve the pain, but more importantly, it would help her to feel like herself again. She looked to the window where two jackdaws were sitting on the ledge, eating the seed she had put there, and nodded in acknowledgement. A Crow was outside the training room door. She could taste feathers.

'Boss?'

Aiden knocked and opened the door of the training room at the same time. Lydia grabbed her bottle of water and nodded for him to speak. Every day since she had taken over as the official head of the Crow Family and reinstated the truce between the four Families, every day since Charlie Crow had died with a crossbow bolt through his skull, there had been something for Lydia to take care of. Aiden was a brilliant second-in-command and had really stepped up, but there seemed to be a never-ending list that required Lydia's direct input.

Aiden ducked his head, as if sensing Lydia's irritation at being interrupted. 'We've got a situation.'

FOLLOWING HER SECOND-IN-COMMAND TO A FLAT near Camberwell Green, Lydia listened to Aiden's report. The Crows ran a string of betting shops around their territory. One of the managers had been found dead in his home by his girlfriend. She'd let his boss know, and he had passed the info up to Aiden.

'I was going to clean it up,' Aiden finished, 'but I wanted to check with you first.'

Lydia knew that she ought to call the police. Fleet was police and she had to keep her nose clean if she wanted him to be able to rehabilitate his career. But she was the head of the Family now, and that brought responsibility to the Crows and their businesses. And to Camberwell.

She could have delegated this one, she knew. She could have asked Aiden to call the cleaning service and marked it as 'done'. But she was still enough of an investigator that she wanted to see the scene. And it felt important to handle things with a personal touch. There were rumours in the Family that she wasn't fully engaged. It didn't seem to matter how many tasks she handled, how many people she met or favours she gave out. There were whispers that she was 'no Charlie'. She couldn't put a feather wrong.

Jez McAllister had lived in a small block of flats in a row that had been built in the nineties. Stocky, large, brown bricks and matt-silver scrolled metalwork on the balconies. The communal stairwell was freshly painted and there was a neat bank of post-boxes inside the front entrance.

Aiden used a key to let them into Jez's flat on the second floor.

'He let his killer in,' Lydia said.

'Must have done,' Aiden agreed. 'Door is intact and the lock hasn't been messed with.'

The flat smelled strongly of coffee. The main room was typical London. Not a lot of square footage, but packing a lot into the space available. It was an open plan layout with a kitchen shading into a living room.

There was a small dining table shoved against the back of the sofa with a couple of chairs tucked underneath, and a chunky IKEA bookcase was being used as a room divider and storage unit.

'Bedrooms?' Lydia had found the source of the smell. A bag of fresh coffee grounds had been spilled over the floor and not cleared up. It looked out of place in the otherwise-neat environment. She pointed at it. 'He doesn't seem the messy type.'

'This way,' Aiden said. 'He's in the main one. There's a spare.' He opened a door near to the front entrance and Lydia clocked a room barely bigger than the low double bed. There was a pile of laundry, a gym bag, and a few bags from clothes shops that looked as if they had just been put down after a trip. She checked a couple and found a box of Nike trainers, a silky dress from All Saints and leggings from Lululemon. She glanced at the receipt for the leggings and, without really knowing why, put it in her pocket.

Aiden didn't comment, just waited until she had finished and then led the way to the main event.

The door was ajar. 'Is this how you found it?'

'I think so.' He shot her a worried look. 'I'm not sure. Sorry, Boss.'

'That's okay. We know his girlfriend already disturbed the scene. What's her name again?'

'Jade.'

'So Jade has a key?'

He nodded. 'She says she spoke to Jez at lunchtime and he seemed fine. She went shopping with her mates in town. Got in about five and found this...'

'Bit of a shock for her,' Lydia said. 'Did she use the kitchen before she came through to the bedroom?'

'I dunno. It didn't come up.' Aiden pushed the door open and stood back to let Lydia take in the room.

Jez was lying on the bed with his head on the pillow and arms relaxed by his sides. He was very dead. That's always the thing about seeing a corpse, in Lydia's experience, your brain insisted on screaming at you that the person was dead. As if you didn't know. As if it wasn't the only thing you had noticed. She wasn't shocked anymore, had seen enough death, but it was still something significant. She supposed that if it ever stopped being significant, she ought to start worrying.

The second thing that hit Lydia, after the deadness and the way his head was tilted back as if he had been snoring, was the blood. There was a lot of blood and it had soaked into the duvet. He was lying on top of the duvet, fully dressed in t-shirt and jeans. He wasn't wearing shoes, but this wasn't a surprise as Lydia had seen a neat line of shoes by the front door, so he obviously had the habit of taking them off the moment he got inside. His socks were black and looked new.

Forcing herself to stop fixating on Jez's feet and how poignant they appeared in their new black socks, socks that would no longer be required to keep his extremities warm and comfortable as he no longer went about his daily life, Lydia made herself look at his face. She scanned it in sections, rather than taking it in as a person. His light-brown skin looked soft and well maintained, like he moisturised or had excellent genetics. No signs of injury. She continued to his limbs. She had expected to see wounds, something to account for the blood loss, but the skin beneath his t-shirt sleeves was intact. Perhaps he had been cut underneath his jeans? But then the killer would have had to re-dress him and that seemed unlikely.

'He was stabbed in the back,' Aiden said.

'You looked?'

'Nah, but it makes sense, innit? He looks fine from here.' Aiden waved a hand to indicate the visible parts of Jez's body. 'But he's bled out from somewhere.'

Lydia had been taking shallow breaths through her mouth, but the iron scent of blood was getting overwhelming. She wasn't going to be sick, but she was looking forward to getting away from the smell.

'I need to see,' she said, stepping closer.

She could sense that Aiden wanted to argue, but he dutifully followed her to the bed and helped her to roll Jez's body so that she could see his back. It felt all kinds of wrong, but they didn't have to worry about contaminating the crime scene.

Swallowing back nausea and taking shallow breaths, she examined the wound. His t-shirt was matted with dried blood, but intact, and the entry point was smaller than Lydia expected from the amount of blood. That was about all she could say about it. She wasn't a forensics expert and she was in danger of losing her breakfast if she looked any closer.

'We done here, boss?' Aiden was also clearly not enjoying himself.

Turning away from the dead man, she scanned the room. It was painted whatever shade of white property developers bought by the gallon and the carpet was grey. There was one bedside light that was bendy and functional and one that looked more like a nightlight. It was shaped like a toadstool and seemed more like something you would find in a kid's room. No books, but there was an iPad and a pair of glasses next to the reading lamp. The curtains were dark blue and Lydia was pretty sure they had matched the duvet cover, back before it had been soaked in several pints of Jez's blood.

Lydia dropped to the floor and peered under the bedframe. A couple of dusty cardboard boxes, which had probably been in situ since Jez moved in, waiting to be unpacked. And a messenger bag. Lydia hooked it out. It wasn't particularly dusty.

'Shall I call the cleaners?'

'Yes, please.' She looked at Aiden, who had moved away from the bed. He was shifting his weight as if desperate to leave the murder room. 'Reception will be better outside.'

Aiden fled, and Lydia turned her attention to the bag. It was probably the one Jez took to work. She couldn't imagine he dealt with much physical paperwork, but it was possible he had stuff to bring to and from the shop. Or he just used it for his water bottle and lunch. Maybe his iPad and specs too.

The bag was dark-brown canvas with leather straps and buckles. Inside, Lydia didn't find a lunchbox. Just a lot of cash.

She closed the flap of the bag and looped the strap around her body. She regarded Jez for another long moment and, before she could second guess herself, took a series of pictures with her phone. The point of the cleaning service was to eradicate any evidence. Jez would simply disappear. Jade would be paid off to keep her mouth shut. Any other friends or family that came asking questions would meet with stonewalling, bribes and intimidation. No police, no murder, no problem. Adding pictures of the dead man to her phone's storage wasn't a smart play. She was already regretting it.

Aiden was outside the flat, sucking the life from a cigarette. Lydia didn't blame him. She knew she would be seeing Jez's sightless eyes and all that blood every time she closed her eyes.

He didn't ask her about the messenger bag, which just went to show what a good second-in-command he was. She answered the unspoken question anyway. She wanted Aiden to feel trusted and valued. Trust was tricky in their Family, but Lydia was determined to try. 'Can you think of a reason why Jez would have ten grand stashed under his bed?'

Aiden's eyes widened slightly and he glanced at the bag. 'Ten gees?'

'Thereabouts. I haven't counted it yet.'

He whistled through his teeth. 'You reckon that's why he was...' Aiden drew his finger across his neck.

She shrugged. 'If the killer was looking for money, they did a piss-poor job of it.'

CHAPTER THREE

Lydia had arrived back at Charlie's house to find that Angel had been in. She had stocked the freezer with her homemade meals and packed a grocery delivery away into labelled canisters. Lydia had employed Angel on her old salary as a stop-gap measure after The Fork was burned to the ground. Ten months later and she was still acting as Lydia's personal chef and housekeeper and was showing no signs of getting a different gig. Having seen inside the Crow Family finances, Lydia knew she could afford to keep the arrangement going, but part of her felt a bit weird. It was one thing to mooch food from Angel at The Fork, but another to pay the woman to act like a housekeeper. On the other hand, the fridge was fully stocked, and there was a basket of freshly baked muffins on the counter.

It was late now. Past ten o'clock and there was no sign of Fleet. Lydia had been working in the living room. She didn't like using Charlie's office, still thought of it as his, and had been curled up on the sofa with her laptop and a blanket. Jason had been sitting on the other end, until Lydia had complained about him making her cold, so he was now sulking in his bedroom. She would make it up to him later. They had been snappy with each other since The Fork had been destroyed. Both of them were discombobulated and unsettled. Jason was dead, though, which was surely the worse deal. She ought to be more understanding.

Lydia picked at a lemon-and-poppy seed muffin while she zapped an individual portion of lasagne, and then ate standing by the counter in the enormous open-plan kitchen-diner. The garden was a wall of black on the other side of the bifold doors and she knew that she would be lit up inside for anybody looking in. She flicked the switch for the electric blinds and watched them slowly descend as she chewed. Everything here had been chosen by Charlie. Or one of his people. None of it was hers. Of course, The Fork hadn't been properly hers, either, but that had felt like home. This was Charlie's. And it always would be.

Lydia checked her phone before switching off the bedside light. The last message from Fleet had come in an hour earlier, telling her not to wait up. He had been busy at work over the last ten months, rebuilding his reputation and impressing the latest new management team. Lydia didn't resent the time it took. She understood his drive to succeed and knew that his career had taken a blow from his association with her. Not to mention the few weeks he had been overcome by visions of the future, unable to tell reality from hallucination. That had coincided with the appearance of his father in the city and had led to him having to leave London for a time. All of which had fuelled the rumours about his mental stability and suitability for his role in the Met. He hadn't been demoted, not officially, but she knew it had affected his standing. While she kept herself out of legal trouble, things could go on as they were, but she didn't know how long it was sustainable. That wasn't something she wanted to think about too hard, so she shut her eyes and started counting her breaths instead. When that didn't work, she pictured a crow in flight and counted its wingbeats.

When she woke up, the lights on the clock told her it was almost three. She had heard the front door and recognised Fleet's tread on the stairs. A crack of light showed around the bedroom door as he crept inside.

'I'm awake,' she whispered.

'Sorry, sorry.' Fleet's voice was soft in the dark.

'It's all right.'

Once he had shucked off his clothes and climbed into bed, wrapping cold arms and legs around Lydia's warm body, she tried to regulate her breathing again. She was wide awake and worried that she wouldn't be able to get back to sleep.

Fleet's breathing was already slowing down.

'Anything new on your scum bucket?' Fleet had been working on a murder case. A man called Craig Johnstone had been stabbed to death. Sadly, not a particularly unusual event for London.

Fleet was happy to have a serious case, but was very

aware that it wasn't prestigious or high profile. He had explained it to Lydia when he had first been appointed to head the team. 'It's not that nobody cares. I mean, it's murder and we're all doing our jobs, but nobody is crying into their pints. Not even the guy's grandma is upset that he's gone.'

'You spoke to Johnstone's gran?'

'I was speaking metaphorically. I reckon if his granny was alive and I told her that he was dead, she would have danced a jig.'

'His metaphorical gran is happy he's dead. Harsh.'

Fleet had shaken his head. 'He was a pimp. Used trafficked women.'

'Oh,' Lydia said. 'Fuck him, then.'

'My feelings exactly,' Fleet said. 'Unofficially.'

Now Lydia waited for him to answer. He shifted, kissed her temple, but didn't respond.

'Fleet?'

A pause. 'Another body. Same MO.'

'Stabbed?'

Fleet mumbled his assent. She waited to hear more, her whole body awake, but he didn't say anything else and soon she realised he had fallen deeply asleep. Exhausted.

THE NEXT DAY, LYDIA MADE COFFEE AND SAT AT THE kitchen island to drink it. Fleet had already left for work. He had got up while Lydia was still asleep and left without saying goodbye. He couldn't have had more than a couple of hours of kip, but she knew he was happy to be on a murder case. To have something to sink his teeth into after months of busywork in the office equivalent of Siberia.

Jason was scrolling on his iPad. One of the many gifts she had bought him over the last ten months. It wasn't technically her fault that his home had been destroyed, but she couldn't help feeling responsible. And while he had adjusted to living at Charlie's, she could tell that he felt the same as her. Unsettled.

'They found a body last night in Whitechapel. Suspicious death,' Jason said, reading from the screen.

'Fleet said there had been another death with the same MO as his case. I wonder if that's it?'

'His case is Craig Johnstone, right? The stabbing?' Lydia had talked to Jason about Fleet's murder case. She missed her investigation work, and talking about Fleet made her feel involved in his life, even if they hardly saw each other. He was coming back to Charlie's to roost, but even that had started to get less regular.

She distracted herself from that depressing thought by asking a question. 'Was it a stabbing?'

'Doesn't say. Just that the death is being treated as suspicious. He looks like the sort to be in a knife fight, though.'

'What do you mean?' Lydia leaned across the island. 'Rough?'

'You shouldn't judge on appearances, I know, but yeah.' Jason angled the iPad so that Lydia could see the news site.

The image of the deceased showed a puffy-faced man with small eyes and a shaved head. It had been taken while he was somewhere warm as there was sea and a palm tree in the background. 'Hang on,' Jason said, reading further. 'Sometimes you *can* judge on appearances. Raymond Price. Previously been convicted of human trafficking, apparently. Is this what Fleet's working on?'

'Maybe. I mean, I don't know for certain if this is his new case. But it's possible.'

'News got it quick,' Jason said. He was tapping away on the screen. 'Looks like whoever found the body went on social media, so there wasn't much hope of keeping it quiet.'

Lydia knew how frustrated Fleet would be by that. It made his job harder if the world and his wife knew all the details before he had a chance to question key witnesses.

'Send me the links?' Lydia asked. Then she tapped a message to Fleet. *'This yours?'* It was good to show an interest in each other's work. And it felt easier for her to ask about his than for him to ask about hers. Keeping their interactions focused on Fleet's charmless dead guys smoothed the way between them. Maybe other couples wouldn't count murder talk as bonding, but normality was overrated in Lydia's opinion.

A few minutes later, she got a one-word response. 'Yes.'

ONE OF LYDIA'S LEAST-FAVOURITE PARTS OF HER role as the new Charlie involved meeting with her counterparts in the other Families. The truce had been renewed, but if they had learned one thing over the last couple of years, it was that none of them could take it for granted. The truce was only strong if it was alive and well: a living, breathing agreement, not a dusty old concept.

Lydia had suggested that they meet once a year. Check in with each other, renew their commitment to playing nice. Maria Silver had countered with once a month. Lawyers bloody loved to talk. Paul Fox had said twice a year would be more than sufficient and they had compromised on every quarter.

Lydia had destroyed The Pearl King. As far as any of the Families knew, his power had been dissipated above ground. Probably into the many descendants with Pearl blood. Hopefully, harmlessly giving a little more juice to some Instagram influencers and the like. Lydia's best guess was that Rafferty Hill, an actor, was the heir apparent. She had been waiting to see what this meant for the truce and the Family. Rafferty had stood in as the de facto leader during the restatement of the truce that had left Charlie Crow dead on the floor with a crossbow bolt in his skull, but he hadn't attended a meeting since. Always sent his apologies, but it was clear he didn't want to be in the same room as them ever again. Lydia couldn't exactly blame him, and as long as he was truly disinterested in Family politics, then it shouldn't matter. By all appearances, he had been concentrating on his career as an actor and didn't seem to be a threat. She had light surveillance on him anyway, just in case. One of the plus sides to her new role – she had funds for that kind of caper.

Lydia had chosen three neutral locations for the meeting and invited the other two to choose. Paul had gone for Queen Mary's Rose Garden in Regent's Park, but requested the cafe nearby. Maria had chosen the bar at Claridge's in Mayfair, as Lydia had known she would. Maria was a sucker for a nice hotel. She sided with Paul and tried not to think too much about what Maria would read into that. Three was unbalanced. In the absence of Rafferty, they needed to find a representative for the Pearl Family, as ballast for the meetings if nothing else.

Maria was easy to spot. She was surrounded by a group of suited people. One of them broke away and circled the outdoor seating before selecting a chair for Maria. Paul Fox had already arrived and was eating a sourdough pizza at a central table. The suited woman who had chosen a seat for Maria approached him and Lydia watched her try to get him to move to Maria's table. His head was tilted back and he smiled at the young woman with a Fox magnetism that Lydia could feel from her vantage point a hundred metres away. She pocketed her scope and went to join the fun.

CHAPTER FOUR

After Paul had finished his pizza and been convinced to move to Maria's chosen table, Maria had a glass of white wine which she was inspecting with a dubious expression, and Lydia had ordered a portion of double-cooked chips with garlic mayo, more to annoy Maria than out of any true hunger, the meeting could begin.

'You brought people,' Lydia said, addressing Maria. 'To our top-secret meeting.'

Maria flapped a hand. 'I trust my staff completely.'

'I don't,' Paul said. 'And this is supposed to be just us three.'

'And a Pearl,' Lydia said. 'Anyone got any ideas about that? Rafferty emailed his apologies again. He is in Canada shooting a TV pilot.'

'I've not finished with Maria and her entourage,' Paul said. He was staring at Maria with open hostility. 'Not a good start.'

Maria put a hand on Paul's forearm. 'I sincerely apologise. It won't happen again.'

Paul pulled his arm away and leaned back in his seat.

Lydia blinked at Maria in surprise. She had sounded contrite. Serious. But then, the woman was a Silver. The bright tang of metal was cutting through Lydia's thought processes and probably messing with her judgement. Silvers could sell any lie, that was the problem. They were believable, they sounded reasonable, they made sense. And before you knew it, you were agreeing to things you would have never thought possible and accepting the unacceptable. Back in the bad old days, a Silver could convince you it was safe to walk onto the tube tracks and have a nice lie down.

'If I'm honest,' Maria said, still sounding suspiciously sincere, 'I felt some trepidation about this meeting. And this location didn't help. I would have been far more comfortable at Claridge's. And the cocktails are to die for.' She took a sip of her white wine and winced.

'We'll meet at Claridge's next time,' Lydia said. She didn't really care, but she saw Paul scowl at her words. Feathers. This diplomacy business was a pain in the arse.

'So, what do we do?' Paul was still leaning back in his chair. He looked good. Something that Lydia had been trying to ignore since she first sighted him through the scope. 'Is this it? Or do we read a pledge not to go for each other? Shake hands? Pinky swear we won't wage war?'

'Sounds good,' Lydia said, keeping her tone light.

'I've got no intention of warmongering. I've got enough on my plate.'

'How is the Crow empire?' Maria asked, red lips stretching into a sardonic smile.

'Yeah, Little Bird. Is it all you hoped for?'

Lydia wasn't about to tell them the truth. That she hadn't hoped for it. Didn't want it. And didn't have a bloody clue what she was doing. 'You know how it goes,' she said instead. 'Keeps me busy.'

'I like that,' Maria said. 'Stay busy on your side of the river and we don't have a problem.'

'Come when I call and that's true,' Lydia shot back.

Paul was watching them, not smiling. 'Stay away from my den, stay out of my business, and don't even think about calling on me.'

'Lovely,' Lydia said after a moment of silence. 'This all sounds about as trucey as it's ever been. Job done, do you reckon?'

Paul was already standing. 'Claridge's in three months.' He looked at Maria. 'You're paying.'

LYDIA LEFT JUST AFTER PAUL, DELIBERATELY walking in the opposite direction so that Maria wouldn't think they were colluding. It wouldn't look good to appear too cosy with the head of the Fox Family, especially given her rocky history with Maria.

The day was warm and the huge rose beds were blooming. The air was thick with floral scent, cloyingly sweet and undercut with fresh-cut grass. The box hedges were neatly clipped and there were healthy-looking ornamental trees lining the wide paths. Regent's Park was a royal park and a prime tourist attraction; it was the city in its finest clothes, all the dirty linen hidden away.

She was just passing a large pond, big enough to have its own small island, when a warm earthy scent cut through the heady floral aroma of rose. On a curved wooden bridge that led to the island in the pond, Paul Fox was waiting for her. At least, she assumed that was what he was doing. Unless he was a bigger fan of ornamental gardens than she had hitherto realised.

When she drew level with the bridge, he tilted his chin in invitation.

She took the few steps to join him and looked out at the view. It was safer than looking at Paul. She was having the vertiginous sense of déjà vu.

'What do you think, Little Bird? Can we trust Maria?'

Lydia stiffened. She liked Paul saying 'we', liked feeling less alone, and that made her wary. She *was* alone. She couldn't afford to lean on anyone. Especially not Paul Fox. He had protected her in the past, but that didn't mean she could rely on that in the future.

'I heard you had a bit of bother with one of your shops,' Paul was saying, looking over at the island that had been done out in the style of a traditional Japanese garden. 'Didn't you lose a manager?'

'Staff turnover. You know how it is.'

'I know that a gangster from Brixton was looking to take a cut back in Charlie's time.'

Well, that was news to Lydia. She didn't let it show, though, as Paul was clearly fishing. 'You don't need to concern yourself with Crow business. How are your clubs? I heard Vixen got raided three times last month.' She clicked her tongue. 'Sloppy.'

Paul flashed a smile that was mostly white teeth and no longer friendly. 'Is that how it's going to be?'

'I don't know what you mean.'

'There's no Charlie. You are free—' he stopped. 'There's no Charlie. You're the new Charlie. I thought things would be different.'

'They can't be,' Lydia said. If she was too different, the various contacts and gangs and businesses, the interconnected contacts in both the political and criminal world, would sense weakness. If there was blood in the water, the truce with the Silvers wouldn't hold. Maria Silver was not the charitable type.

'We were friends once,' Paul said, his voice low.

The way that he was looking at her was sending all kinds of unhelpful signals to unprofessional parts of her body. She had to shut that down. It was his Fox magic, clouding her mind. She turned and walked away without answering him. But she could feel his gaze on her back like a brand.

There was no 'we' with her and Paul. That was ancient history. And although he had helped her since she had arrived back in London, they had greater loyalties. And, Lydia reminded herself, a second too late for comfort – she was with Fleet. Still. His eyes held a promise, and one she knew very well he could fulfil. Paul Fox aged twenty-one had been a revelation. She wondered what else he had learned in the intervening years.

· · ·

31

BACK AT THE HOUSE IN DENMARK HILL, JASON WAS waiting to speak to her. He made her a coffee and put a pastry onto a plate, putting them both onto the desk. Lydia loved seeing him so solid. It had taken a few months before he had been able to move objects reliably, starting with touchscreens and moving onto typing, before getting back to pouring cereal and finally, confidently handling the kettle.

He had also placed the iPad on the desk, and Lydia peered at the screen. It showed a black-and-white photo, blurry and old-looking. A row of houses, women outside doors scrubbing the steps. 'What am I looking at?'

'Camberwell in 1878.'

'Okay...'

'You remember the little boy I met at The Fork?'

Jason had seen a ghost that had been little more than an echo, repeating the same pattern over and over, and it had upset him greatly.

'What do you think has happened to him?'

He meant now that The Fork was destroyed. It appeared that ghosts were anchored to the place they died or the place they had a strong emotional link. Jason had been able to leave The Fork by 'riding' in Lydia's body, anchoring himself to her. After The Fork was destroyed, Lydia managed to tether him to Charlie's house by revealing the details of his death at Charlie's hand, provoking a strong emotional reaction. 'I don't know,' she said. 'I'm sorry. I know you wanted to help him.'

'There must be thousands. I want to help all of

them. I don't want to leave them stuck and alone. Frightened.'

'I know.' Lydia touched his arm.

Her phone dinged and she checked WhatsApp. A message from Emma. *Feathers*.

CHAPTER FIVE

London, Then

Lydia had been Christmas shopping with Emma. They had started in Covent Garden, dodging the street performers and tourists, and browsing the market. Emma had already bought dark-pink socks with tiny embroidered butterflies and handmade soap that looked like a lump of crystal for her mum. Lydia had bought some posh fudge and had almost finished eating it. She offered the bag to Emma, who shook her head. 'I'm not allowed.'

'Sugar?' Lydia was horrified.

'Sticky stuff like that. Fudge, toffee, chewy sweets. Dentist said I've got weak enamel.'

Lydia extracted a lump of fudge from her back molar with her tongue. She thought about saying 'go on, live a little' but knew there was no point. When Emma had decided to do something – or not do something – she

35

stuck to it. It was one of the many things Lydia admired about her friend.

As well as being iron-willed, Emma liked skate clothes and skater boys, so they stopped at the shop in Neal's Yard to eye up the soft hoodies in washed-out colours and the slouching clientele. Lydia couldn't see the appeal herself. But then, this was an ongoing concern in her life. Since fancying boys had become a 'thing' at school, she had been waiting for it to happen. She just seemed to be missing the essential component. She liked some of them well enough. The quiet nerdy ones who weren't throwing their lunch around or bullying other people, but she didn't remotely want to kiss them. Emma, on the other hand, had had a series of intense crushes that had, in the last couple of years, graduated to a succession of boyfriends.

Lydia didn't think it was a case of mistaken sexuality. She didn't fancy any of the girls, either. And she felt stirrings for the male form on occasion, when watching a film or rock star. She just didn't seem to be able to work up any kind of reaction to the real-life boyfriend candidates she encountered. She had even, in a moment of madness, revealed this to her mum. It had been in response to a long campaign of 'bonding', but still. What a lapse.

'Don't worry, darling,' her mum had said. 'Boys aren't all that attractive. When you're older, you'll start meeting men and then you'll see what all the fuss is about.'

Lydia didn't want to see what all the fuss was about. She liked that she wasn't distracted and swooning. It gave her a sense of control and superiority. Emma aside, who was steadfastly sensible and completely herself regardless of her boyfriend of the moment, Lydia watched her classmates lose their minds. They changed things about themselves, becoming sporty when they hadn't been before or dropping interests entirely, or changed friendship groups, or started smoking and cutting school. And the evidence from literature and film was even worse. No thank you.

They dipped into Oxford Street. Tried on clothes in Top Shop and got a Starbucks. As they left the cafe, Lydia heard the distinctive sound of a wingbeat. Once, twice. She looked around, expecting her dad to have materialised, checking up on her. He wasn't there, of course. He didn't follow her in central London. And she was allowed to be here. Camberwell was off limits, unless accompanied by him, which very rarely happened, but Oxford Street was neutral. Still, there had to be a distant cousin or something nearby. Lydia was a Crow, but her only power lay in sensing which Family a person came from. It wasn't very useful and she wasn't even very good at it. Unless the person was main bloodline and standing pretty close, she didn't sense anything at all. She had spent her early teens waiting eagerly for something better to show up. Waiting for her own metaphorical Hogwarts owl to show up and tell her she was special, but it didn't. Her father had chucked in leadership of the Crow Family, passed the crown to his brother and retreated to Beckenham to raise Lydia and live in suburban bliss with her mum. He had been special and he had thrown it away.

'You all right?' Emma had her head tilted in concern.

'Yeah. Good.' Lydia knew she had a reputation as odd, not helped by the knowledge that she was a Crow. Beckenham kids might have been in the suburbs, but it wasn't the moon. They had heard the rumours. Emma had never seemed to care about any of it – Lydia's awkwardness or her Family – and had always accepted her as she was.

'Liberty's?'

'Liberty's.' Lydia confirmed.

Emma was a design-freak and a homebody. She had the most stylish bedroom, created with handsewn cushions and curtains, framed pictures from magazines and a way of arranging unusual objects that made it all tie together and look meant, rather than just jumble. Emma always spent ages in the fabric section of the department store, they both laughed at the expensive designer clothes with their ridiculous shapes and colours, and Lydia liked the fragrance room with its dark-blue ceiling, painted with stars.

The familiar black and white building came into view and Lydia felt a bubble of happiness. The Christmas decorations were up, so they looked at the window displays before diving past the doorman and into the sparkling world of sumptuous goods and arts-and-crafts glamour.

Lydia was going through the scents in the fragrance room. It was a circular space, packed with ornate glass bottles on shelves that glittered and glowed. She had been picking up heavy glass bottles and sniffing, lost in a heady world of exotic aromas. There were strips of card to take away sample sprays and she sprayed one that she thought Emma would like and put it in her pocket. She wasn't going to buy it, the bottle she had just sniffed cost almost eighty quid, but it smelled of fresh air and sea spray and tickled something in her brain. She sprayed it onto her wrist and waited for it to warm up before lifting her arm and inhaling. The fresh air scent mingled with her skin and made something else. It was green. Woody. No, earthy.

'Found something you like?'

Lydia turned to tell the assistant that she was just browsing, her shoulders tense in case he was going to ask her to stop sampling expensive perfumes she had no funds to buy, when she realised it wasn't a Liberty employee.

He had close-cropped dark hair and the kind of cheekbones that ought to be illegal. He was probably the most good-looking man she had ever seen in real life. Certainly this close. His black t-shirt was stretched across a muscular chest and an excellent pair of shoulders. Lydia's brain was short-circuiting, and all she could think was 'Fox'. The earthy smell. Green. A flash of red fur moving through trees. The urge to reach out and put a hand onto that firm chest.

'Hello, Little Bird.'

She was clutching the perfume bottle like a lifeline. 'Have you been following me?'

He laughed, low, and the sound reverberated in her body. 'Why would I be doing that?'

Why indeed? She shouldn't let him know she knew he was a Fox. Her ability, such as it was, had to remain a secret. Her dad had made that clear. She forced a shrug. 'You give off a creeper vibe, I guess.'

He put a hand to his chest. 'Harsh.'

She managed to turn, put the perfume bottle back in its place.

'I'm Paul,' he said, 'and you're Lydia Crow.'

'How do you know that?'

He flashed a devilish smile. 'I've been following you.'

London, Now

LYDIA DIDN'T KNOW WHY SHE HAD BEEN THINKING about Paul Fox. She had seen him at the meeting, of course, and maybe that was enough. She was also feeling restless, pacing the house that would always be Charlie's. Trapped. And maybe that reminded her of how she had felt as a teenager.

She looked at her phone, trying again to formulate a response to Emma's text. The message from Emma had also pulled her back to the past. Emma was her constant, along with her parents, her friend from before she was Lydia Crow and all that entailed. But she was also sealed in Beckenham. A link to Lydia's relatively normal childhood and teenage years, but something that was essentially separate.

She would do anything to keep Emma and her family safe, and that meant keeping Emma at a distance. She had solemnly promised to keep in better touch and had set herself a recurring notification on her phone to make sure she kept the letter of that promise. She knew she had withdrawn further emotionally, though. She couldn't share the new normal of her daily life. Didn't want to infect Emma's life with the unseemly side. It had been bad enough when she had been a PI, on the outside of her infamous Family. But now she was their leader. She had no one else to blame for the morally grey waters she swum in every day.

She re-read the message from Emma.

Tried that ballet class I told you about. Have pulled every muscle in body. Send help.

And a smiley face, a grimacing face and a laughing emoji.

Lydia forced a light response. And ignored the way her heart ached.

CHAPTER SIX

I t was Saturday morning and, in theory, Fleet didn't have work. He was asleep in their bed at Charlie's house, on his back and snoring very lightly. Even though he was resting, his face looked tired. He had been working overtime and Lydia fully expected him to end up back at the office later on. She had mixed feelings about this. On one hand, she knew they weren't spending enough time together and she missed him. On the other, her brain was itching to find out what happened to Jez McAllister and to work out why he had had ten grand stashed under his bed. And that wasn't a case she could chat to Fleet about.

After Fleet's father had turned up in London, almost taken Fleet away with him and then drained Lydia's power, Lydia had realised that she and Fleet had to go all-in. She had to stop being guarded and to trust Fleet with everything. Every part of her. And he had to do the same. He had been so busy trying to protect her and her feelings that he had nearly left London forever without even discussing it with her.

Of course, all of that was easy to say. 'Let's trust each other'. 'Let's be more open.' What was hard, it turned out, was to overcome the habits of a lifetime. Especially when their lives were so different and so busy. Lydia had been working twenty-four-seven as head of the Crows, making sure that she didn't show a sliver of weakness. Now that she could no longer reach out and move people like they were puppets or even produce her coin, she wasn't going to give anyone in the Family, or the gangs and factions that were always on the make, looking for what they could get in Camberwell, a moment to wonder whether she was up to the job. And now she had a murder on her patch.

Fleet had been working his arse off at work, trying to make up for the double whammy of having been off his game while his visions were uncontrollable and the associated rumours about his mental fitness that had started to fly around his colleagues and superiors, and the fact that he was seeing the head of an infamous crime family. Everything was digitised now, of course, but the old files on the Crow Family were inches thick.

Fleet moved, stretching in his sleep and then rolling onto his side. His arm reached across her body and pulled her against him. 'Morning,' he mumbled against her neck.

'Morning,' Lydia said back, pushing against his body and snuggling into his arms.

She was just remembering how pleasant it was to

wake up with Fleet, to feel his body pressed against hers, when his phone rang, interrupting them.

He lifted his head and hissed through his teeth. 'I have to get that.'

'I know,' Lydia said. She was still breathing heavily and pushed her hair away from her face with a frustrated movement.

Propped up one elbow, phone pressed to his ear, he almost growled his greeting. 'What is it?'

Lydia could hear the voice on the other end, but not make out the words. She lay where she was, guessing this probably meant game over for their lie in, but waiting just in case.

Then Fleet sat up and began looking for his clothes as he listened. He shot her an apologetic look.

Feathers.

LYDIA CAME OUT OF THE SHOWER, EXPECTING TO find Fleet gone. Instead, he was waiting for her.

'You know I told you there had been another stabbing?'

'Raymond Price,' Lydia confirmed. 'Is it linked to Craig Johnstone's murder, do you think?'

He nodded. 'Looks possible. But there's something I didn't tell you. Before.'

Lydia had just been happy that he was on something more suited to his rank, and out of the community-policing purgatory he had been exiled in since his time off work. 'Okay,' she sat on the edge of the bed, still wrapped in her towel. 'What is it?'

'We've kept it out of the news so far, but that's been easy because there wouldn't be much interest. Johnstone isn't considered a great tragedy.'

'You indicated as much.'

'Yeah.' Fleet ran a hand over his head. 'I didn't tell you that he was killed in Whitechapel.'

'Two bodies in the same area? Okay.' Two stabbings in London were, sadly, not a surprise. But two in Whitechapel and in such a short timeframe... Something else occurred to Lydia, something she should have thought of before. She really had been distracted. 'Whitechapel's not your manor.'

'No,' Fleet agreed. 'I've been assigned to a central murder team. We pick up the cases for the city, regardless of borough.'

'Is that what you want?' Lydia was still stuck on Fleet's career and whether this was a step back towards where he wanted to be, or further punishment. It took her another beat to realise that he was watching her very carefully. 'Johnstone and Price were in a similar line of business, right?'

He nodded. His expression strange.

'What?' Her bare skin had goose bumps, even though it wasn't cold in the bedroom, and she had the urge to stretch out her wings.

'Have you been in touch with the Foxes recently? Anything going on that I should know about?'

'This is not Family business,' Lydia said firmly. Whitechapel was Fox Family territory, but that didn't mean they had anything to do with these deaths, and the last thing the truce needed was Fleet stumbling into their den.

'You seem very certain.'

'That's because I am.' She hadn't recognised either of the two victims and knew the Crows didn't have anything to do with human trafficking. At least, nothing in her lifetime, at any rate. And she had no knowledge of it being anything to do with one of the other Families. So that was fine. There was no need to remind Fleet that, under the terms of the truce, she wouldn't tell him if she did.

'Right,' he said. 'Okay, then. I had to ask.' Fleet made to leave.

Lydia didn't know she was going to ask until the question was already out. 'Where in Whitechapel was the first body dropped? Johnstone?'

'Gunthorpe Street.'

London, Then

Eighteen months had passed since Paul Fox had approached Lydia in Liberty's, and it wasn't an encounter that she thought about anymore. She was in town, celebrating her nineteenth birthday with a crowd of new friends. Friends was probably pushing it. New acquaintances. She had been tilting off the rails for a while and hanging out with different groups of people. Anyone who seemed to offer the danger she was looking for. Although she wasn't exactly sure what sort of danger she wanted. Emma had been at the pub earlier, but had left an hour ago. She wasn't a fan of Lydia's self-destructive phase or the random company she kept gathering. They were good, though. She was still Lydia's best friend and part of her hung onto that. If Emma was still by her side, things hadn't become too seriously out of control. They had plans for a cinema trip on the weekend and Lydia was looking forward to that return to the safe part of her life. Her old self.

She knew what had sent her out with this random group tonight. What had her jumping on the train into town with her head buzzing and a desperate need for distraction. She had argued with her dad again. He wanted her to go to university. She wanted to join the Family business. What was the point of being a Crow otherwise? Why did he want her to do life on hard mode, when there was a whole ready-made empire waiting for her to slot into?

'You can have a normal life,' he kept saying. 'Do whatever you want. I've worked hard to make sure you're free and you want to throw it all away.'

'Free means free to choose. And I choose the Family business.' Her mum wasn't in the room, but she could sense her presence nearby. Probably waiting in the kitchen, putting candles onto Lydia's homemade birthday cake, and 'giving them a moment'.

'You don't know what you're talking about. I've kept you from it for a good reason. Why do you think I left?'

Lydia wanted to say 'because you couldn't hack it', but she stopped short. Her dad was not a scary man. He never raised a hand and rarely raised his voice, but he still exuded authority. Lydia might have been in her rebellious phase, but she wasn't an idiot. 'I'm going out,' she had muttered instead, banging the front door on her way. She felt bad that she hadn't said goodbye to her mum. Hadn't waited to blow out her candles or eat a piece of cake. Her parents were good people, and they were good to her. She knew that, and the guilt churned in her stomach. What was wrong with her? Why was she so angry all the time? When was she going to get her shit together?

The man she was sitting with now had the wiry skinniness of a drug addict. His left leg hadn't stopped jiggling up and down throughout their conversation, and his gaze kept darting around the pub, as if searching for his next fix.

Lydia had given up making conversation and was playing with her coin, practising flipping it over the back of her knuckles.

'That real gold?' The guy asked suddenly. She realised that she had forgotten his name. Danny?

She pocketed the coin. 'Nah.' She looked at his mouth and saw bad teeth. Suddenly, she wanted to be anywhere else. The group she had joined meant nothing to her, she realised. They had seemed edgy and exciting, but they were dull. Maybe-Danny had no conversation, the woman with the frizzy blue hair just seemed to want to pick fights, and the guy she had met first, with the sweet baby face and floppy blonde curls, had been enthusiastically kissing another girl for the last half an hour.

Lydia rose from the table. Maybe-Danny stuck out a

49

hand and grabbed her arm. His grip was surprisingly strong. 'Don't go.'

She forced a smile. 'Need a piss.'

He pulled her back down. 'You'll be all right.'

'Don't be weird,' Lydia said, peeling his fingers from her arm and standing again.

'Come right back,' Maybe-Danny said, eyeballing her. There was something worrying in his expression. Something lurking behind his eyes. Lydia was getting out of this pub and making for the nearest tube station. In all her ill-advised adventures, she relied on her instincts. They told her who was fun-dodgy and who was just psycho. Her gut told her when things were turning nasty. When to cross the street and when to get out of the pub. Maybe-Danny was about to turn, she could feel it. So she went.

Outside the pub, night had fallen. She tilted her head and looked at the slice of navy-blue sky, edged with spilled light from the city. There were glowing yellow bulbs strung across the narrow street, and there was an enticing scent of garlic coming from the restaurant next door. Lydia set off in the direction of Aldgate. The high street turned into Whitechapel after the site of the old defensive gate, but she wasn't going that far. Whitechapel was Fox territory, but she would cross the river at Tower Bridge and get a bus back to Beckenham.

She passed a closed barbershop called Abdul Scissorhands and a 'bit of everything' shop with boxes of apples outside the door.

Once she joined the main road, there were tall glass

buildings next to the Victorian ones and a long line of hoarding, covered in graffiti and posters, hemming a construction site. A crane was silhouetted against the sky. She was almost at the station, and she could feel her senses screaming. Whitechapel road began a few feet away and she knew she shouldn't be anywhere near it. The Family territories had been drummed into her since she was a toddler. The city divided up as part of the 1948 truce. Each of the four Families agreeing to stick to their areas.

She was almost at the entrance to Aldgate when her senses went into overdrive. A figure peeled away from the wall just ahead and stepped into her path. She stopped walking and a woman detoured sharply around her with a muttered oath.

Paul Fox, wearing a fitted black t-shirt, stood no more than a foot away from her. Her brain was scrambled. Dark woods. Red fur through trees. Warm earth. Safe underground. Soft, thick fur brushing along her side, making every nerve ending quiver. She gripped her coin in her hand and squeezed until the impressions slowed. Once she could shove them to the back of her mind, she was able to focus on the fact that Paul's mouth was moving. He had been speaking. She had no idea what he had said, so she shrugged.

'That a fact?' Paul said.

Still none the wiser, Lydia pointed behind him. 'I'm heading home.'

'I've got a better idea. Come for a drink with me.'

'No. Thank you.' Lydia added the 'thank you' to be

polite. She hadn't had dealings with the other Families, had barely dealt with her own, but she knew they were dangerous. And she wasn't an idiot. You didn't antagonise a wild animal. Not unless you were carrying a weapon, and she was defenceless.

'Ah, come on. Let me buy you a birthday drink.'

'How do you know it's my birthday?'

His lips twitched. 'My father knows all kinds of things.'

'He sent you to look for me?'

A dark look crossed Paul's face. 'My father would beat me senseless for speaking to you.'

That wasn't quite an answer. And it was probably calculated to form a bond, and she definitely couldn't trust a single word that came from a Fox, but Lydia felt herself drawn toward him, nonetheless.

'I'm not on Whitechapel Road,' she said. 'It starts over there.'

'You're close, though. Just a few steps. You can stand on it, you know. You won't burst into flames.'

'I know that.'

'Come on, then. I dare you.'

She hesitated.

'Not so brave, then.'

'You dare me? How old are you?'

'Thought as much,' Paul said. 'I had heard the Crows had gone soft.'

Lydia felt a thrill of excitement. She was a Crow. She also felt irritated. 'You think that's going to work? Call me names and I'll do what you want?' She shook her head in mock disappointment. 'And I thought the Fox Family were supposed to be clever.'

He flashed a white smile that she felt all the way down to her toes. 'Drink then? We can stay on neutral territory. I know a place.' He turned his head to indicate a side road. His profile was as ridiculously attractive as the front view, and Lydia's mouth had gone dry with a longing she had never felt before. Bloody Fox magic. All the stories were true, and she wasn't even sorry. He was intoxicating.

'You been down Gunthorpe Street?'

'No idea. Why?'

'It used to be called George Yard. Martha Tabram was killed here by Jack the Ripper. We know she was one of his, even though she doesn't get counted in the history books.'

Well, that was good for dousing her lustful feelings. 'Going to visit the site of a murdered woman is not the pull you think it is.'

'I thought you were looking for a walk on the wild side?'

'Dead women aren't the wild side,' Lydia said flatly. That was the problem with boys. Men, whatever. They always disappointed you.

'I agree, as it happens,' the Fox said. 'But the street is part of our history. It's important to learn from the past. That's all I think.'

The drag of disappointment was battling with her hormones. Added to that was the self-destructive mode she couldn't seem to shake. And the fact that she was excited to be in the city, away from the suburbs. It felt like truly living.

Paul Fox tilted his head. 'So, Little Bird. You coming for a drink then?'

Against all her better judgement and her trusty gut instincts, Lydia followed him.

CHAPTER SEVEN

Walking on a deserted back street, narrow and cobbled with windowless buildings in old London brick, felt like the worst idea Lydia had ever had. Her gut wasn't screaming danger, though. It was probably clouded by her awareness of the man loping alongside her. If sex had been anything other than a quick disappointment, Lydia would have said he was pure sex. If he had been anything other than a Fox, she would have said he was a dodgy geezer. If she had been able to think straight, she would have got the tube at Aldgate as planned.

'Here we go,' Paul said. He pushed open a wooden door that led into a small pub garden. More a yard than anything worthy of the name, with scuffed wooden barrels as tables and a metal bucket overflowing with cigarette butts. It smelled of old beer and pot. A couple with matching pale blonde dreadlocks were sitting at one of the tables, their heads bent close together.

They looked up as Lydia and Paul passed and she

realised they were identical twins. Wearing contact lenses, no doubt, to give them that unusually bright-blue eye colour.

The pub was a typical London boozer, half-filled with drinkers of all ages. There was no reason for Lydia to feel a gut punch of fear. She looked around, trying to locate the danger. The back of her throat felt clogged and she couldn't breathe. She was choking on earth. Could smell greenery. Sharp sap and rotting leaves. The sensation of thick fur was back, sliding over her skin. Muscles under red fur, surrounding her. Her vision was black at the edges and she felt herself tip.

'Steady there, Little Bird.' Paul's voice seemed to be coming from far away. She squeezed her coin and closed her eyes, willing her balance to return. When she opened her eyes, Paul Fox was filling her vision. 'How much have you drunk?'

'Whisky.' Lydia's mouth was filled with saliva and she swallowed hard. She was *not* going to throw up in front of Paul Fox.

'What?'

'I'll have a whisky. Single malt, but I don't care which one.'

A beat. 'Right.'

He steered her to a table and she slid into the seat with her back to the wall. Her senses were still screaming danger, but she had got the other impressions under control. Again. Maybe this was why her dad had told her to stay away from the other Families. Maybe he knew she would react like this. Or was it something that all Crows experienced? Butting up against the walls of her ignorance was a familiar frustration. Now it switched to anger. How was keeping her in the dark keeping her safe? What was her dad thinking?

He wouldn't be thrilled to see her in a bar with Paul Fox, that was for sure. Something that gave her a frisson of excitement. And something else. Triumph? She watched Paul at the bar. He looked relaxed. Confident. She couldn't help but find it attractive. Was it what happened when you were brought up as part of your Family? Or was it just the difference between being an insanely hot man and a slightly awkward girl? He had to be around her age. Maybe a year or two older, but still. He shouldn't be so unbelievably assured. It wasn't fair.

Watching him chat to the barman, her gaze fell on a wooden sign hung on the back wall. The White Hart. With a stylised painting of a white deer rearing up on its hind legs.

The White Hart was on Whitechapel High Street. She knew this because she had double-checked her landmarks before going out near to Fox territory. She thought back to the route. It had been deliberately twisty, and Paul had taken her via the back roads, talking shit about showing her historical landmarks, when all he had wanted to do was to confuse her sense of direction and then bring her into Whitechapel. No wonder her senses were going haywire. No wonder she felt surrounded by Foxes. *Hell Hawk.*

He had brought her in through the back of the pub deliberately. Why? What was his game? Just a show of power? Or was this an elaborate ambush? Was his Family on their way? Cold fear ran through her body.

Paul was turning back already. He had two tumblers of amber liquid, and was looking at her with a lop-sided smile that promised good times. It was a lying smile.

She forced her shaking muscles to obey and got to her feet. Front or back? If she went out the back, she could get lost in Fox territory. Out the front led to the high street. She consulted her mental map of the area. As long as she turned right, she would be out of Whitechapel in minutes. Seconds if she flew.

She wasn't going to run. Prey ran. She forced her shoulders to relax, looked around as if she was looking for a sign. Paul was at the table, he raised his eyebrows in a question.

'Toilet?'

He put down the glasses. Pointed to the back of the pub, near where they had entered.

'Back in a sec.' Lydia was grateful that she hadn't taken off her leather jacket yet. And that she didn't carry a handbag. Taking her bag would have looked suspicious. She made her way to the toilet. She glanced over her shoulder and saw that a man had stopped at the table and was leaning down to speak to Paul.

Could she get past them without being seen? Or should she go out the back and brave the back streets?

A split second later, she had made her decision. If she had learned anything from Paul's little history lesson, it was that back streets in Whitechapel spelled dead. She wasn't going to be a modern-day Ripper vic. She wasn't going to compound her poor choices with a worse decision. She spun on her heel and walked quickly to the front of the pub, pushing through the door without a backward glance. On the high street, she turned right immediately and, despite her vow to herself, broke into a full sprint. She passed a building under construction and a sports shop, a Burger King and the entrance to the Aldgate East station, she dodged into the road to get around a group of people congregated around a bus stop, and again when there were bins blocking the pavement. Her feet were flying over the concrete and her breath was getting tighter, a stitch starting to threaten under her ribs, but she kept running until she felt herself cross the Whitechapel boundary.

Aldgate Station was on her right and the trees of Aldgate Square up ahead. Still feeling as if a pack of Foxes were on her tail, she veered into the station and took the stairs at speed. Flinging herself onto the train just before the doors locked, she finally allowed herself to look behind as the train pulled away. Paul Fox was standing on the platform, looking straight at her. He didn't even look out of breath.

It was only a couple of weeks before Paul Fox showed up again in Lydia's life. Things had been smoothed over at home, but Lydia was still restless. The arguments about what she was going to do with her life had died down, but she knew they weren't over. Her dad was biding his time.

'I've got nothing to say to you, Fox.'

'I think we got off on the wrong foot.'

'You tricked me.'

Paul spread his hands. 'I'm a Fox. Can't say you weren't warned.'

'And I'm a Crow. Which means I'm not stupid enough to talk to you again.'

'Come on, Little Bird. Where's your sense of adventure?'

He wasn't going to goad her. She was in control. Just because he made her insides go funny was no reason to lose her mind. She was better than that. Stronger than that.

'Live a little.' Paul's voice was low and inviting.

'I intend to live a lot. And that means staying away from you.'

He frowned then. 'I'm not going to hurt you.'

'So what was The White Hart?'

He glanced away, thinking for a beat. Then he looked her straight in the eyes. 'A bet.'

'What?'

'I bet my brothers that I could get a Crow into Whitechapel.'

'Right,' Lydia said flatly. 'Well done. Hope you won something decent.'

Paul dug into his pocket and produced a thick roll of banknotes. 'Want to help me spend it?'

'No,' Lydia said. She took a step back.

'Dinner. My treat. Anywhere you like.'

'I'm not going anywhere with you.'

'The bet was an excuse, really,' he said, looking almost contrite, but not, Lydia noticed, actually apologising. 'I approached you because I like you. I want to get to know you. See where things go. But I'd made the bet ages ago. It was still in place, and I thought I may as well kill two birds with one stone.' He stopped. 'Poor choice of words. I meant...'

Lydia's arms were crossed, her coin tight in her hand. 'And you thought that if you pretend to be all open and tell me about the bet that I'll be disarmed by your honesty. I'll think, "why would he tell me something he knows will piss me off?" He must be on the level.' Lydia fixed him with a look she had been practising in the mirror. One she had seen her terrifying Uncle Charlie use. 'How stupid do you think I am?'

London, Now

When he arrived home from work that night, Fleet was wired. 'I was worried they would find a way to take me off it now there has been a second body and there is attention online, but I was hauled in for a chat with the guv and she said she was pleased with the progress so far.'

'That's good.' Lydia grabbed two beers from the fridge and opened them, passing one to Fleet. 'Have you eaten?'

'It might be,' Fleet continued. 'But the emphasis was on the "so far".'

'Sounds standard,' Lydia said, trying to be reassuring. 'She's always been light on the praise.'

'Maybe. I felt like it was a reminder that I'm on probation.'

'Not officially, so they can't—'

'Not officially is worse,' Fleet interrupted. 'Officially, there are procedures. You need evidence and to give clear markers and performance indicators. Unofficial is just people looking at me funny and my boss sounding like I'm doing surprisingly well for a nutter, but that she isn't taking any chances.' Fleet took a long swig from his beer.

'I'm sorry. That sucks.' Fleet had been the golden boy at work, been promoted to DCI in record time. His work had been his life for many years, the place he felt most at home. Now all that had changed and Lydia knew it had started when he had met her.

He must have caught something in her expression, because he crossed the kitchen in a couple of strides and wrapped her in a hug. 'It's not your fault.'

Lydia pressed her face into his chest and inhaled the good Fleet smell. The burst of sunshine that came with his presence was no longer jarring. For a little while after his father had taken her power and left her for dead, she had found it difficult. It had reminded her of a very bad moment of total helplessness, when she had truly thought she had been going to die. Maybe a tiny, irrational part of her had felt angry at Fleet, too. For the nature he couldn't help. But now it was just Fleet again. That meant safety. 'I'm still sorry,' she said into his chest. If he hadn't met her, maybe his innate power would never have manifested. He wouldn't have seen visions, wouldn't have been driven half-crazy by them.

He squeezed her tighter for a moment before moving away. 'I need to eat,' he said, half-apologetically. 'Didn't stop today.'

Lydia leant on the counter and watched him select a container of chilli from the fridge and whack it into the microwave.

'So, they are linked? Your murders?'

'Looks that way.'

'Don't keep me in suspense.'

He pulled a face. 'You know it's not a prestigious case. Craig Johnstone?'

'Not pretty either,' Lydia said. Fleet had described how Johnstone had died, stabbed multiple times and his throat cut.

'Yeah. He was found in the stairwell of a small block of flats. I can show you the scene, if you want?'

Now he was talking. Lydia missed working with Fleet more than she cared to admit. She held her hands out for his iPad. 'Gimme.'

The photo showed a stocky white man. He was splayed on the ground, head resting on the bottom step of a flight of stairs. His arms and legs outstretched like he was in the middle of making a snow angel from the detritus blowing around the landing, and his front was a mess of blood. His head was thrown back, showing the deep gash across his neck.

'It seems as if he was easily overpowered,' Fleet said. 'So we are looking at a physically larger or stronger man.'

Lydia estimated Johnstone was average height, but with the dimensions and flexibility of a fridge. In his younger days he had probably been light on his feet, most East End wide boys were, and she didn't imagine he was one of the big thinkers. If you couldn't think fast, you had better be able to sprint. 'Hard to defend against a knife, though. Especially if he was caught by surprise. Do you have the weapon?'

'Not yet. Postmortem confirmed a blade, approximately six inches in length, but we haven't picked it up.'

She handed the screen back to Fleet. 'So. The link? Did they move in the same circles? Him and Price? Have a handy mutual enemy?'

Fleet smiled at her. 'Nothing's jumping out.'

'Shame.'

Fleet took a swig from his beer before continuing. 'Johnstone was a nasty piece of work and successful in his own way, but Price was on another level. Known to have connections to human trafficking. Convicted back in the nineties and served time for it.'

Lydia was quiet for a moment. 'Reformed character?'

Fleet pulled a wry face. 'Unlikely. He's not been convicted since, but he is known to us.'

The phrasing covered a lot.

Lydia tilted her head. 'Bit of a coincidence, them both working in sex trade. Is that the only link?'

'The stabbing pattern is the same. Frenzied attacks with multiple wounds. Twenty on Craig, thirty-nine on Price. Price's was even more of a mess than Johnstone's.'

'Like Martha Tabram.'

'What?'

'One of the Ripper's suspected victims. She was stabbed thirty-nine times.'

'Is that a fact?'

'Sorry. I don't know why I said that—'

'It's okay.' Fleet smiled, but Lydia had seen the

frown that had crossed his face first. As happened so often these days, she felt out of step with him. That they were misunderstanding each other. What had felt easy and safe was now spiky and filled with traps. She tried another tack. 'Frenzied attacks are usually either panicked or motivated by anger.'

'Or eroticism. Emotion for sure, though. Neither of these were clean kills.'

'So it's personal?'

Fleet shrugged. 'I'm not going to read too much into it. Need to keep an open mind at this stage.'

'I wasn't suggesting the Ripper had come back from the dead.' Suddenly, it felt important for Lydia to clarify that.

'I know,' Fleet said. He smiled, but it didn't quite reach his eyes. 'It's just weird you mentioned it. Gunthorpe Street used to be George—'

'Yard.' Lydia broke in. 'I know. It's where Martha Tabram was killed.'

He frowned. 'I didn't know that until one of the team mentioned it today. Apparently, there's a walking tour that visits all the murder sites.'

'And Raymond Price was killed in Whitechapel too?'

'Side road near Durward Street. He had been for a curry and was walking back to his car when he was attacked.'

'You said he was stabbed, right? Are we talking a knife? Same as Johnstone?'

'Broken bottle,' Fleet said. 'Left at the scene and

drenched in blood, but we don't have any prints. Killer must have been wearing gloves.'

'CCTV?'

Fleet shook his head. 'We have him leaving the restaurant, but there isn't coverage in the side street. Whoever jumped him must have got really close before he was worried. There's no sign of him running. And he wouldn't have had to go far to get picked up on CCTV again.'

'Someone he knew, maybe?'

'It's a definite start.' Fleet was digging into his chilli like a starving man. He chewed and swallowed before adding: 'But it's early days. And we don't have evidence that Johnstone and Price knew each other. Or that they both knew someone in common.'

'The killer.'

'Exactly.'

'You think it's the same guy?'

'I hope so. One deadbeat murder is a case, two by the same murderer is a pattern. And if there's a pattern, it increases our chances of finding him.'

'A serial killer.' Lydia smiled at him. 'You're going to end up on a podcast.'

'I'd better bloody not.'

CHAPTER EIGHT

The following week passed by in a now-familiar blur of meetings and physical training. Lydia saw Fleet briefly, either late at night or early in the morning and, for a few days, not at all. He had been crashing at his flat with increasing regularity as he didn't want to disturb her or because it was closer to work or easier to park. A selection of reasons that were perfectly logical. Besides, as Lydia got dressed and walked down the thickly carpeted stairs to the shiny kitchen-diner, she didn't blame Fleet for not being entirely comfortable at Charlie's house. She wasn't.

Jason was in the kitchen. He had made her a mug of coffee and was whisking pancake batter. 'You need to eat,' he said, anticipating the words that had been about to fly from her mouth.

'I really don't have time,' Lydia said. She had been hoping to look into Jez McAllister's death all week, but Aiden had kept her schedule full. There were a couple of hours before she was expecting him today, and she was determined to make some progress. If she could even remember how to investigate, it felt as if it had been so long.

Jason ignored this and turned the burner on underneath a frying pan.

Knowing it was pointless to resist and realising that she actually was hungry, Lydia sat at the breakfast bar. The glass doors to the garden revealed a drizzly morning. A line of jackdaws stood sentry just outside and four crows were sitting on a telephone wire. However ambivalent Lydia felt about taking over Charlie's place as head of the Family, she found the sight comforting. Just as the birds had come to help her during the violent meeting of the four Families, they hadn't abandoned her now.

'There's something I wanted to talk to you about.' Jason flipped the first pancake with an expert flick of his wrist.

Lydia was enjoying the strong coffee and hoping it would help her work out where to start. She should interview Jez's girlfriend, Jade. See if she knew anything about the cash. Speak to people who worked with him, find out if there was any tension at the betting shop. Her instinct told her that the death had nothing to do with Fleet's two stabbing victims, the style of attack was too different, but the puzzle of it itched at her mind. She wanted to be certain that she wasn't withholding something vital from his case.

'I've met a girl.' Jason put a plate in front of Lydia and a bottle of syrup.

Lydia focused on Jason. 'Romantic-styles?'

'No!' His face was comically horrified. 'Not like that! Another echo.'

'Here?' Lydia looked around the bright kitchen. It was sleek and modern and very shiny, but the building underneath was old. Victorian? Georgian? Lydia didn't really know her architecture well enough to say.

'Sometimes,' Jason said. 'Not the kitchen, but in the garden. She does this,' he mimed carrying something and tipping it out. 'Like she's emptying a basin of water or maybe veg scraps onto a compost heap.'

'Can she speak?'

'She's starting to. She talks about her work mostly.'

Lydia doused her pancakes in syrup and began eating.

'I think she was a maid,' Jason was saying. 'I've been looking at historical clothing online and I reckon she's from the late 1800s. I thought if I could remind her who she was, is, it might help.'

She swallowed a mouthful. 'I thought you said echoes just repeated a single pattern? They aren't sentient, are they? Not like you.'

'That's the thing, I don't think she's just an echo anymore. I've been chatting to her every day and this morning she stopped what she was doing entirely. And she remembered our previous conversation. It shows she can learn new things.'

'That's good,' Lydia said weakly. She knew that Jason wanted to help the ghosts he met and she could understand that. But she didn't want him to get hurt when it turned out this ghost was another echo. Stuck in a place she had never chosen and doomed to repeat the

69

same old actions over and over again. Not really here at all.

Lydia felt unsettled and unfocused. She went for a run to burn off some energy, aware that she had been sitting still in too many meetings. It didn't suit her. She would get to Jez's death once she had run off this antsy feeling.

There was no sign of Jason when she got back to the house. Or the ghostly maid he was worrying about. She made a post-run snack and tried to push aside the feeling that she was using somebody else's kitchen. That she was an interloper.

The first few months in Charlie's house had been rough. Lydia had moved furniture, donated boxes of stuff to charity, and considered getting the whole place redecorated. But that involved hassle and decisions, so she had shoved it down the list, and told herself she would get used to the house. That she would stop expecting to see Charlie sitting at the breakfast bar or on the sofa. That it would feel like her home eventually. She just had to be patient.

Patience had never been her strong suit, but she was lucky enough to be distracted constantly. There were the day-to-day demands of being the head of the Family. The business details, of course, and the Family stuff that seemed to involve her meeting and greeting relatives and their families, mediating spats, and fielding endless requests for favours.

The undercurrent to this new life was a constant

hum of anxiety. Her tattoos were at least trying to move again and Jason was getting more corporeal day by day, which suggested her powers were returning. The River Man had drained her, but she was a battery and it seemed she was able to recharge herself as well as others. But progress was incremental and she felt vulnerable. If the River Man had been able to drain her like that, could other people? She had dystopian nightmares of being locked in a tiny white cell, wires attached to her as some unseen machinery drained her power like a knock-off Matrix movie.

Fleet had tried to talk to her about it. Back in the early months, when they were still spending enough time together to have deep conversations, but she hadn't been able to articulate it to him. Not then.

People weren't their parents. Feathers-knew she knew that. But Fleet's father had looked into her eyes with all the compassion of a butcher viewing a slab of meat. He had reached into her and taken her power, draining her energy and leaving her for dead. And Fleet's closed-in demeanour over the subsequent months had widened the gap between them.

It didn't help that people wanted her to demonstrate her powers. The rumours had spread around the Family about her defeating Charlie after he had killed Daisy and John, and the methods she had used becoming more and more fantastical. Of course, now that the River Man had drained her, she wasn't in a position to put on a show for every curious Family member. Worse was the bubbling hope that was infusing the Family. The Crows had always been the strongest of the Families but, along with the other three, their powers had dwindled down the generations to a handful of parlour tricks.

Now, there was real excitement that the glory days were returning. Aiden summed it up. 'They think that you will be able to train us all. Power us up so that we can fight anyone.'

'What do they want to do?'

'They are saying you called the crows and they came to help. That you control people with your mind. That you can create a thousand coins and fling them like bullets. That you can fly.'

'I can't fly,' Lydia said. 'That's silly.'

Aiden shrugged, not quite hiding his disappointment.

'Who do we need to fight? I fixed the truce. We're safe.'

Aiden gave her a look that made him look far older. 'We're never safe.'

SHE HAD JUST FINISHED HER POST-RUN SANDWICH when Aiden breezed into the house.

'Boss.' He touched his forehead in greeting. Lydia was never sure if he was sincere or taking the piss, but she didn't really mind either way. Aiden had proved his loyalty to her, and that was all that mattered.

'You're early,' she said, trying not to sound accusatory. She knew he worked too hard as it was and didn't want him shouldering any more than he already did.

'There's some documents from the accountant.' He

got a sheaf of papers and put them onto the kitchen table. 'There are sticky notes and crosses where you need to sign.'

Her phone buzzed with a message from Fleet. They had talked about going to the pub for dinner, but he was cancelling. Overtime had been authorised for his case, which she knew he would be pleased about. He needed time to make progress.

After the paperwork was dealt with, Lydia raised something that had been bothering her. 'I've been talking to you about cleaning up the business. Going legit. Maybe we should have called the police when Jez died? I mean, it wasn't us...'

Aiden gave her a quick look, assessing if she was joking. When he saw that she was serious, his expression turned to confusion. 'We don't call the cops.'

Lydia had no desire to remind Aiden that she had grown up outside of the Family business, but she had nobody else to ask. And she needed to know. 'Talk me through it. Like I'm an idiot.'

Aiden licked his lips, his gaze darting to her tattoos. 'Well. We don't like attention on the gambling side of things. Or on any of our things, to be fair.'

'But the betting shops are legit.'

'Yeah. They've got the permits and all that. The licensing board don't usually get involved, but if there was a murder on the premises, they might revoke the licence for that location. And the council give us permits for the businesses and they would definitely get antsy about a murder. There was that club in Brixton that got closed by the council after there was a shoot-out.'

73

'Jez wasn't killed at the shop. And it wasn't a shoot-out, nobody else was in danger.'

'We don't know where he was killed. His girlfriend found him in his bed, but he might have been moved.'

Lydia nodded, acknowledging the point.

Aiden was still talking. 'We don't know what the police are going to find if they start poking around, so it's best not to invite them through the door.'

'Why aren't we looking, though? It looks bad if someone working for us gets offed.' Charlie had always talked about protecting the community. He said that the Crows had to maintain their fearsome reputation to act as a deterrent. That way, the Family and people who worked for them and even the general population of Camberwell, would sleep safe in their beds. He sold it as a public service. Made it sound like he deserved a bloody medal.

Aiden shrugged. 'He wasn't that important. And nobody seems too upset.'

Well, that was bleak. Unless. 'Isn't that suspicious?'

Aiden pulled a face. 'I've met plenty of geezers you wouldn't piss on if they were on fire.'

'Right.' Lydia was about to tell Aiden he needed a new social circle when she remembered that they shared that circle. And that she was his boss. Her head was pounding again. 'I want you to ask around. Check Jade's story. And I want to know where Jez got that cash.'

'Why? We've got it now.'

'What if someone comes looking for it?'

Aiden shrugged. 'I say we punch that bridge when it comes looking. Boss,' he had that pained expression, the one that meant he was going to say something she didn't want to hear.

'What?' She tried not to snap, but knew she had failed.

'You've got meet-and-greets this afternoon.'

'When?'

'Half an hour ago.'

Lydia popped a couple of paracetamol out of the blister pack and swallowed them dry. She wanted a whisky, but resisted. Now that she felt stronger again, she assumed her alcohol tolerance would be back to its superhuman levels, but she hadn't had time to test it. That was a lie. She hadn't wanted to test it. To find out that it was another thing that she had lost.

'Boss?' Aiden had put on his jacket and was holding the door open for her. She had no choice but to walk through.

CHAPTER NINE

London, Then

Lydia ended up going for a drink with Paul Fox after all. She had refused a meal, that was too much commitment, but he had sent a brand-new mobile phone to her house and then worn her down with funny, flirty text messages. In truth, it hadn't taken that many. Lydia was nineteen years old and in the market for some fun. She didn't trust Paul Fox, but he was beyond smoking hot and, also, forbidden fruit. With hindsight, she was proud of herself for resisting him for even one single second.

The pub was a few streets away from Borough Market. On Lydia's side of the river and safely distant from Whitechapel, but still nowhere close to Camberwell. Neutral territory.

Paul was waiting for her outside, and her heart rate kicked up at the sight of him. He wasn't staring at his phone, like ninety-nine per cent of the population, but was looking around. Alert to his surroundings. It was sexy. But then everything about him was sexy. It was a problem.

Lydia had promised to stay for one drink. By her third, he had her laughing so hard she was in danger of snorting whisky out of her nose.

Outside the pub, he had taken her hand for the walk to the tube station. Just as Lydia was wondering whether he would try to kiss her or whether she would hear from him again, he had asked if she was free on the Saturday. 'We could do this again,' he gestured behind him in the direction of the pub, 'or something else.'

'I'm free,' she said and, putting her hands onto his shoulders to pull him closer, kissed him.

Kissing Paul Fox had been a rush. A heady, terrifying, intoxicating rush. Every sense was heightened, every nerve ending alive, and Lydia wanted more of it. Before long, they were an item. Lydia still refused to go near Whitechapel and neither of them could afford a hotel, so it kept their activity to the things that could be reasonably accomplished in public. Pubs, parks, the cinema, they desecrated them all.

'You could come back to my place?' Paul said, not for the first time. His hands were gripping her hips and she could feel him pressed against her body, short-circuiting her brain. Her resolve was weakening. What difference did it make? She was seeing Paul. Feathers help her, but she liked him. Trusted him. Wasn't it a prejudice against the Fox Family to assume it would be dangerous to go into Whitechapel? And there was a truce with the Families. She had grown up with the stories, she knew that back in the day the Families had agreed to peace. Lydia knew that the peace was based on them all leaving each other alone and respecting the boundaries of their territories, but still. That was ancient history. And she really wanted to be alone with Paul Fox. In a bedroom.

'Maybe,' Lydia said. 'Who will be there?'

Paul's face registered momentary surprise, followed quickly by excitement. It was a little bit adorable and Lydia felt the power of being wanted, desired. It was almost as intoxicating as her lust for him.

'No one.'

'You have your own place?' Lydia had assumed that Paul lived with his parents, same as her. He was twenty-one, and this was London.

'There's a place I can use, it'll be private.'

'That sounds dodgy.'

'We have a few boltholes. For Family use, when cousins come into town, that kind of thing.' He flashed her a quick smile. 'There are a lot of us.'

'Where do you live? I'm not asking to visit, or anything, just curious.'

'With my siblings.'

'What about your parents?'

'My father is currently with his mistress.'

'Oh.'

'Yeah. Don't feel bad for my mum, though. She's shacked up with two fellas. Having a grand old time, apparently.'

'I'm sorry.'

'Why?' Paul gave her a piercing stare. 'They are

adults. And we are carnal creatures. Anyone who says otherwise is lying.'

'Some people aren't that interested in the physical.' Lydia didn't know why she was arguing. With Paul's full attention on her and the word 'carnal' hanging in the air, most of her brain activity had halted. She was alive with sensation, with the desire to find out what it would be like to have his hands on her body.

Paul shook his head. A small smile tugged at the corner of his mouth and his eyes were dark with promise. 'Liars.'

London, Now

THE BETTING SHOP WAS ON A COMMERCIAL STREET near Burgess Park. It didn't take long to walk there, but it was a long way from Denmark Hill. The shop was between a tanning salon and a pawnbroker. There were sprayed tags on the walls and on the closed metal shutters on what had once been the 'FOMO Nail Salon'.

Aiden had told Lydia that the assistant manager had taken over and that the business was running as smoothly as it ever had. Jade had been paid off and Jez didn't have any family to come looking. Nobody local was asking questions. People knew better than that, and Jez hadn't apparently inspired much loyalty of his own. In short, Lydia didn't need to be here. And she had many other things she ought to be doing.

But it niggled at her. Somebody had disliked Jez McAllister enough to stab him to death. A messy, up-close kind of killing. And in his own home. He had let his killer into his home, possibly even gone into the bedroom with them, assuming he had been killed where he had been found.

If he had been skimming, it had gone under the radar. One of the Family accountants had checked the books for the gambling shop and not found anything significant. Which meant he had a mystery bag of money. That the killer hadn't looked for. Even a cursory search would have revealed it.

She pulled out her phone and called Aiden. 'How is Jade?'

'All sorted,' Aiden said after a beat. He was probably wondering why she was asking. Jez McAllister was old news and there were new fires to put out.

'Was it easy?'

'Easy?'

'I mean, the man she lived with, was in love with... she must have been upset.'

'Yeah. Sure. But she knew the score. Knew he worked for us.'

'Right. Okay.' Lydia pocketed her phone and stared into space for a moment. Across the road there was a Caribbean takeaway and a large scruffy shop with multiple signs promising 'food, wine, DIY, locks, electrical'. Nobody would be giving this part of Camberwell a prize for good looks, but it was part of her territory. She felt that deep in her bones. Even with her power nowhere near what it was, that was something that hadn't altered.

She pushed into the betting shop, somehow still

expecting the fug of cigarette smoke, even though it had been banned in 2007. There was a bank of gaming machines showing blackjack, roulette, and poker. A heavily built white man in a high-vis jacket was mechanically stabbing buttons on a fruit machine in the corner. There were a couple more men staring at the horse racing on a television screen bolted high up on the wall, next to a poster advertising Sky Sports.

The young guy behind the desk was scrolling on his phone, but he looked up and greeted her politely when she approached. His gaze flicked over her as if surprised and Lydia wondered whether it was because he recognised her, or that she didn't fit the profile for his usual clientele.

'Is the manager in?'

His face closed. 'Is there a problem?'

'Not yet,' Lydia said pleasantly.

'He's not here,' the guy said.

'Acting manager, then?'

'That's Yvonne. She's at lunch.'

It was almost three o'clock.

He must have sensed her scepticism because he added, 'We always take it late. Busy here at lunchtime.'

Lydia looked around at the almost-empty shop. 'I should hope so.' When she looked back, the guy's expression was nervous.

'I can take a message?' He didn't sound sure.

'How long have you worked here?'

'Eight months.'

'What's Jez like? As a boss?'

Now he was definitely nervous. 'Great. Fine. You

know…' He waved his hands. 'I don't have much to do with him.'

Lydia knew it wasn't kind, but she didn't stop herself. 'Are you expecting him back in tomorrow?'

The nervous look increased. She wondered if he knew Jez was dead or whether he just knew something was wrong and that he had been told to keep his mouth shut. She decided to put him out of his misery.

'I'm Lydia Crow. Your boss's boss's boss.'

He swallowed. 'I'm sorry, I didn't know—'

'Now you do. Answer my question, please.'

A look of confusion. She could see the gears spinning, so she repeated herself. 'What was Jez like as a boss? On every detail or hands-off?'

'Hands-off, I think,' he said. 'Like I said, I didn't have much—'

'Okay. Did he gamble? Place bets here?'

A hard swallow. 'We're not supposed to do that.'

'It's all right, he's not going to get into any trouble. I'm just concerned. He's missing and I want to make sure he's okay. Did he lay bets? Play on the machines?'

The man was already shaking his head, but Lydia's senses were tingling. She could feel the ink of her tattoos stinging, trying to move. 'Did he get you to place bets for him?'

Another hard swallow. A head twitch that wasn't a shake.

Lydia took pity on the man before he started crying. 'Here's an easy one. Did you like him?' It didn't matter that she couldn't produce her coin, the man was sweating and not in any state to lie to her.

He swallowed, his eyes wide, but his head was already shaking the answer. 'No.'

LYDIA WALKED HOME USING A MEANDERING ROUTE. She knew she was putting off getting back to Charlie's house and that this was something she would have to address at some point. But she didn't know how, so she walked the streets on autopilot, loud music blasting through her headphones and hoped it would magically destress her enough so that she didn't snap at Aiden later.

She discovered she was near The Fork before she had time to change direction. She avoided walking past it, usually, and this was exactly what she got for zoning out.

There was the gap in the street where the building ought to be, the hoarding still up. She could rebuild it. The Crows had the funds and she could delegate the project management, but something was stopping her. She didn't know what. Maybe the stubborn part of her felt like rebuilding would be admitting she cared about the place? It was a sobering thought. Was she regressing to her younger self? The one that would have preferred to cut off her own arm than admit she needed it?

There were sensible reasons not to rebuild, of course. She had a place to live and work and there was no need to spend time and money on the cafe. There were more important things. If she was going to funnel cash into some urban regeneration, some affordable housing or a new shelter or a GP surgery would better benefit the community.

Which led to feelings of inadequacy. She wanted to be a better leader than Charlie. She didn't want to be selfish. She wanted the Crow Family to truly be a positive force in Camberwell, but every single thing was more complicated than it first appeared. And everything cost so much money, she could see it flowing out of the account. There were bureaucrats and politicians, business-owners and residents, activists and anarchists, do-gooders and hate-mongers. And all of them had an opinion and most of them needed incentives. Greasing the wheels was expensive when there were so many damn wheels. Her head hurt thinking about it.

Which was why she forgot to avoid the street and found herself walking past the graffitied boards that deterred folk from climbing around the site of The Fork. The rubble had been cleared. The old London bricks, the ones that had stayed intact at any rate, had been worth a packet and there had been plenty of other salvage.

The sight was a punch. It was just wrong. The gap in the line of buildings, the end of a sentence that ought to be punctuated but was just hanging... It was an itch she couldn't scratch, a thought she couldn't complete. She wanted to stretch her wings out, but they felt pinned to her sides. The feathers all stuck together.

There was a flicker of movement, something peeling away from the hoarding. What might have been a monstrous spirit was instead a familiar figure, shimmering and translucent, but unmistakable in his baggy eighties suit, the sleeves pushed up to his elbows. Jason.

'How—?'

'I was going to tell you.' His face was hard to see, his form was vibrating and Lydia could see the hoarding strobing through his body, but she could sense his anxiety.

'You can leave the house,' Lydia said slowly. 'You can leave Denmark Hill.'

'Not just to here,' Jason said, his words rushing now. 'I've been all over Camberwell. I went to Brixton yesterday.'

Lydia waited for a man to pass by. He didn't give her a strange look. A woman talking to thin air on a London street wasn't all that noteworthy. Besides, this was Camberwell and there was a fair chance he knew exactly who she was and wasn't going to risk giving offence. She focused on Jason. 'What's in Brixton?'

'I just wanted to see if I could. I was going to try getting to the river today.' he glanced at the gap where The Fork ought to be. 'I come here most, though.'

Lydia reached into her pocket automatically. She could understand that. 'Why didn't you tell me?'

He shoved at his sleeves, not meeting her eye. 'I don't know.'

'I've been busy,' Lydia said, wishing she could squeeze her coin for comfort.

'There's that,' Jason agreed. He was looking more solid, and Lydia wondered if it was because she was nearby. She knew she used to power him up and was hoping this meant she still did, that her power was truly returning. Slowly. 'What else?'

'I didn't think you would like something else changing.'

It took Lydia a moment to work out what he meant. 'You're worried about me?'

Jason shrugged, his outline still vibrating. 'You're sad. And tired.'

Lydia knew he was right, but it stung. She prided herself on her strong exterior. And it could be dangerous if people sensed weakness. If people could see through her façade, then what might she give away? 'I'm fine,' she said. 'I have to be fine.'

'Don't worry,' Jason said, looking away. 'I don't think Aiden has noticed.'

CHAPTER TEN

Lydia didn't sleep in Charlie's bedroom. It was huge, by London standards, had an ensuite, and was tastefully decorated in neutral shades. It wasn't his room anymore, she had told herself that a million times, but it didn't make any difference. She just couldn't do it. Luckily, the house had a second bedroom with a comfortable king-size bed, and the main bathroom was next door.

Jason said he didn't mind taking Charlie's room, but Lydia had to wonder if he was being honest. Charlie had murdered him. And killed his wife. That had been an accident, but still. She had yet to see him inside the room but, since he didn't actually need to sleep, it was hard to accuse him of avoiding it. And she didn't know whether to open that can of worms or not, anyway. She had saved his undead life by bringing him to Charlie's when The Fork burned down, and she still remembered the rush of sheer relief she had felt when it had worked. When she had seen his thin and shimmering shape and heard his voice. But she didn't know how he truly felt about it. It was possible she had done something monumentally selfish. Maybe he would have been happier to fade away. Or maybe he would have been trapped in a hellish limbo. She didn't know, and that tortured her.

Lydia had been trying to work, but her arms were cold and it was distracting. She went upstairs to grab a hoodie and was alarmed to find Fleet asleep in the king-size. It wasn't like him to be in bed during the day, and she wondered if he was ill. Or having uncontrollable visions again.

'I'm fine. Needed a power nap,' Fleet said, a touch defensively.

He was fully under the covers and the curtains were shut. The room smelled of sleep and Fleet. She sat on the bed. 'How are you doing?'

He sat up, stretching his arms and giving Lydia a very enjoyable view of his shoulders and chest. 'I thought we agreed you were going to stop asking me that.' He gave her a lop-sided smile.

In the early days after the River Man had left London, Lydia had watched Fleet like a hawk, alert for signs of distress. And if he thought he could shut down a conversation that easily, he had forgotten who he was dealing with. Lydia regarded him for a moment, giving him a chance to answer, then she prodded. 'Visions? Hallucinations?'

He shook his head tightly. 'Nada. All good up here.' He tapped his temple.

'What is it then?'

'Just catching up. I've got to go back in a bit and it will be another late one.'

'Okay.' Lydia couldn't shake the feeling there was something else.

'A podcast has picked up on the locations of the Johnstone and Price murders. It's gathering some steam online.' He reached over and hauled Lydia closer.

He had undressed for his power nap and she found herself pressed against naked Fleet. She tilted her face close to his. 'Hello.'

'Hello.' He kissed her and, for a moment, it made everything else in the world recede. Then he stopped and it all rushed back in. 'Because they're both Whitechapel?'

For a horrible moment, Lydia thought he meant that people were talking about murders being in Fox territory. That could bring repercussions if the Fox Family felt attacked or as if their reputation was being questioned.

'You were right,' he said, releasing his hold on her waist and leaning back. 'The multiple stab wounds and the locations. It's reminiscent of Jack the Ripper.'

Lydia felt bad for Fleet. Media attention was bad news for him, but if the world was taken with the Ripper story, it would keep the Fox Family out of the frame. She checked her phone. 'What was the name of the podcast?'

'It's a non-story,' Fleet insisted. 'Two deaths doesn't mean serial killer. It will be a mutual acquaintance, someone they both pissed off or owed money.' He rubbed a hand over his face. 'It'll fizzle out.'

. . .

THE MOOD WELL AND TRULY BROKEN, LYDIA LEFT
Fleet dressing and went downstairs. He followed not
long after, but before they could resume their conversation, his phone rang.

After pacing up and down and making monosyllabic
responses that told Lydia exactly nothing, Fleet ended
the call and turned to her. 'This can't go anywhere.'

'What?'

'Price's clothes were really cut up in the attack.'

He had been stabbed even more times than Johnstone and Lydia wasn't going to forget the state of that
corpse in a hurry. 'I can imagine.'

'There's a strip of his shirt missing,' Fleet said. 'It
took a bit of time to piece together his clothes and there's
a scrap not accounted for, three by ten centimetres.'

'Could it have blown away? Or landed on the
ground somewhere nearby?'

'Unlikely,' Fleet said. 'Scene of crime check the
surroundings, so unless someone thoroughly screwed
up...'

'It was taken?'

'Probably.' Fleet did not look happy. And Lydia
didn't blame him.

THAT EVENING, LYDIA SENT A MESSAGE TO EMMA,
and they had a quick back-and-forth. It was a window
into another world and a portal into the life she used to
have and, as always, it left her feeling unsettled. She did
what she always did with uncomfortable feelings and
covered them with carbohydrate and research. In the

past, she would have added a generous hit of whisky into the mix, but she stuck with a can of coke from the fridge.

She was just scanning the transcript of the podcast Fleet had mentioned, when Jason wandered into the kitchen.

'Mary's upstairs. It looks like she's cleaning the skirting boards.' He pushed the sleeves of his baggy grey suit jacket up his arms. 'I've told her she doesn't have to do it, but she says it's Thursday and she always cleans the woodwork on Thursday.'

'Is that new?'

'What do you mean?'

'Is it her echoing? Or is she really speaking to you?'

Jason smiled. 'Really speaking. I'm working on getting her to understand that she doesn't have to clean stuff, but she doesn't realise she's free.'

'Maybe she finds her old routine comforting?'

'Maybe. It was her work, though. She didn't have a choice when she was alive. It would be nice if she could suit herself now.'

Lydia imagined being stuck in Crow Family meetings for eternity, repeating the same interactions over and over. She would be insane within a decade, never mind over a hundred years.

'I'm going to find out what happened to her. With or without your help.'

The last bit was said a bit mulishly, and Lydia didn't blame him. She had been zero help. With Crow Family business and training to try to regain her strength, trying to adjust to living at Charlie's house and fending off queries from her parents, trying to keep things going with Fleet despite their incompatible jobs, as well as what felt like a hundred other small irritants, Lydia hadn't had the bandwidth for investigating an old-timey death.

'She needs peace,' he added. 'This isn't right.'

'I know.' Lydia put a hand onto Jason's cold arm and felt the strange buzzing sensation under her fingertips. He was pretty solid these days, and it was a constant relief. 'I'm sorry I've been distracted. I'm listening. What can I do to help?'

'You don't have to do anything. I know you're busy.'

'I want to help.' And she did, but she also wanted to help Fleet with his murder cases. If he solved them quickly, his guv wouldn't have a chance to move him off the team. And it would send a clear message to his work that he was back on form.

'I'm just happy to talk about it,' Jason was saying. 'I don't know what to do next. I've looked up the street at the right sort of time and read the papers, but there wasn't a murder reported. Not that fits.'

Lydia forced herself to focus on Jason's ghost. 'Was her death recorded? Parish records or whatever they used then?'

There was a tapping sound that was distracting Lydia. A crow was standing outside the bifold doors that led to the twilit garden, tapping on the glass with its beak.

'Hang on a sec.' Lydia patted Jason and walked to the door. The crow didn't move. She slid it open and stepped into a light drizzle. The kind of rain that wasn't falling, just sitting in the air ready to saturate your clothes by stealth. She looked at the crow. 'What?'

It cocked its head. Stared.

Lydia looked up at the back of the house. A line of crows were sitting on the apex of the roof, framed by the red sky.

The one on the ground croaked as if it was clearing its throat. And then it let out a sound like a car alarm chirping. Crows were excellent mimics, Lydia knew, but why this one was impersonating a car alarm was beyond her. As mysterious messages went, it wasn't helpful.

'Thank you,' she said. No harm in being polite. Especially when speaking to a corvid with a wickedly sharp beak. 'Anything else?'

The crow hopped away and watched her from its new position on the square of lawn. Lawn that needed cutting.

'Right-o.'

Back in the house, Jason was making a mug of hot chocolate. Lydia felt relief that he had forgiven her for not being more helpful with his cold case, but with a sense of foreboding. He made hot drinks when he was upset or worried.

'I'll ask Fleet. I don't know how far back the Met's records go, but he can do a search.'

'Would you?'

'Course.' Fleet wasn't going to be thrilled. He had explained to her that every search was logged and he had to be able to justify every single one if questioned, something to do with data protection, but she knew he would look if she asked him. 'Have you got a surname?'

If Jason had been alive, he would probably have blushed. As it was, he looked away briefly. 'Not yet.'

Lydia didn't point out the obvious, that 'Mary' wasn't going to narrow things down too much. 'I'll ask him,' she repeated.

'What's on your schedule tomorrow? Meetings?'

'So many,' Lydia replied. She picked up the hot chocolate and took a sip. 'Shoot me now.'

'You shouldn't joke about that.' Jason was filling the kettle.

'I just miss The Fork. And I miss working.'

'You're working.'

'Meetings aren't work. Not real work. People just want to talk to me.'

'They want an audience with the big boss.'

Lydia sighed. He was right. But it sucked. She had never wanted to be at the top of the tree. Never wanted Charlie's role. Aiden wanted it, she was pretty sure of that. She had high hopes that he could do it, too, but the Family wouldn't accept a change of leadership right now. There had been too much upheaval. Maybe in a year or two.

'Is there anything I can help with?' Jason was looking at her like he was worried.

Lydia shook her head quickly. Then reconsidered. 'Actually, could you set up some search alerts for Fleet's case? Craig Johnstone and Raymond Price. I want to keep an eye on the chatter, see if anything useful gets shared.'

Jason lit up as Lydia had known he would. The ghost loved the internet and was already reaching for his iPad. 'There's an episode called "A New Ripper" released yesterday.'

'That's the one.'

'Fleet must be furious.'

'He's not best pleased, no.'

FLEET'S MOOD DIDN'T IMPROVE. BY THE FOLLOWING afternoon, the media coverage had exploded, and the pressure from his superiors had increased. As he explained to Lydia, he expected to be removed from the team any moment, 'they'll call it re-organisation, but that's what it will mean'. She could hear the frustration in his voice.

'It's still your case right now, though, right? Make progress. Then they can't take it from you.'

'I appreciate the vote of confidence,' Fleet said, a brief smile tugging at the corners of his mouth. 'But I can't just snap my fingers and solve it.'

Lydia wondered whether he was hoping for a helpful vision. She knew first-hand what it was like to know you had certain powers, but to find them shy when you needed them most. 'Can I help?'

A hesitation. 'I shouldn't really tell you this—'

'Another body?' Lydia couldn't help but jump in. She knew that expression of Fleet's, had seen it so many times. A mix of seriousness and excitement. He loved the chase, the puzzle of a case, as much as she did.

A longer pause. 'Was that a lucky guess?'

Lydia wasn't going to dignify that with an answer. 'Where?'

'Cerberus. Underground club and music venue not far from Brick Lane.'

What he didn't say, although she assumed they were both thinking it, was that it was possibly another Whitechapel location. Depending on how far from Brick Lane.

She sighed. 'You think it's Family business?'

'Could be. Looking at the locations, it could be the Foxes—'

'It's not.'

Fleet shook his head gently. 'It worries me that you're so certain.'

'Okay,' Lydia amended. 'I don't think it's the Fox Family. But I could take a look, see whether something jumps out?'

Fleet hesitated. 'I would like your opinion.' He unlocked his iPad and found the crime scene photographs. 'Brace yourself.'

CHAPTER ELEVEN

The man in the picture was over ten years older than the last time Lydia had seen him, but she recognised him immediately. He still had long, dark hair and hollow cheeks. The kind of bone structure that made him striking. Not conventionally handsome, perhaps, but with a brand of dangerous good looks that made you assume he was the lead singer in a band. The kind of man, in short, that she would look twice at in a bar.

She had looked twice, she remembered. Even though he had been much older than her nineteen years and those years counted more at that age, she had watched him sitting in the corner of the club, his arm slung around Aysha Fox and one leg crossed over the other at the knee. Long legs and a slim physique. Enough muscle to stop him from seeming just skinny, but with the definite whiff of nineties heroin-chic. He had to have been at least thirty-five then. With hindsight, it was dodgy as all hell that he had been seeing Paul's seventeen-year-old cousin. But, somehow, Lydia hadn't thought like that when she had been nineteen. It had been a bit weird, perhaps, but not outright wrong. Not a red flag of gigantic proportions. She shook her head at the follies of her youth. How little she had known. An uncomfortable moment of self-realisation crept across her mind. How little did she know now? What was happening now that she would be shaking her head over in ten years' time? Since she couldn't know future-Lydia's thoughts and she had enough of present-Lydia's to contend with, she shrugged off introspection and got to work.

In the photograph, Perry was lying on his back, his arms spread wide. He was wearing tight black jeans and a billowy black shirt that looked like silk or satin. Chunky silver rings on his fingers, thin leather wrapped around one wrist and a couple of necklaces, one with smooth dark beads that might have been onyx or tiger's eye. The front of his body was a mess. The multiple stab wounds had bled copiously, so had been inflicted while he was alive. The floor around him was dark with blood, but she couldn't see any footprints. She wondered if it was just the angle of the photos and whether they were visible in situ. The killer had to have left a bloody trail, unless they had cleaned up behind them.

Fleet was frowning, watching her study the picture. 'You know him?'

She shook her head, still cataloguing the details. 'I don't think so,' she lied. 'He seems familiar, but he looks a bit like Richard Ashcroft, so it might be that.'

He looked at the picture, his shoulder brushing hers. 'I don't see it. Wait. I might be thinking of someone else.'

Lydia Googled the singer of The Verve and showed the image to Fleet. 'See?'

He looked at her phone for a long moment. This was work-mode Fleet. Thorough. Measured. Even when he was weighing up how much a corpse looked like the singer from an indie band. Eventually, he said. 'A bit I suppose.'

'Do you have a name?' It would be tricky if he didn't. She would feel worse about withholding the information.

'Tyler Baxter. He worked in promotion. Booking bands, mainly, but some comedians.'

'In London?' Lydia was scrambling to cover her surprise at Chris Perry's change of identity. And it would be odd for Perry to be working venues in the city. Even with his new name, the Fox Family would have found him in a heartbeat.

'Manchester.'

She wondered why Perry had felt safe to come out of hiding. Did he think the Fox Family would have somehow forgotten what he had done? Or because he had been living as Tyler Baxter for so long, he had become confident. 'What was he doing here?'

Fleet leaned back against the sofa cushions, letting his head tip back and his eyes close. 'No idea. Maybe visiting old friends. He grew up in Camden.'

If she was going to tell Fleet she had met the man, way back in the day, this was the time to do it. She could say, quite naturally, that the face had just clicked and that she had known him under a different name. Instead, she asked, 'who found him?'

'Cleaner. He has keys and was the only one here.'

'He called the cops right away?'

'We believe so.' Fleet was angling his head, thinking. 'Why do you ask?'

'No reason. Just getting a feel for the timeline.'

'First officers arrived on scene at four-thirty-three. Found the lock broken on the back door. The cleaner hadn't noticed as he let himself through the front with his keys.'

'He had been dead for a while, though, right? And someone has cleaned up the area.'

Fleet flashed a grim smile. 'You caught that? Yeah. He's a real mess, as you can see, but the surrounding area is oddly clear. No prints, no blood, nothing. I wondered whether he was killed elsewhere and the body was moved into the club, wrapped in plastic sheets or in a body bag. Then all of that could have been taken away.'

'Lot of effort. Moving a body.' Lydia was still looking at Perry. 'Usually that's to hide a murder, not put it somewhere public.'

'Unless that's the point. To send a message of some kind. Or to get attention quickly.'

'If he was killed elsewhere, it would have to be some-where private.'

'We're reviewing all the CCTV in the area and I reckon we'll find something. Not easy to move a body of that size and in that state without getting caught by at least one camera.'

They looked at the picture and then at each other. Lydia knew that Fleet was wondering about the Fox Family and whether they were involved and whether she knew anything about it. Despite the circumstances, it was nice to feel that closeness, to feel connected to him and as if she could see his thoughts. She felt a spark of excitement. It felt like old times. Unfortunately, she needed to put Fleet off his idea that it was the Fox Family, but seeing the victim made that a distinct possibility. If anyone would want to kill Chris Perry, it would be Paul Fox.

London, Then

LYDIA AND PAUL HAD USED THE FOX SAFE HOUSE several times without incident. It was always clean and tidy, with fresh sheets on the bed. It wasn't a large flat, but it was filled with mirrors and low lighting that gave the illusion of more space. A warren that seemed to go on further than was possible from the size of the building. The walls were painted in velvety dark colours and there were sections of richly patterned wallpaper. The furniture was antique or, at least, vintage, and every square inch was filled with soft cushions, lamps, thick throws, and jewel-coloured rugs. Lydia had prepared herself for the onslaught of Fox as she had crossed into Whitechapel, but no amount of deep breathing or mental fortitude could stop the overwhelm of red fur and warm earth as she stood in the Fox flat. Her reflection, in several mirrors, showed how pale she had become and her eyes looked wild and panicked as she focused on getting oxygen past her frozen lips. On breathing in and out. On not letting the cascading sense impressions short-circuit her brain completely. She wasn't going to pass out. That was her goal.

'Are you all right?' Paul led her to the sofa and got her to sit. 'I'll get you some water. Put your head between your knees if you feel faint.'

Lydia closed her eyes and gripped the velvet material of the sofa, connecting herself to the real world through that sensation. Over time, she had become used to the onslaught, and it ceased to overwhelm her. She still felt the same, but knowing it was going to happen and that it would ease, meant that she got through it much more quickly.

And it was worth it. While the entire flat was sumptuous and comfortable, the bedroom was pure luxury. There was a giant ensuite with stone tiles, underfloor heating and brass fixtures. The king-size sleigh bed was made of burnished dark wood, and the copious bedding was a quality that Lydia had never experienced before. It was so soft and pillowy, it enveloped you and made you feel safe and more comfortable than seemed possible. It was so instantly relaxing that it almost made Lydia want to just curl up and sleep rather than get naked with Paul. Almost.

She and Paul had been seeing each other properly for a few months, but it had been longer if you included the long dance they had done in the lead up to that first date.

Time seemed expanded, too, with the intensity of it. The feelings were stronger than anything she had experienced before, and the physical side was enough to make her feel as if a few hours with Paul in that gigantic sleigh bed clocked as weeks in normal time. Consequently, when they had been awoken from a post-coital slumber by the sound of screaming and hammering on the front door, Lydia had turned to Paul for direction. Looking at her past-self, Lydia could hardly believe she had been so trusting. So gullible. How could she have forgotten his essential nature? Been so unguarded with Paul Fox?

But in that moment, her past-self had felt so comfortable and safe with Paul Fox that she had looked to him. He was already getting out of bed, pulling on his discarded clothes. Lydia followed suit and was just behind him as he motioned for her to stay in the bedroom. He slipped from the room, pulling the door almost closed behind him.

She waited. Listening to the sound of the front door opening. The screaming had turned to a garbled yelling and then abruptly cut off. With her ear to the crack in the door, she heard sobbing. A woman in distress. Whatever this was, it wasn't physical danger. Somebody, somebody who knew this place existed, was extremely upset.

Once she had finished dressing, Lydia pulled the bedclothes straight to disguise what she and Paul had been doing athletically for the past few hours.

In the doorway to the living room, she saw Paul's back first. He was blocking her view of whoever was sitting on the sofa. If they were still crying, it was silently, apart from the occasional sniff.

Lydia felt the intense feeling of being unwelcome. She shouldn't be here. She opened her mouth to offer to make tea or to tell Paul that she was heading off, but found she couldn't speak.

Paul shifted and she saw a young woman, her head bowed and shoulders curved inward. She was cradling her right arm and crying steadily.

Lydia turned to leave, but Paul's voice stopped her. 'Lydia?'

She was just about to ask if there was anything she could do, when Paul said 'I'll call you later, yeah?' without looking at her.

Lydia didn't see Paul for three weeks after Aysha had turned up at the Fox's safe house, shaking and crying. He had messaged her and they had spoken on the phone once, but it wasn't the same. She had hated the needy note in her voice and he had sounded distracted. Hard, somehow, like he had put on armour. She knew that something bad had happened to Aysha and all Paul would say was that it had been 'that bastard'. She knew he meant Perry. He had been looking for him. Him and his siblings. Tristan, their father, had set them the task. Not that he had needed to. Paul had been ready to walk to the ends of the earth and tear the man limb from limb the moment he had seen Aysha crying.

At nineteen, Lydia had found that thrilling. But

she had enough sense to realise it wasn't a rational reaction. And that it meant she was in deeper than she had ever intended. That was the worst thing. She cared. She missed Paul. She was worried about him and what might happen when he caught up to Chris Perry.

In the end, it was her dad who convinced her to leave London.

'There's trouble with the Foxes.' As an opener it had got her attention. Her dad rarely referred to the London Families. Not in the present tense, anyway. He told her stories of the past, and of myths and lore, but he was firmly out of that world.

'What kind of trouble?'

The snooker was on the television and he watched it while he spoke, not looking at her. 'I think you know.'

And there it was. Her dad didn't have to spell it out. Lydia felt a shot of icy cold from the soles of her feet to her scalp. He knew that she was seeing Paul Fox. Lydia thought she had been careful. Thought that there was no way anybody in the Family, least of all her clueless dad, could find out. Mouth dry, she tried to think of what she could say.

'It will get messy,' he said quietly. 'You need to distance yourself.'

'I'm not involved,' Lydia said, finally able to speak. 'I haven't seen him for three weeks. Not since it happened. I don't even know what happened.' She snapped her mouth shut to stop herself from babbling further.

Still looking at the TV, Henry Crow spoke. 'They will find him and they will kill him. Probably in a violent and public way as a warning to the world. You need to be far away when that happens.'

'I...'

'And while you are far away, perhaps you can think about whether Paul Fox is the kind of man you have a future with. There are no half measures with the Families. You are in or you are out.'

'It's not serious... It's just...'

He looked at her then. Henry Crow was still there, but she could see her familiar dad, too. The gentleness was back in the lines of his face, softness in his eyes. 'Lyds, I'm sorry. There is only serious when it comes to Paul Fox. You can't play with him. There will be consequences. Tristan will already be working out how to use you.'

'I haven't even met Tristan. He doesn't know...'

A sharp shake of the head. 'Don't be foolish. I raised you better than that.'

Lydia felt the admonishment like a slap. She nodded her understanding, not trusting herself to speak.

'Think of something good to tell your mum. She doesn't know about this Fox business, and I don't want her upset.'

'I will.'

'I don't care what you do with your life. I just want you to be the one choosing.'

As long as it isn't staying in London with Paul Fox, Lydia added silently.

'The change will do you good,' he was saying. 'You're stuck in a rut here, anyway. You could travel.

That's a thing, isn't it? Interrailing? And you can come home in a few months. Six months, maybe. A year.'

'Okay,' Lydia said. She didn't love being told what to do, but she knew he was right. There wasn't a happy ending to this thing with Paul Fox, and it was only going to get harder to walk away.

'I just need to keep you safe,' her dad said. 'This is for the best.'

CHAPTER TWELVE

London, Now

N ow that there was a third Whitechapel body, the media attention on the case ballooned. And even though the nightclub didn't map exactly to one of the Ripper murder locations, it was close enough for the stories to gain traction. There were enough true crime buffs and fans of historical crime to pick up on the similarities of the cases – the locations, the timing, the frenzied stabbings – and the rest of the public seemed keen to go along for the ride. Jack the Ripper had been a public sensation in Victorian times and, over the almost one hundred and fifty years that had followed, the popularity of the case endured. Partly because it was never solved and partly because the things that made it famous at the time, were the same things that appealed to people now. The catchy name. The mysterious letters to the police and press. The sheer horror of the murders themselves.

The murder of Chris Perry had kicked up the pressure on Fleet's team. He was an events promoter, not a gangster or a pimp. He had journalists and talent agencies in the contacts list on his phone, he paid his taxes and he played squash at a health club. His live-in girlfriend in Manchester was devastated and already threatening to speak to the press, despite a police warning not to do so.

'They wanted to give it to another team, but the similarities are too striking. They would have to justify that decision at a later date if it turns out to be the same killer, so I've got it for now.'

'Will you get more bodies?'

'Couple of PCs and a detective.'

'That's something.'

Fleet shrugged. 'Yes and no. More resources means more pressure for results. Something DCI Moss was very keen to point out to me.'

'Moss?'

'Dominic Moss,' Fleet said. His mouth twisted in distaste. 'Absolute arsehole when we were training and he hasn't improved with age. He's been leading the unofficial "Fleet's a nutter" campaign.'

'Have you considered violence?' Lydia's hands were curled into fists.

Fleet smiled gently. 'He's not wrong. We're stretched for funding, everything is cut back to the bone. Where money is allocated is a big deal for management and we have to deliver results or they'll be answering uncomfortable questions in a tribunal.'

'I don't know how you do it,' Lydia said, thinking of

working within a system like that. The rules and admin and restrictions.

'It's better than the alternative.'

'Is it, though? Wouldn't you rather work for yourself?' Lydia was genuinely curious.

'I wouldn't be a copper. I would be another rat jumping off the sinking ship.'

'You're not a rat.'

'Okay.' Another quick smile. 'But if all the decent cops leave, what will happen to the force? It's not exactly stellar at the moment, but I know plenty of decent people in the Met. I owe it to them and to the community to stay put. To do what I can.'

'You're too decent.'

'I don't know about that,' Fleet said seriously. 'And I wouldn't want to work for myself, either. It doesn't look all that easy,' he gestured to her.

'I like being my own boss,' Lydia said. As she did, she realised the truth of it and how much she missed being a PI and her own person. Not the head of the Family, not stuck in Charlie's house with all of his expensive things. The gilded nest that wasn't her true roost, filled with things she hadn't chosen. She felt instantly guilty for the thought. There were thousands of people struggling to make rent payments or buy their own homes, thousands with no home at all. What kind of selfish person complained about the roof they had over their head? She had a nest and she would make the best of it.

. . .

The next morning, Fleet was back at work and Jason was out in the garden, talking to his ghost. He came through the glass doors without opening them, his face lit up. 'I think she's going to come inside. I told her you're here.'

Lydia was sitting at the breakfast bar, scrolling through the news on Jason's iPad, but she put it face down and tried to look unthreatening.

Jason was watching the garden intently and Lydia couldn't help but pick up on his nerves. After a long, tense minute, she saw Jason's shoulders relax. He shoved up the sleeves of his baggy grey suit and smiled at what appeared to be empty space.

'She's here.' Jason was looking to the left of Lydia. He addressed the space. 'Don't be afraid. Lydia's on our side.'

Lydia felt her heart squeeze at his words. She raised a hand in greeting. 'Hello.' She realised this had to be how Fleet felt when she told him Jason was in the room.

Jason seemed to be listening, so she kept quiet. Just looking at the space and trying to see if she could see anything in the air there. Maybe if the ghost stayed for long enough, she would power her up in the way that she did with Jason. Was that a shimmer? Or were her eyes playing tricks in the half-light?

'She says she met a man,' Jason said. He glanced at the shimmer and added, 'a gentleman. He worked as a barber.'

The shimmering air was becoming something else. A silvery shape that she didn't have time to decipher before it disappeared. Lydia closed her eyes for a couple of seconds and then looked again. The space appeared empty. 'Can you remember your full name, Mary? Your family name?'

A shudder in the air. Lydia's stomach rolled and she swallowed hard to contain the nausea, not letting herself look away. 'It's all right,' she said. 'I'm sorry to ask. I don't want to upset you.'

'Who was the gentleman?' Jason asked. 'Can you remember his name?'

The shimmer was back. It skimmed the outline of a figure. Lydia wasn't tall, but this woman was tiny. Way under five foot. There was the suggestion of a long skirt and some sort of shawl. Lydia couldn't make out Mary's features, but she could see the lines of a head covering, maybe a bonnet. And then it was gone.

'Anything?' Lydia turned to Jason.

'She's gone,' Jason said.

'I know. I saw her outline for a moment, just before she disappeared. That's progress.'

'She said the name George,' Jason said. 'She was very proud that he had a trade. I think he lived over the river. Or maybe worked over the river.'

'That's good,' Lydia said, even though it hardly seemed like any information at all. 'Gives us something to work with. Was he her boyfriend?'

'She says he was courting her. Gave her a posy, whatever that is.'

'Little bunch of flowers.'

'Get you,' Jason said and fluttered his hands.

'Shut up.' Lydia threw a dishtowel at his head and watched it sail right through.

LATER THE SAME DAY, FLEET CALLED. 'HIGHER-UPS are willing for me to connect Tyler Baxter with the Johnstone and Price murders, but they have made it clear that if it goes south, it's my name on the docket.'

This wasn't news, but Lydia could hear the tension in Fleet's voice. 'Anything I can do?'

A slight hesitation. Then he said: 'I wondered if you would take a look? See if you can spot anything I've missed.'

She knew what he meant by that. Fleet wanted her to see if there was a Family signature hanging about on the victim or general area. She didn't know if her senses were back up to scratch or not, but she wasn't going to refuse to help Fleet. Apart from anything else, it was better than the prospect of an afternoon of 'meet-and-greets'.

Lydia checked the location on Google and grabbed her jacket. Aiden arrived just as she was leaving. 'We've got—' he began.

'I know, I know,' Lydia said, trying to make herself at least sound a little bit apologetic. 'Can you handle things for me? I've got somewhere I have to be...'

The entrance to the club was past a cash and carry and behind a swanky bar and arts space, housed in a redeveloped brewery. There was plentiful graffiti, but it was the artistic type and made what would have been a bleak industrial backstreet a little livelier.

'I don't know if there will be anything here,' Lydia said, as Fleet pulled aside the police tape and unlocked the door. 'It's been a couple of days.' What she wanted to say was that he should have asked her to check for Family vibes when the body was in situ, not days later once the police had tramped all over it and the body was neatly stored in a mortuary drawer.

'I know it's not ideal,' Fleet said, handing Lydia plastic booties to pull on over her DMs. He waited for her to do the honours before leading the way in through the foyer of the club, past the ticket booth, and into the main room. 'I couldn't bring you in straight away.'

Not without word reaching his superiors. She didn't blame Fleet for wanting to protect his career, but it was a reminder of their separate lives.

The walls were painted black and the front of the bar was painted in a graffiti style. As with all places designed to be seen under the influence of mood-altering chemicals, and with colourful lights and loud music, the club seemed dingy and strange in the daytime. A bare waiting room with the cold light of day highlighting the questionable stains on the floors and walls, the ripped-up furniture, and mould patches. The place smelled of bleach, cigarette smoke, and blood.

'Where was—' Lydia caught herself just in time before she used Perry's real name. 'Baxter found?'

'Here,' Fleet led the way to the middle of the dancefloor.

Lydia realised that she needn't have asked Fleet. The thick dried bloodstain showed exactly where Chris Perry had died.

She stood still and closed her eyes. She breathed in and out slowly, reaching out her senses. There was a musty smell underneath the bleach, probably from the black mould she had clocked creeping up the walls. There was no earthy Fox or fragrant Pearl or sharp Silver. She couldn't taste feathers or hear the beating of wings. No signature of Crow.

She opened her eyes and shook her head. 'Nothing.'

'Ideally you'd see the body, but I don't know—'

'It's all right,' Lydia said. 'I told you I didn't think these were Family related deaths and this just confirms it. There's nothing here.'

'It might have faded.'

'True.' Lydia thought about asking him why he had asked for her opinion if he was going to instantly dismiss it, but she didn't want to argue.

'But thank you,' Fleet said. 'I appreciate your help.'

'You're welcome.'

He was looking at her intently. 'What?'

'You're sure you don't get anything? This is Whitechapel.'

She knew what he meant. He meant 'this is Fox territory'. Lydia ignored that and refocused on the blood-stained floor. 'Show me the body again.'

Fleet opened the image on his iPad and passed it across. She squinted at the gory mess that had once been Chris Perry, holding the picture up so that she could imagine it in situ. There was so much blood on the ground she expected to see bloody footprints leading away from the murder site. Or, if not clear footprints, then at least some sign of movement. Whoever had killed Perry had not been tidy about it, the multiple wounds had torn flesh and sprayed blood. There was a trail of blood visible in the image, shiny in the lamp lights that appeared to lead toward the far wall. She moved the iPad around until she matched the background, getting the correct angle, then dropped to a crouch to get a better look. The dried trail was still clearly visible, but it was shorter than she had expected from the picture. The trail of gore reached a couple of feet and, apart from a few droplets of blood, it just stopped. Lydia straightened up and turned in a slow circle, checking the evidence of her eyes.

'You see it?' Fleet was watching from the side of the dancefloor.

'The killer walked in this direction,' Lydia said, indicating the trail, 'and they were dripping blood. They had to be covered in the stuff.' She looked around. 'But what were they heading toward?' The exit was on the opposite side of the room. Presumably, they had managed to stop dripping blood before they reversed direction and made their way out. But what had brought them to this part of the room in the first place? She examined the trail of blood. 'If they walked back, there would be footprints in the blood.'

'There is still more analysis to be done, but the team didn't find any more blood after where you're standing.'

'So, they managed to get to the exit cleanly? Maybe they put bags over their shoes?' Lydia pointed at the plastic covering her DMs. 'But it seems weird after making this kind of mess. Why did they want to hide the way they left?'

Fleet replied with his usual restraint. 'It's unusual.'

· · ·

Lydia brought two pints to the table and slid onto the bench seat, her back against the wall. Fleet was still tense, but he raised his glass and clinked it against Lydia's. He even attempted a smile, but it wasn't one of his best.

Lydia wasn't relaxed, either. She had chosen the Rose and Crown because it was just out of Camberwell. The extra travel was worth the anonymity in her mind. She didn't want to be known, to have people eying her with fear or interest. Or, worse still, wanting to sidle up for a 'quick word' or to fawn over her as if this would buy some kind of future favour. She was being grumpy, she knew, but it had all just got too much.

Halfway down their drinks, Lydia thought she had made an error and not gone far enough away from Camberwell. A young woman kept glancing over at their table. She had brown wavy hair and was wearing a green jumpsuit. She was sitting with another woman, and a man with sideburns and a fitted seventies-style shirt.

'Don't look,' Lydia said quietly, 'but I think I might have been recognised.'

Fleet managed not to do the first thing that everybody did the moment they were told not to look. He raised his eyebrows slightly and drained half of his drink in one long swallow.

'I thought if we came out of Camberwell...' Her voice trailed off as the woman in the jumpsuit got to her feet. 'Here we go.'

'Excuse me,' the woman said once she arrived at their table.

She had pale-pink lipstick and her eyes were magnified by her red-framed spectacles. Lydia had never felt more like a crow in her black jeans, black boots and black t-shirt. 'How can I help?' She tried to make her tone kind, but not too welcoming. She ought to be able to have an evening off, for feather's sake.

The woman hardly glanced at her, her eyes on Fleet. 'Are you DCI Fleet?'

'I'm sorry, have we met?' Fleet's tone was polite, but distant.

'You're working on the New Ripper case, aren't you?'

'New Ripper?' Fleet's face creased in displeasure.

'The murders are identical, aren't they? To Jack the Ripper. They have all got multiple stab wounds and Craig Johnstone's neck was slashed deeply like Mary Ann Nichols' was. Do you think you are dealing with a copycat?'

Fleet leaned back. 'As opposed to?'

Lydia knew he was pointing out that the alternative was the ghost of Jack the Ripper back from the dead and terrorising London's men, just for a change of pace. Unfortunately, she thought he had misjudged the woman's capacity for sarcasm-detection.

'You think the original is still active?' Her eyes were wide. She pulled a small notebook from her pocket and flipped it open. Lydia would have laid money that she had practised the move several times. 'Mind if I take notes?'

'Yes,' Fleet said, a snap in his voice. 'This is off the record.'

The notebook was flipped shut with another smooth

movement. The pink lips curved in an anticipatory smile and Lydia almost felt sorry for her.

Fleet fixed her with a blank stare, his whole face shutting down to a mask of pure professional nothingness. 'No comment.'

There was a beat before the disappointment registered, and then she nodded tightly. 'Well, thank you for your time.'

'That wasn't very diplomatic,' Lydia said, once the woman had returned to her own table.

'I thought I was very restrained.'

'Have you been getting a lot of it?'

Fleet was already on his feet, pulling on his jacket. 'Let's go somewhere else.'

'That's a yes, I take it.'

Fleet met her eye, just for a second, and she saw his gleam. Then it was gone. 'The frustrating thing,' he said, marching out of the pub and onto the busy pavement, 'is that no one is looking at the Foxes.'

'Be glad,' Lydia shot back. 'A media campaign focusing on the Fox Family would not be conducive to peace in the city.' She knew that Fleet's hunch was likely right, but that he would never be able to prove it. The Foxes were too tricky. And dragging them into a police investigation would threaten the truce. No matter that Lydia didn't control the Metropolitan Police, the fact that she lived with the lead detective on the case would be considered Crow involvement.

Fleet slanted an unreadable look in her direction. 'They prefer to stay in the shadows, true enough.'

CHAPTER THIRTEEN

Nowhere in Whitechapel could be called quiet, but Aysha's flat was on a relatively calm street running alongside a small park. The terrace was well kept, and the small front yards were neat. Outside Aysha's building, the dark-blue front door was flanked by several potted plants, none of which were chained to the fence or kicked to smithereens. Either this was an unusually law-abiding area, or the locals knew this building housed a Fox.

After she was buzzed in, Lydia climbed the stairs to the first floor. Aysha opened the door, her hair in a messy topknot and looking like it needed a wash. She had changed from the pretty teenager Lydia remembered, and she tried not to let the shock show on her face.

'I already heard,' Aysha said, but she let Lydia in anyway. Lydia wondered how much Aysha knew about her and what she assumed Lydia was doing. She didn't seem alarmed or all that surprised to see her, but she also didn't seem 'all there'. Her pupils were dilated and she dragged her feet as she walked, almost shuffling, as if her legs felt heavy.

Lydia followed the woman into the small living room. It had a big window and a comfy-looking sofa, covered in brightly coloured cushions. Every available surface housed a plant pot and the curtain rod had a trailing plant twisting all along it. Macramé holders hung from the ceiling, dripping with more greenery. Behind the odour of green leaves and a floral scent from the orchid collection on the coffee table, there was the faintest smell of pot.

Aysha sank onto the sofa. 'I already know,' she said again. 'I saw it.'

Lydia assumed Aysha meant the news story that was doing the rounds. Although he was named as 'Tyler Baxter' and the picture on the BBC article was only a year old, there was no way Aysha wouldn't have recognised Chris Perry. It didn't seem likely that Aysha was going to offer a cup of tea, so Lydia asked if she could use the bathroom.

The small room housed more plants. Frilly leaved ferns and other green things that Lydia wasn't certain about identifying. The cabinet over the sink yielded dental floss and a packet of Diazepam with a prescription sticker on the front. Half of the tablets had been taken and it began to make sense of Aysha's eerie calm. Lydia pulled the flush while making a quick scan of the rest of the room.

Outside the bathroom, with the living room on her left, there was a closed door to the right. Lydia opened it and confirmed that it was Aysha's bedroom and that it looked like only Aysha lived in the flat. There was a jumble of stuff on one of the bedside tables, but she didn't have time to go in and look properly. She closed the door and re-joined Aysha in the living room.

'I know who you are,' Aysha said, seeming to sharpen up. 'What's this got to do with the Crows?'

Lydia wondered whether Aysha remembered seeing her that day in the bolthole. She had been very upset and Paul had been standing between them, and it wasn't likely to be the most important detail of the experience. 'I wanted you to know that the police don't know about you and Chris Perry. Not yet, anyway. I'm not going to tell them, but they might find out elsewhere.'

Aysha's narrow shoulders were slumped and she wasn't making eye contact. 'S'okay. I won't talk to them either.'

'I know that,' Lydia said. Aysha was a Fox. They weren't in the habit of sharing anything with the cops. It was one thing the Crows and Foxes had in common. 'But I wondered whether you would consider it? Just this once?'

She straightened. 'Why would I do that?'

Lydia held up her hands. 'It's Fleet's case. I want to help him solve it. But I'm not going to tell him about you. Not unless you say I can.'

Aysha's gaze flicked to Lydia's face and then away. Downward. 'Well I don't.'

It was little more than a whisper.

Lydia could feel the fragility of the woman and felt the sting of guilt. She probably shouldn't be speaking to her about this. But then, Aysha had been through hell and she was still here, so she had a core of strength. And her Family would look after her. The Fox sense was subtle, but if Lydia focused, she could taste earth and feel the gentlest brush of fur. Besides, she had a job to do. She needed to look into Aysha's eyes and see whether she had prior knowledge of the killing. If she did, that increased the chances that a Fox was responsible. What Lydia would do with that information was still unclear. She would worry about that later.

'Did you know he was back in London?'

A slow shake of her head. Her eyes were glassy, and Lydia didn't know if that was the tranquillisers or emotion. 'I didn't think I would have to see him again. Just you saying his name...' she trembled, her thin frame convulsing. 'I would say it brings it all back, but it's never left.' Her sudden smile was too wide, her eyes wild. 'It never bloody leaves.' She cocked her head as if hearing something and her fingers groped for a tin on the table.

'I'm glad he's dead,' Lydia said.

Aysha frowned. She had opened the tin and lit up a ready-rolled joint. 'You don't get to say that.'

'It's still true.'

Aysha's eyes narrowed as she inhaled the smoke. 'I remember you. You were with my cousin.'

'We've all got a past.' Lydia hesitated, but felt she owed some honesty. It had been ten years since Chris Perry had fled London and it was shocking just how messed up Aysha still appeared. 'I left London, and Paul, after it happened.'

'What did it have to do with you?'

'My Family didn't want me mixed up with Perry's

murder.' Which was true. But not the whole story. Lydia wasn't going to share that she had recognised her path was a self-destructive one, heading nowhere happy. She and Paul didn't have a future, but she was falling for him. Truth was, she had welcomed the excuse to run away. 'And I could see things were going to get messy.'

Aysha took another couple of long pulls on the joint. She didn't offer it to Lydia, grinding it out on the surface of the tin instead. 'Why is that do you think?'

Lydia was confused. 'What?'

'That the bad things never leave and the good things...' she fluttered a hand into the air. Her baggy sleeve fell down to her elbow, revealing a pattern of scars on her forearm.

'I don't know.'

Aysha leaned back against the cushions. She looked as if she was going to drift off to sleep, but then her gaze found Lydia's face. It seemed to take a great deal of effort and Lydia felt a surge of protectiveness. She shouldn't be alone. And she shouldn't be with a Crow.

'Was it you?' Aysha's voice was barely more than a whisper.

'No. I thought it might have been you.'

Aysha's eyes drifted shut.

Lydia waited for a few minutes, listening to Aysha's breathing get deeper. Then she stood and quietly let herself out of the flat. She still wasn't certain that the Fox Family hadn't been involved, but she knew one thing: the woman inside was not an avenging angel. Aysha had not risen up with a flaming sword and cut down Chris Perry. For starters, she had truly meant it when she had asked whether Lydia had done it.

Lydia had just closed the main front door, making sure the lock clicked into place, when an angry voice startled her.

'What the fuck are you doing here?'

A wall of Fox slammed into her, but the impressions weren't sexual. Instead of soft inviting fur and dark warm earth, she felt sharp teeth and crunching jaws. Paul was a couple of paces away, even though it felt as though he had made physical contact. Her body was tingling and she blinked, checking that there really was air between them. He was holding himself in place, visibly furious and shaking with tension. It was terrifying.

'Speak.'

Lydia weighed the situation for a second and decided not to lie. 'I wanted to see if Aysha was capable of killing Perry.'

'And?' Paul snapped the word, as if he wanted to smack her with it.

'I don't think so. No.'

'You said his name?' Paul's hands were flexing and his eyes were wild with fury. 'You walked into my cousin's den and spoke that piece of shit's name?'

'I told her he was dead. I thought she would want to know.'

'Bullshit. You thought she already knew. Don't pretend this was anything else.'

Lydia swallowed. Paul might have looked intimidating, but it wasn't just anger in his eyes. He was upset. She thought about how she would feel if he had gone barging in on a member of her family who was struggling the way Aysha clearly was. 'You're right. I'm sorry. I was narrowing down the suspects.'

He looked away, the muscle jumping in his jaw. 'You are so bloody single minded.'

'That's the job,' Lydia said automatically.

'You're not a PI anymore. And this isn't your case.'

'I am,' Lydia said. She thought about saying that Fleet's job was on the line, but wisely realised that Paul wasn't likely to be swayed by that bit of info.

'You're leader of the Crow Family. You're dreaming if you think you can carry on with your own little business venture,' he sneered. 'Your life isn't your own. You're a puppet for the Crows. And you're kidding yourself if you think you can marry a copper. You're just stringing that man along, which is cruel, even for you.'

He was trying to hurt her. It seemed like he was stopping himself from throwing a punch by flinging verbal shots instead. 'I didn't come here lightly. I want to keep the Fox Family out of this.'

'You want to find Perry's killer? That's not a good reason to upset Aysha. She has suffered enough because of that piece of poisoned meat.' Paul gestured at the door with a stabbing motion. 'You saw her. It's been ten years. Ten years and she's still not right.'

'I would have thought you would be interested in finding him.' Paul frowned at that, like he was thinking about punching her, so she rushed on. 'So that you could throw him a party, I mean.' She held up her hands. 'I've got no problem with that. Whoever killed Perry did the world a favour.'

Paul wasn't placated. 'I don't care about the world. I care about Aysha. She's been through enough. Perry messed her up and that was just the start.'

Lydia kept quiet. Her brief visit with Aysha had shown her that. Aysha had clearly been struggling for many years with poor mental health and likely drug abuse, and it seemed Paul held Perry responsible for her downward spiral. She still wasn't sure if Paul was going to lose control and she was ready to run. Tensing the muscles in her legs ready.

'I wanted to do it,' Paul said. His hands were fisted and he wasn't looking at her, his gaze seeing something else. 'I wanted to look into his eyes and know that he had suffered. Whoever did this took that away from me. From my Family.'

It was hard to know how to respond to that. Lydia went with, 'I'm sorry.'

He took a deep breath and let it out slowly. Some of the tension had drained, but he still looked devastated. Lydia would have laid money that this had been a Fox hit, but now she wasn't so sure. Foxes were tricky and Paul wasn't their de facto leader purely because he was Tristan's son, but she couldn't help believe him. He was genuinely distressed. It reminded her of the first time she had met Aysha.

As if she had planted the thought in his mind, he raised his eyes to hers and she felt the jolt of Fox animal sensuality. She had buried the memories of the time they had spent together, but when he looked at her like that, they came fighting to the surface. Blood rushed to her face and her breathing quickened.

Abruptly, his face hardened. 'You left.' The words ripped from his throat, close to a snarl. 'After.'

'I had to,' Lydia said. 'And it wasn't as if I could do anything to help.' The words sounded pathetic, and she wished she had a better excuse. He was right. Leaving London had seemed like the right thing to do at the time, but she had never considered that he would have been upset. Paul had been so casual, so confident. She had assumed that, from his point of view, she had been a mild diversion, nothing more. For her, it had been an obsession that had frightened her. She had felt her sense of control slipping and knew that she was falling head-long for a man who could offer her no future, no happy ever after. Leaving had been an act of self-preservation, but she had never considered that Paul would have been hurt by it.

'You just left,' he said, now, his voice softer. His gaze was boring into her, as if searching for something.

'I'm sorry,' Lydia said. 'I should have said goodbye.'

A shudder ran through his body. When he looked into her eyes, his assured Fox swagger was back, rolled over the emotion like a thick layer of snow on the ground. 'You can say it now.'

'Goodbye, Paul.'

CHAPTER FOURTEEN

L ydia was satisfied that Paul Fox hadn't killed Chris Perry. Which meant there was a different link between Perry, Raymond Price and Craig Johnstone. She also knew that Fleet wasn't going to see past the Fox Family without a solid alternative theory.

She had spent the afternoon reading about Jack the Ripper and making notes. When Fleet arrived, carrying Chinese takeaway in one hand, a bottle of red in the other, she gave him her notebook to read while she sorted cutlery and poured two large glasses of wine. There was something about spending the afternoon with a series of violent crimes against women that gave her a terrible thirst for oblivion.

She watched Fleet reading. It was soothing and, thinking about how much she loved the way his forehead creased when he was concentrating, eased away some of the darkness. The wine and food helped, too, and by the time he had turned the last page she was feeling more sociable. Other couples probably talked about... Well, actually, she didn't know what other people talked about. That had always been one of her problems. She liked solving puzzles, though, working out why and how, and she knew that Fleet did too. Solving murders was their love language. She decided not to say that out loud.

'You have started with Martha Tabram. George Yard Buildings,' he said. His tone suggested a question.

'Mary Ann Nichols was next and most of the sources I looked at count her as the first Ripper victim, but there isn't a consensus. I thought it was best to include the plausible possibles, given the case wasn't solved and the considerable time that has passed. We can't know anything for certain.' She didn't add that Paul Fox had called Tabram a Ripper victim when he had walked her along Gunthorpe Street and that was part of why she was included it in her timeline. It made no sense. Paul Fox hadn't been alive in 1888, had no more knowledge than any of the Ripper scholars she had been studying, but she couldn't shake the conviction that he was right. Whitechapel was his den, after all. 'Martha was found on a landing in the building. They were dark at night and known to be used for illicit activity.'

'Johnstone was in the stairwell,' Fleet mused.

'Mary Ann Nichols was found in a doorway on Buck's Row.'

He snagged a spring roll and gestured with it. 'Which is now Durward Street. Building site behind Whitechapel Station.'

Lydia nodded. She had bookmarked the sites on Google maps, as well as writing down the description in her notebook. Raymond Price was found close to

Durward Street, but not in the exact location. He had been for a curry at a restaurant nearby and had, apparently, been walking to his car, which was parked on Underwood Road, when he was attacked. It was a CCTV blackspot.

Fleet had been very polite, engaging with the Ripper research and entertaining the possibility of a copycat killer. But now he got to the thing he had been clearly waiting to say. 'You know all this ignores the most likely suspects?'

Lydia didn't know how to convince Fleet. She couldn't tell him about Aysha Fox and, even if she could, it would hardly help to prove Paul's innocence.

She decided on half-truths. 'I went to see him. Paul.'

Fleet's expression was carefully neutral. 'And?'

'He had heard of Baxter. Through club business stuff. Same circles.'

Fleet leaned forward slightly.

'He didn't like the man. Thought he was a creep. Didn't like that he was always with young women. Girls, really.' This was as close to the subject as Lydia wanted to get. 'He's protective about what happens in Whitechapel and in his clubs. He said he didn't have anything to do with Baxter, and I believe him. If anything, he's angry that he didn't get the chance to kill the man himself.'

'So he's told you he would murder Baxter and you take that as evidence you should trust him when he says he didn't murder him.' Fleet's tone was thick with disbelief.

'Truth isn't always pretty,' Lydia said. 'So, yes. It

makes me believe that he didn't kill Baxter. It doesn't make me forget that he's a Fox.'

Fleet shook his head.

'What?'

'You've always had a blind spot when it comes to that man.'

THE NEXT MORNING, LYDIA WOKE UP THINKING about 'Tyler Baxter' and his penchant for very young women. She wondered how his girlfriend was holding up. She had lost the love of her life, but worse than that, she had discovered that he wasn't the man she presumably thought he was. It had to be bad enough discovering that he was having an affair, but the news that it was barely legal had to make it so much worse. Perry had been seeing a sixteen-year-old girl called Lauren. She worked as a glass collector at a club in Manchester and had met Perry three months earlier. That he hadn't been topped in Manchester was part of the mystery. Of course, Lydia had an idea about that, but revealing it to Fleet would mean she would have to explain how she knew, and that she had recognised the man immediately. And had withheld Perry's change of identity, too.

Fleet was showering and when he walked into the room to get dressed, his hair wet and a towel wrapped around his waist, she asked him about the Lauren lead.

'It isn't enough of a motive. If it had happened in Manchester, we would be looking closely at the girl's family and friends, but it seems like a stretch for them to follow him to London.'

'But wouldn't you choose to kill someone out of your manor? What's that phrase? Don't shit on your own doorstep?'

Fleet looked dubious. 'Maybe. But I don't see it. Lot of effort.'

'Have you interviewed Lauren's family?'

'This week,' Fleet said. He was dressing with efficiency, becoming DCI Fleet with every item. 'They didn't think there was anything wrong with the relationship, but they weren't thrilled to learn he had a live-in girlfriend. They were at great pains to emphasise that Lauren wasn't a "home wrecker" and hadn't known about Baxter's live-in girlfriend.'

'They weren't worried about the age gap?' Lydia hauled herself out of bed and started rooting around for clean clothes. Clean-ish would have to do.

Fleet shrugged. 'He had visited the house, brought gifts, played the big man. There's only a mum and siblings at home, and she was of the opinion that Lauren could do a lot worse than a man with a car and a decent job and no obvious drug problem. Can't say I blame her. It's tough living around there.'

Lydia paused. She had pulled on a stretchy vest top, only to discover it had a grease stain on the front. She stood in front of the mirror, trying to assess how obvious it was. 'Sixteen, though.'

'Not illegal, not my jurisdiction,' Fleet said robustly. He stood behind her and leaned down to kiss her lightly on the neck.

'Without your copper hat on, though?' Lydia didn't

know why she was pushing it, but it suddenly seemed very important.

He caught her eyes in the mirror. 'Oh, fucking disgusting. There was something wrong with him.'

She breathed an inner sigh of relief.

ONCE FLEET HAD GONE TO WORK, LYDIA WANDERED into her office. Jason was in his accustomed position on the sofa. She had offered to get him a desk, now that he was an official member of Crow Investigations, but he said he preferred the sofa. And that one of the perks of being dead was that he didn't need to sweat the bad ergonomics.

Jason looked up from his laptop. 'I think I might have found Mary's gentleman caller. He's called George, anyway, and it's around the right time. And he worked as a barber. I found him in the court records. Did you know they have transcripts from all the trials in there?'

Well, that didn't bode well. 'Let me guess, he wasn't a gentleman?'

'Terrorised his wife and lived with three different mistresses.'

'At once?' That sounded crowded.

'Sequentially,' Jason said, not in the mood for levity. 'He lived with them as if he were married, calling them "wife" although they weren't actually married. He beat them, but that wasn't how they died. Poisoned with something called antimony, small amounts given regularly over time. It gave a slow and painful death.'

'Hell Hawk. Please tell me he was convicted.'

'Hanged for it. Well, one of them. They could only put one murder on the indictment, apparently. I don't understand why, evidence was given for all three.'

'That's something.'

'You're a fan of the death penalty?' Jason sounded surprised.

Lydia hesitated. 'No. But I'm a fan of revenge.'

Jason shook his head 'That sounds like a contradiction.'

'I just don't trust the court system. Don't like the idea that it could result in something so permanent. And it feels wrong to mete out death in such a cold-blooded way. But I can respect someone taking revenge of their own. When it's personal.'

'You sound like Charlie.'

Well, that hurt.

A moment later, Jason closed the computer and got up from the sofa. He drifted to the kitchen and filled the kettle. Hot drinks were his love language, so she knew he was apologising for the Charlie comment. Lydia decided to meet him in the middle with an olive branch of her own. 'I'm sorry about Mary. I know you care about her. I don't want this man to be her George, but it might give her closure.'

'You don't think I'm jumping to conclusions? I mean, she might have died a simple natural death and have nothing to do with this man at all.'

'How likely is that, though?' Lydia knew she was being brutal, but she knew Jason must have been thinking this way. Otherwise, why would he have been checking court records? 'She's a strong echo and she lived well over a hundred years ago. That suggests something traumatic happened.'

Jason gave her a small, sad smile. 'It's good I've got something to tell her, but I don't know what it will do. Assuming I'm right, will telling her about the man who hurt her unlock her memories? Will she remember her life? Will she remember him?'

What Jason wasn't saying was 'will she remember her death?'. And what Lydia wondered was where this new obsession to help ghosts had come from. She knew that he wanted purpose and liked helping with her investigations, but since moving from The Fork and her new role as Charlie's replacement had taken up most of her time, there hadn't been much going on in that area. He missed it. And, of course, he could relate to the lost spirits.

'Do you think about yours?'

'My life?'

She had meant his death, but didn't want to say so. 'Your old life, yeah.'

'I can't picture her face.'

Lydia knew he meant his wife. Amy Silver. 'I'm sorry.'

He shrugged, his outline vibrating. 'Honestly, I'm glad. I can't hear her voice or picture her face and it makes it a bit easier. If I dreamed, I feel like she would visit me there, but I don't, so I haven't seen her in forty years. It's all faded. The feelings. All of it.'

'They do say time heals.' Lydia immediately wanted to kick herself for saying something so cliched.

He gave exactly the look she deserved. 'It's not healed.'

'No. Sorry. Right.'

'It's washed away. I hate that it's all... dissolved. It was the last thing I felt. With my body and my breath and it's leaking away. What will happen when it's all gone? I don't want to be like...'

Lydia thought she knew what he was going to say, but she asked the question anyway. 'Like who?'

Jason turned away. He opened a cupboard and got mugs down, even though there were already two on the counter.

Lydia waited while he measured spoonfuls of hot chocolate powder, poured hot water into all four cups and stirred each one. When he spoke, the vibrations of his outline had calmed and he seemed thoroughly solid again. 'Mary. I don't want to end up like Mary.'

CHAPTER FIFTEEN

When Fleet had been unofficially demoted, he had been marooned in the Safer Neighbourhoods team. It was a police enterprise that included a count of crimes by category displayed on the website, along with the stated priorities of the team and a handy-dandy table with 'priorities' such as 'antisocial behaviour in Denmark Hill area' and the reassuring word 'issued'. The other side of the table was a list of 'progress'. This, invariably, read, 'no update available' and made the whole thing rather less reassuring than was probably intended.

Fleet had had the whole thing explained in tedious detail during a training day. 'It's part of the "building trust through transparency" initiative.'

'What if it just confirms the public perception that the force is drowning and nothing is actually getting done?'

Fleet shrugged. 'I assume the idea is that at least we

will be seen to be being honest about our failings. That's a step in the right direction.'

Lydia wasn't sure. Someone had to maintain the website, issue and update the actions. She knew that most victims of crime would prefer a properly staffed station, rather than a table on a computer screen. It hit her why her days were so full of face-to-face meetings and visits in the local community. People needed to see her. The Crows didn't have a website. She had to be out and about, letting the community – and the worst elements of that community – know that she was paying attention. It didn't mean she had to enjoy it, though.

The man sitting opposite Lydia was trying to be charming. It wasn't in his wheelhouse, but he was giving it a go. Perhaps he had watched a YouTube video on the subject, because he kept using Lydia's name and making an unusual amount of eye contact. Lydia guessed the video had told him about mirroring, so she leaned forward and rested her chin on her hands, just to see if he copied her movement. He did. 'That looks uncomfortable,' she observed after a moment.

He straightened up, looking put out. 'Can I count on your support?'

'In what?' Lydia had given up waiting for him to get to the point and had been thinking about other things for the last few minutes. She was only halfway through the day's meetings and already at the end of her patience.

'Saturday night. We're expecting a gang from Brixton. At my pub.'

'They warned you?' That seemed oddly polite.

'Not directly. But someone knows someone who is friends with one of the girlfriends. They passed it along.'

'What have you done to this gang?'

'Nothing.'

'I'll ask again.' Lydia wished she could produce her coin. These meetings would go a lot faster if people started telling the truth from the beginning.

'There was a spot of bother at one of their pubs last week,' the man said. 'Some bird got glassed.'

'Some bird?' Lydia gave the man her full shark-smile. The one that promised things were about to get nasty.

'I didn't mean... I meant someone got hurt. It was an accident.'

'Want some advice?'

'Please,' the man said, ducking his chin and speaking to the table.

'Stop making trouble in Brixton pubs.'

AFTER THE MAN HAD LEFT AND LYDIA HAD SAT through another four meetings, it occurred to Lydia that she wasn't even pretending to learn people's names now. She had met a lot of people when she had been working as a PI, and she had never felt like this. Disconnected. Disinterested.

She had also been wondering about the cash that she had found underneath Jez's bed. Had he been killed for it? If so, why hadn't the killer searched his room? Was it a principle thing? The Brixton gang was coming to make trouble in a Camberwell pub because the owner of that pub had made trouble in one of theirs. An eye for an eye and all that tiresome, dick-measuring macho jazz. If you kept on giving back what you got, taking chunks out of each other in a cycle of retribution, you both ended up losing. If you kept on taking pieces from each other, eventually there was nothing left.

Fleet had been working long hours all week and, when he had been home, he was quiet. When Lydia asked him if he was okay, he had said 'just tired' and that had been that. She had resorted to reading the news for updates on his case, but the few stories available had nothing added. One guy, who said he worked for The Guardian, but Lydia had her doubts, had found their address. He turned up one evening and stood on the doorstep, saying he was looking for 'background' and that he would only name Fleet as an anonymous source. Fleet ranted about being a DCI in the Met for ten minutes before sending him on his way.

'Why would he think I would speak to him?' He said, running his hand over his head as he marched into the kitchen.

'As a strategy?' Lydia was saying the first thing that came to her mind that wasn't 'because he thinks you're a bent copper because you're shacked up with the head of an infamous crime family', but Fleet frowned as if taking the suggestion seriously.

'Like baiting the killer? Or trying to communicate with them? I'm not sure what that would achieve at this stage...' He trailed off and resumed his pre-journalist activity of staring into space, not speaking.

Lydia wondered when he was going to come back to her. She knew the hallucinations had been a living hell, but he had assured her that he was no longer suffering. She knew it had been a rough time at work, with suspicion and ignominy. He hadn't been rank-stripped, but he described his new team as the 'lame ducks' of the department. This being London, there were plenty of suspicious deaths to investigate and Fleet's new team had been given the dregs. The cases that were either essentially box-ticking exercises to ensure that the Met were filling their quotas for investigation or, as in the case of Craig Johnstone and Raymond Price, murders that nobody would much care whether they ever got solved. It gave the office jokers plenty of ammunition, too. 'Gang hit? Better ask your girlfriend.' That kind of side-splitting repartee.

When Fleet arrived home that afternoon, Lydia was surprised to see him so early. Angel had left brownies, but he said he wasn't hungry. She went to the coffee machine and made them both fresh cups. The sun was shining through the bifold doors, highlighting streaks on the glass. There was the shape of bird wings where a medium-sized bird had smashed into the glass. Not a corvid, they were too smart for that, probably a pigeon.

The crows that roosted in the trees at the bottom of the garden were cawing loudly. Lydia waved at them through the glass and transferred her attention back to Fleet. He wasn't staring blankly into space anymore, but appeared to be waiting for something. 'Sorry. Did you say something?'

'Do you think I'm really bad at my job?' Fleet was not looking happy.

'What are you talking about?'

'Jez McAllister. One of your employees.'

'He runs one of the shops,' Lydia said. 'I don't employ him as such.'

'He doesn't run anything anymore. As I'm sure you're aware.'

She looked at him levelly. 'Is there a reason you are angry? Because I don't appreciate your tone right now.'

'Well, I don't appreciate being lied to.'

This was dangerous territory. Lydia waited. She had always been good at waiting and it was something Karen had emphasised when she was doing her training. Leave gaps in the conversation, don't be afraid of silence. If you wait, the other person will fill the dead air with all kinds of interesting detail. Even when people don't think they're saying anything important, the way they say it or the filler they choose is all information. It was a technique Lydia had honed to a fine art.

'Missing, but I'm guessing he's dead,' Fleet said after a short silence.

'Jez? I haven't heard anything, but I can ask Aiden. He's hands on with the retail side of the business.' Another silence. Lydia cracked and said, 'You're not on missing persons, you're on the Johnstone stabbing case.'

'Funnily enough, my colleagues couldn't wait to tell me that a man employed by my girlfriend was missing in suspicious circumstances.'

Lydia's mind was racing. They had cleaned up the

148

scene, there was no body to be found. Jade had been paid off and wouldn't have reported him missing.

Fleet's eyes were narrowed. 'His dad reported him missing. Usually got a payment to help with his rent, apparently, and this didn't come through. He couldn't get hold of him on the phone and then turned up at the flat, where he discovered his son's girlfriend living on her own suddenly.'

'What did she say?'

'That Jez had left and that she hadn't heard from him. Said they had split up.'

'That doesn't sound so unlikely.'

'According to Jez's dad, it was. His words were something along the lines of Jez never making a decision that would cause him to have to get up off his arse.'

'I'll look into it,' Lydia said. 'He's probably just skipped off on holiday. Maybe he won big and is off spending it.'

'Your employees have gambling problems?'

'No,' Lydia said, frustrated at his judgemental tone. And that he had a point. Crow policy stated that employees shouldn't use their shops, but she had got the impression that Jez hadn't been following the rules. And there were plenty of other options in the city.

Lydia knew she shouldn't say anything else, knew she was inviting an argument, but she couldn't stop herself. 'Why do you presume McAllister is dead?'

Fleet looked tired suddenly. 'He works for the Crows. He has disappeared. It's not a difficult equation if you've a passing familiarity with the files on your Family.'

'Circumstantial at best, then.' Even though he was right, she felt annoyed at being judged.

Fleet shook his head, frustrated. 'You can't keep this stuff from me, we have to be a team, or this won't work.'

'You want me to tell you every detail of my business? My Family? What happened to plausible deniability? I'm protecting your career.'

'I want you to tell me when someone dies.'

'Okay.' Lydia took a long, slow breath. She loved Fleet. She loved him in a way that went through to her bones and made her ache if she thought about it with any honesty. But it had been a hard eighteen months and they both bore scars.

'Okay?' His lips were a straight line and there were lines of tension in his face.

He had been distant. He had lied to her. Lydia would be the first to admit she had trust issues and things changing so fast, for her and with Fleet, had sent her into defensive mode. She knew this logically, and she knew that trust was the foundation of a healthy relationship. The urge to tell him that she knew about Jez, that she had seen his body and ordered a clean-up crew, crowded in her throat. But the certainty she had felt with Fleet had gone. And she could taste feathers. She had been raised not to talk about the Family business and now she *was* the Family business. She ignored the urge to clear her throat, knowing that the feathers would subside if she heeded the warning. 'If someone dies, I'll let you know.'

. . .

JASON WALKED INTO THE ROOM JUST AFTER FLEET had left. 'I wasn't listening in,' he said, 'but what was that about?'

Lydia didn't want to talk about Jez McAllister. She shrugged. 'There's just stuff we can't say. We are living in two different worlds and it's tricky.'

'You two need to talk.'

'We talk all the time,' Lydia protested. 'We live together.'

Jason pushed the sleeves of his suit up. 'You sort of live together.'

Lydia paused. 'What's that supposed to mean?'

'Fleet still has his flat.'

'He stays here most nights, though.'

'You haven't bought any furniture together.'

'We don't need any furniture,' Lydia said. She gestured around the room. 'We've got all of this.'

Jason pursed his lips, gazing at her in a way that she really didn't care for. 'Do you like Charlie's stuff?'

Lydia winced. She hated to hear it said out loud. 'Charlie's'. It just reminded her that this wasn't her home and that she was living a life she hadn't intended.

'It doesn't take a genius to see that something is off with the two of you.'

He was right, of course. But she wasn't going to admit that. 'We're fine,' she said out loud.

'Everyone you know is going to die,' Jason said flatly.

She started. 'What?'

'It's just a fact,' Jason said. 'I'm not trying to be morbid, but it's hard to escape the facts when you're—' he broke off and gestured to himself.

'What has that got to do with—?'

'Fleet will die one day and so will you. And Emma and Aiden and everyone you know. This is it. This is your moment and if you and Fleet don't talk now and get things back on track, you're just wasting time. And you don't have a lot of it. Not from where I'm standing.'

Jason wasn't so much standing as floating. He was emotional, and when that happened, he tended to forget to anchor himself to the floor like a living human. 'I hear you,' Lydia said, because she didn't know what else to say and one of the podcasts she had listened to recently had said it was important to make people feel heard.

The ghost gave her such a withering look that she felt judged to the tips of her feathers. And then he disappeared. It wasn't a fair way to win an argument, but it was pretty effective.

CHAPTER SIXTEEN

As much as Lydia missed working for herself, and her old Crow Investigations office above The Fork, she didn't often think about where it all started. Training as an investigator, back in Aberdeen, belonged to her life before she had returned to London. Before she had joined the Crow Family in more than name. Once she arrived in London, her Uncle Charlie had manipulated her into looking for her cousin Maddie, and that act had changed the course of her life forever. She couldn't bring herself to regret it. For all the bad things, the danger and the death and the betrayal, Lydia now knew who she was and wasn't running away from it. And she had a purpose in life. Something that she had been looking for without realising it was missing.

Now she had more purpose than she knew what to do with. She had so much purpose she barely had time to think about anything else, so when her phone rang and she recognised Karen's number, her only thought was to hope whatever Karen wanted wasn't going to take too long.

Her old boss and mentor had a whisky-soaked voice and a straight-to-the-point style of communication that Lydia had always liked.

'Do you remember Brad Carter?'

The lecherous problem that had forced her to leave Aberdeen in the first place. The honey-trap gig that had gone wrong when she had let herself get cornered in a hotel room. The wife that had initially commissioned the job, but had sided with her philandering husband, giving up the agency details and putting Lydia at risk. She had needed to get away for a few weeks, just until the man calmed down. That was what had led her to accepting a temporary place to stay, and a job, from her Uncle Charlie. 'Vividly.'

'His wife is in hospital.'

'Hell Hawk.' Lydia could guess what had happened, but Karen explained anyway. Apparently, Carter had been abusive to his wife for years. Emotional and psychological abuse that had morphed more recently into physical attacks. Slaps and punches that had escalated, with a sickening inevitability, until he had apparently broken her leg, wrist and pelvis by pushing her down the stairs in their five-bedroom new build.

'The polis are involved now. Mrs Carter is ready to give evidence against her husband.'

'Good.' Any irritation that a young Lydia had felt with Mrs Carter was long gone. She had met too many frightened women, beaten down until they had no more self-preservation instincts and, worse, were stripped of the belief in their right to live.

'He is claiming a momentary madness due to work stress and alcohol. Prosecution want to establish a pattern of behaviour to support the manslaughter charge, as well as the multiple abuse charges. I need to turn over your notes. The tape. Everything from that operation.'

It took Lydia a second to realise that Karen was asking for her permission. 'Of course.'

'Thank you,' Karen said crisply. 'You might get called as a witness, but hopefully not. The Prosecution Service has plenty of other testimonies. The case looks solid.'

'Anything I can do to help?' Lydia remembered the feel of Carter's hands on her body, his strength as he hauled her against him. The fear in that moment, even though she knew back-up was seconds away.

'Thank you,' Karen said, suddenly sounding tired. 'I appreciate that, hen.'

Hearing her voice, Lydia was transported back to Karen's office. It always smelled of good coffee and the vanilla and cinnamon diffusers she had dotted about the place. It had been a few years since she had seen her old mentor and she wondered, suddenly, whether she would ever retire. It had seemed impossible, but nobody went on forever. 'Are you all right? You sound done in.'

'Not really,' Karen said. 'I'm sick of seeing women in the hospital.'

. . .

Lydia hadn't seen Fleet since their fight, so she wasn't sure what to expect when his name flashed up on her phone.

'Are you free at all today?' His tone was formal, which didn't bode well.

Lydia said she could make time. 'Lunch? Pub?'

'I was thinking a walk and talk.'

They agreed to meet at Burgess Park in thirty minutes. Lydia pulled on joggers and trainers so that she could run back after. Blow off steam if necessary.

Fleet was waiting at the park entrance, looking good in his work suit. 'Chris Perry,' he said after a brief hello. No kiss.

Lydia's heart stuttered. 'Who?'

'Tyler Baxter's old name. He changed it ten years ago, when he moved from London to Manchester.'

It made sense that the police would find out, so it shouldn't have taken her by surprise. She realised that she had been expecting more on Jez and was further distracted by Karen's phone call, bringing back the spectre of Brad Carter. 'That's interesting,' she said, keeping her tone neutral. 'Wonder what prompted that?'

They had started walking and Lydia could feel Fleet staring at her. She glanced his way. 'What?'

'I think Perry was lured to the club on the day he died. We've looked through his phone and he'd used Google maps to find the club. Plus, there was a call from an unknown number at three o'clock the day before.'

'What does the owner of the place say?'

'That he had never heard the names Tyler Baxter or Chris Perry and that he categorically did not telephone him to arrange a meeting. He also has an alibi for the time of death, which we've narrowed to between nine and eleven that morning.'

'Credible alibi?'

'Owner's wife says he was at home with her. So, whoever called him and, presumably, specified the meeting place, could have broken into the club first.'

'A nightclub in the morning would be conveniently quiet. If you were sure the owner didn't come into the place to do his taxes or whatever. Are there cameras at the club?'

'Mainly outside and around the till areas. There are a lot of blind spots, but I still don't see a person carrying a body-size bag into the place without it being caught on camera. Which means we're still stumped by the strange blood pattern at the scene.'

'So, no leads,' Lydia said. 'I'm sorry.'

A pause. 'Just the Fox Family.'

'It wasn't Paul,' Lydia said, side-stepping a man pushing a buggy and puffing on a vape.

Fleet's mouth twisted in displeasure and Lydia didn't know if it was in reaction to her words or the cloud of fake candy floss scent that the man's vape had left. 'Even if I take your word on that, that leaves a lot of other Foxes. And it would explain why nobody is talking.'

'If it was another Fox, Paul would know about it. His Family is even closer than the Crows.'

'You think he would tell you? Just incriminate one of his own?'

It was a fair point. He certainly hadn't thought it was

157

a Fox when she had spoken to him outside of Aysha's flat, but he might not have had all the information. It wasn't like he would call her to update her if he'd subsequently found out one of his siblings or cousins had done the deed.

'Lyds,' Fleet said. 'The murder happened in a club in Whitechapel. The victim left London and changed his name, which suggests he was running away from something here. If it looks like a Fox and sounds like a Fox, it's probably—'

'They aren't stupid,' Lydia argued. 'Why would they leave a body in their territory?'

'Sending a message? Because they're fearless? They know no one will give witness statements.'

Well, she didn't have a good answer for that. Was she being blind? She had history with Paul, and he had picked her up off the street after the River Man had drained her and left her for dead. He had hidden her in a safe place in case she was still in danger, fed her soup. But that didn't mean she could trust everything he said. He was a Fox first and foremost. Still. 'Cerberus is barely in Fox territory. Paul's family doesn't own it.'

'I know that,' Fleet said, 'but you were arguing a moment ago that they wouldn't kill someone in one of their own places. You can't have it both ways.'

Lydia stopped walking. He had a point.

Fleet steered them to a bench. Once they were sitting, Lydia closed her eyes and felt the words she couldn't say backing up in her throat.

'I'm bringing Paul Fox in for questioning. I thought I should warn you.'

Her head snapped up. 'You don't have enough evidence for that.'

'I have three bodies.'

Lydia's mind was whirling. 'I told you, if you focus on the Foxes, it will threaten the truce. You are considered an honorary Crow. Your actions reflect on my Family.'

'I can't help that,' Fleet said, looking away. 'I have to do my job.'

'But I'm telling you he didn't do it.' Her frustration and fear was clear in her voice and she hated it.

'And you always tell me the truth?' Fleet didn't have to say the name 'Jez' to make his point.

'Hell Hawk.' Feeling strangely disloyal to Paul, she said, 'if you want Paul to talk, don't bring him to the station. Visit him on his territory. Even better, let him pick a meeting spot.'

'He's a suspect in a murder case,' Fleet said. 'I'm not letting him dictate jack shit.'

'He's not your man. And he won't say a word if you go about this like police.'

'I am police.' Fleet was staring at her, his gaze boring deep.

'Paul did not do this. But it is his territory and there is a chance he knows something.' Lydia spread her hands. 'You want a chance of finding out what that might be...'

'Fine.' Fleet tilted his head.

Paul still wasn't going to talk to Fleet or any other copper, but at least she had stopped him from being taken to a station. Hopefully she could spin that as special treatment and use it to avert a diplomatic incident. The truce had barely been reinstated, she couldn't have it fall apart already. She would never be able to step down as head of the Family if things weren't stable.

FLEET STAYED AT HIS FLAT THAT NIGHT, AND LYDIA was glad. She was angry that he was endangering the truce over the deaths of three terrible men. It didn't feel like justice, and she didn't understand why he didn't see that. She had texted Paul to warn him, explaining that Fleet was going to speak to him in Whitechapel as a mark of respect and that he wasn't in danger of being arrested.

Paul hadn't responded yet, so Lydia wasn't sure how grateful he was, whether it was enough to prevent a bigger problem. She would find out soon enough, she supposed.

'GEORGIE.'

Lydia had been asleep when the female voice had said the word. Gently, lovingly, and right into Lydia's ear, startling her awake. She opened her eyes and found a shimmering shape standing right by the bed. Thankfully, she was more used to ghosts popping up next to her than the average person, so she didn't immediately go into cardiac arrest. 'Mary?'

The shape shimmered as Mary nodded.

Lydia looked to her left and found that Fleet's side of the bed was empty. Either he was in the bathroom or he

hadn't come back from work. Then she remembered that
he was staying at his flat and wasn't in the house at all.
She had spent the evening reading about the Ripper
murders and drinking whisky alone. Old habits.

'Georgie,' Mary said again.

'I'm sorry.' Lydia scrubbed at her face, trying to wake
up properly. 'I don't—'

'Where's my Georgie?' Her face was a mask of
misery.

Lydia opened her mouth to say something comforting. Luckily, Mary disappeared in the following instant,
as Lydia realised she had no idea what that something
would be. Georgie's long dead? And so are you?

'Your friend nearly gave me a heart attack
last night.' Lydia was drinking coffee and trying to ignore
the crows cawing from their roost in the garden. One of
them could mimic a voice that very much sounded like
Uncle Charlie saying 'Lyds'. She didn't like it.

It took Jason a second to catch on. 'Mary?'

'Can you explain to her that I'm no use to anyone
dead.'

She saw him think about arguing that she wasn't
much use to Mary alive, either, but decide against it.
The near-psychic rapport that she was missing with
Fleet was still perfectly strong with Jason. Which meant
that the person that she was closest to in the world was a
ghost. Was that a problem? It didn't sound like the sort
of thing she could explore in therapy, even if she was
inclined to go.

'How are you getting on with your search? Any other possible Georges? It has to be a common name, like Mary.' Lydia was hoping for a nice normal man, not a murderer. It would be nice for Jason if he found a happy ending to Mary's story. But, given Lydia's experience of investigative work, it didn't seem likely.

Jason didn't answer her question, but instead started telling her about an algorithm he had written to comb through the results on his behalf. As was usually the way when he started speaking maths, he lost her about three words in.

'It hasn't thrown up any other Georges,' Jason said. 'Nobody that fits.'

'So you're stuck with the killer from the court records?'

'And I didn't need the algorithm for that,' Jason said, looking a little bit put out. 'George Chapman's got a Wikipedia entry.'

'Really?'

'He killed at least three women. A Scotland Yard detective at the time thought he was Jack the Ripper. Some people still think he was, but his method of killing was different. Poisoning, not stabbing.'

'Bloody Jack the Ripper,' Lydia felt a rush of irritation. It felt like the case was stalking her.

'I mean, we can't be completely certain he's Mary's Georgie, but it seems likely,' Jason said. 'He worked as a barber. The timing isn't spot-on, but he could have met Mary before the murders he was tried for.'

'So, she's an unknown victim? That would be enough to keep her hanging about, wouldn't it? Does it mean she was killed here? Is that why she's anchored here?'

'Perhaps she's in denial about her death?' Jason said. 'Knows but doesn't know, kind of thing? Maybe she needs to accept it before she can move on?'

'This sounds like ghost therapy, not investigative work. I'm not any good at that stuff.'

Jason shook his head, the motion making Lydia feel sick. 'You're not so bad.'

She felt a rush of warmth at his words. Maybe they could help? And nobody else could hear Mary. 'We're all she's got, anyway.'

'Better than nothing,' Jason said cheerfully. 'You should put that on your business card.'

CHAPTER SEVENTEEN

Lydia tied her hair in a ponytail and put on her trainers. She hadn't heard back from Paul, and Fleet had sent a quick message to say that he would probably stay at his flat again that night as it would 'be a late one'.

She cued up one of the true-crime podcasts that had been discussing the case and headed out. The two hosts, Ellen and Jo, knew an unhealthy amount about Jack the Ripper, but Lydia supposed she wasn't one to talk.

> Ellen: One of the mysteries central to the Ripper murders centres on his escape after the Eddowes killing. Rather than running left into central London, he went deeper into the East End. The theory is that he lived in the area or knew of a hiding place, and was heading for this bolthole. It added fuel to the vigilante fire that was raging in the East End as a result.

Jo: That's true, but it's also true to say that a string of dead women wasn't exactly unusual in this part of London at that time. These deaths were used to fan the flames of antisemitism, and we have to remember that there was more going on with the investigation and the coverage of the case than simple horror for the murders and fear for public safety.

Ellen: That's right. We are talking about an impoverished and vilified group of people, used to being ignored by the establishment. Maybe a bogeyman like the Ripper was the only way to get attention and police action for otherwise tolerated violence against women.

Jo: You're suggesting the letters to the press were from desperate locals, wanting to keep the gaze of the police focused on murders that might have otherwise been functionally ignored.

Lydia was in Camberwell, her rookery, and she had been focusing on the podcast, so it took her longer than it ought to realise she had a tail. Whoever it was, Lydia knew they were wasting their time. She was going to run a lap of the park and then head back to Charlie's house.

Just as she finished her circuit, she changed her mind. If she took her shadow on a bit of a tour, it would give her time to gather some details. She headed to the main road, slowing to a jog as if she was winding down. Outside a chemist with a big glass window, she stopped and stretched as if fighting a stitch. Her tail was across the road, visible in the reflection of the window. He looked vaguely familiar, but was too far away for Lydia to check for a Family sense. With her power not at full strength, she would need to get closer.

She straightened up and took off in the direction of the nearest station. There was a chance it was one of Sinclair's staff checking in on her or wanting to remind her that she was a person of interest. Sinclair had taken over Mr Smith's shadowy government department, which lay somewhere between MI6 and MI5. They were the only official people who seemed truly interested in the four Families and Lydia could do without their attention.

Kennington was on the northern line, and Lydia arrived just before a train. She had clocked her tail as she entered the station, but she wished him good luck once she got off at Leicester Square. If he could track her in that tourist hellhole, then he was seriously underpaid.

She got onto the train and hoped he missed it. If he got onto the same train, he was trapped in a separate carriage for the journey, but she didn't relish the bottle-neck of leaving the station. She took out her ponytail and finger-combed her hair. It wasn't a cold day so she hadn't brought a hat, but she untied the thin sweatshirt from around her waist and put it on. She collected an abandoned newspaper and rolled it into a cylinder, tucking it under her arm when she left the train.

Outside the station, Lydia ducked into the first souvenir shop she passed. It did travel accessories and luggage storage, and was probably a front for money laundering, but most importantly however, it sold tourist clothing. She bought a pink baseball hat which said 'Keep Calm and Carry On' and put it on before stepping back out onto the street.

She debated heading into one of the casinos, but didn't know their layout and didn't want to get trapped, so she headed for theatreland instead. Plenty of crowds, plenty of CCTV.

She hadn't seen her shadow for a few minutes, but kept going, taking a twisty route on streets clogged with tour groups gawping outside theatres, sometimes doubling back. Eventually, she found herself passing the portico pillar entrance to the Lyceum, flanked by yellow posters for The Lion King, and she knew she wasn't far from Waterloo Bridge. The urge to be on the other side of the river was too strong to resist and she headed towards the water.

As soon as she saw the Thames open up, she felt her chest expand. The traffic on the bridge was typically busy and sun caught the glass and metal of the tall buildings along the river. She hadn't seen her shadow since theatreland, so wasn't expecting to see him standing right in front of her on the pedestrian walkway. For a second, her vision was filled with red fur, dark earth, and tangled undergrowth. The smell of green things growing and the coppery tang of blood.

It wasn't one of Paul's brothers, but Lydia guessed close family, probably a cousin.

'What do you want?' For a moment, she thought he might say that Paul had been taken into custody and her body tensed to absorb the blow.

He clicked his teeth. His gaze raked over her body as if assessing. She couldn't tell if it was sexual or violent. It felt like both.

'Is Paul all right?'

'That's none of your business, Crow.'

'You're the one following me,' Lydia said. 'Why bother, if you don't want to talk?'

He gave her a long, disgusted stare. 'You come to our den, we come to yours.'

The threat landed and Lydia tasted blood, felt sharp teeth grazing her skin.

The Fox tilted his head in a way that reminded her of Paul and then moved forward suddenly, brushing past her as he walked back to his side of the river.

CHAPTER EIGHTEEN

Back at Denmark Hill, she found Jason on the street outside. 'I just saw Mary,' he said.

'Out here?' Lydia looked up and down the pavement.

'I've been tracking her routine. You know I told you she does the same things at the same times, like she's still working?'

Lydia nodded. 'I remember.'

'She's not stuck to the house. She told me she had free time between four and six, but I thought she just disappeared. You know, the way I do sometimes? But I just saw her out here, walking up the road.'

'Did you ask where she'd been?'

'Looking for Georgie.'

'Is it time? To tell her what you've found out?'

Jason looked unhappy. 'I don't want to hurt her.'

Lydia felt her chest squeeze. She remembered how she had felt, carrying the information about Jason's death, and then choosing to use it. She had hurt him to help him to anchor to Charlie's house, to make sure that he could continue his afterlife in Camberwell. 'Cruel to be kind,' she said.

THEY FOUND MARY HALFWAY DOWN THE GARDEN. She was holding her arms out as if carrying something and Lydia assumed this was another of her echo-routines. The crows were so loud that Lydia asked if Jason could encourage her to come indoors. She nodded politely to the black corvids before retreating into the kitchen.

'Can we talk to you about your George?' Jason was already asking, his voice gentle.

'Georgie loves me,' Mary said.

'Did he bring you food?' Lydia asked. As well as beating the women he lived with, George Chapman had poisoned them. Jason's theory was that he had done the same to Mary.

Mary shimmered, going translucent for a moment and then flicking back to solid. 'He brought me all kinds of gifts. He is a good man. A real gentleman.'

'Is this George?' Lydia lifted the lithograph of Chapman. It was an illustration they had found online and printed, just in case Mary was too freaked out by a screen to focus on the picture.

Mary stopped shimmering. For a moment, she was completely solid and still. It was as if all the energy that went into making her present beyond death was now focused on the piece of paper that Lydia was holding.

She reached out a hand as if she was going to touch

Chapman's likeness, but her fingers stopped short. 'Georgie?' She whispered his name and it sounded like wind blowing through the tops of trees.

'I'm sorry,' Lydia said, feeling wretched.

Mary's gaze didn't leave the image. 'Is that my Georgie?'

Lydia looked to Jason for help.

He was watching Mary with an anguished expression. When he glanced at Lydia, she saw pain in his eyes and she felt even worse. The victims of crime. The dead. Their anguish and their sorrow. Their impotent rage, the frustration and grief of all they had lost.

'This man is called George Chapman,' Jason said. 'Was that Georgie's name?'

Mary's gaze flicked to Jason. Her expression didn't change for a moment, and Lydia wondered if she hadn't heard him properly. 'Georgie?' Mary moved closer, her feet skimming the floor. Her face creased into a frown as she peered at the piece of paper.

'George Chapman wasn't a good man, I'm afraid,' Jason said. 'I'm sorry.'

Mary was still staring at the image. She blinked and looked at Jason. 'His whiskers look different.'

Jason tried again. 'Was your Georgie called Chapman? Mr Chapman? He worked as a barber in Whitechapel.'

Mary bit her lip, still staring at the picture. There were tears in her eyes. 'I don't... I don't remember. Why can't I—?'

'It's all right,' Jason said, his voice soothing. 'It will

come back to you. And this might not be your Georgie. I will keep looking. I think you would be sure.'

The tears were tracking down her cheeks, but she tried a weak smile. It showed small uneven teeth and made her look even younger. 'I think I would know his face. My Georgie. I would know him—'

'I'll keep looking.' Jason reached a hand out as if he was going to pat Mary's shoulder, but she had already gone.

When Fleet got in from work, he was too keyed up to sit down. Lydia had been chatting to Jason before he walked in, and now they both watched him pacing the kitchen and wondered what had happened. 'Have you been taken off the case?' Lydia asked eventually.

'Not yet,' Fleet said. 'It's warming up, though. Dominic Moss has been working on the Guv.'

'That's not how it works.' Lydia hoped that was true.

Fleet stopped pacing long enough to give her a sympathetic look. 'If only.'

'He looks stressed,' Jason observed. 'Are you two still fighting?'

'Dunno,' Lydia said. 'Maybe.'

'I got the postmortem results today. Perry's kidney was removed.'

'Grim. Left at the scene or taken away?'

'Taken,' Fleet said.

'Trophy?' Jason asked. 'That's some proper serial killer action.'

'It's weird,' Lydia said to Jason. 'And disgusting. And it's the second trophy. Material was taken from Price's shirt.'

'Is he here?' Fleet was looking around the room, his gaze settling in the opposite corner to where Jason was standing.

'Yeah, Jason just said taking trophies is classic serial killer.' She nodded at Jason to help Fleet look in the right direction.

'Don't say that.' Fleet shook his head.

'Serial killer?'

'It makes people lose their minds. Even if these murders are the same man, he is just a criminal. Not special, not clever, not scary.'

'I'd be scared,' Jason said. 'If I wasn't already dead.'

'Why take a kidney?' Lydia asked. 'Is he deliberately emulating the Ripper murders? If so, why are his victims male?'

'I like my kidneys,' Jason said, patting his torso. 'Always have.'

'And another thing,' Fleet said. 'We're assuming the killer is male because of the violence and mutilation. But it could be a woman. Have to be physically strong or very lucky with the first slashes, but it's certainly possible.'

'Lucky or skilled,' Lydia mused.

'Jack the Ripper killed prostitutes, didn't he?' Jason asked.

'Not exclusively, but yes. And we say sex workers now.'

Jason was pacing, his feet not always touching the

floor. Lydia couldn't watch him too closely or she started to feel nauseous. 'And these men have all been bad people, right? Is this a vigilante thing?'

'You think this is revenge for the Ripper murders? A hundred and fifty years later?'

Fleet waited as she talked to Jason, and then she recapped it for him. 'Jason asked if the killer might be doing this to make a point. The Ripper victims have been dismissed as sex workers for years and the first two deaths in your case were connected to that trade. Jack the Ripper targeted women, as if they deserved violence because of their occupations, maybe this copy-cat is targeting the real villains of that industry?'

'Maybe,' Fleet said. 'But Perry wasn't a pimp or a trafficker. And I know violence against women is still a major problem, but most people write a letter or sign a petition. They march with a placard. They don't start killing people.'

'Unless they're really angry,' Jason said. 'What if they've already tried all the other things?'

LYDIA COULDN'T STOP THINKING ABOUT MARY. SHE had died in likely violent circumstances. She was trapped in the present day, looking for her Georgie and repeating her last days over and over again. Even though she hadn't recognised Chapman, there was every chance that she was one of his victims and that her mind was too addled by the intervening decades to recognise him. Or her psyche was protecting her from the truth. She had loved her George, that was obvious. Maybe the depth of his betrayal was too much for her to comprehend?

And if she hadn't been killed by George Chapman, but by some other, unknown man, what remained true was that her murder had not been solved. There had been no justice. No resolution for her. She was a just a working-class woman and nobody had cared enough about her death to find the person responsible.

She had been so caught up in the truce and her role as the head of the Crow Family that she had lost sight of that.

'THERE'S SOMETHING I NEED TO TELL YOU,' LYDIA began, once Fleet was back from work. 'But you can't tell your colleagues. It can't be official.'

Fleet was sitting with his feet on the edge of the coffee table. He was freshly showered after a run and wearing t-shirt and sweats. Off-duty. She felt bad interrupting that mode, but knew she couldn't put it off any longer. Jason was right. Emma was right. If she kept hiding everything from Fleet, they weren't going to make it. And this could help him solve his case. She knew she wouldn't forgive him if he kept vital information from her in the same circumstances.

'What is it?'

'I need you to promise me that it will go no further. You cannot hear this as a cop. You cannot act on it.'

He tilted his head. 'You're scaring me.'

'Good. I'm serious.'

He sat forward. 'All right. I am not a cop right now.

And I will not repeat this information to the police citing you as the source.'

Lydia narrowed her eyes. 'No loopholes.'

He sighed. 'Fine. No loopholes. Just tell me.'

'Ten years ago, Chris Perry abused a young woman he was dating. Like Lauren, she was much younger than him. You won't find it in the system because the victim didn't go to the police.'

'How do you know this?'

'I can't tell you.'

Fleet watched her, thinking. Then he asked. 'Not Emma?'

'No.'

'Okay.' After a moment, he added: 'Did you just find this out or have you known for a while?'

'I recognised Perry when I saw his body.'

Fleet tensed up. 'Did he hurt you?'

Lydia warmed at his concern. 'No. Nothing like that.'

'Is there anything else you can tell me? Anything that might be relevant?'

'Just that I'm not crying over his death.'

Fleet nodded. 'Okay. Thank you for telling me.'

'It's a link,' Lydia said. 'Another man with a history of abusing women.'

'He's hardly in the same league as Price.'

'I don't particularly want to get into a Top Trumps conversation,' Lydia said. 'Isn't it enough that they're all abusive scum?'

'Of course,' Fleet said, his tone conciliatory. 'But from an investigative point of view...'

She sighed. He was right, of course. The details mattered. 'They might have crossed paths. Nightclubs and adult entertainment. There could be a link there.'

He nodded. 'I've got something to tell you, too.'

She waited.

'As you predicted, Paul Fox didn't say a thing.' He lifted his chin. 'But I'm not so certain he was involved.'

'What changed your mind?'

'The kidney that was taken. I don't like the man and believe he would be capable of violence, even torture, but the kidney was removed after Perry's death. That's mutilation for its own sake.' He locked eyes with Lydia. 'I know you two have a history. From back in the day. I think you're a better judge of character than that and can't believe you would have been romantic with a complete sicko.'

'Thank you,' Lydia said. She climbed onto Fleet's lap. 'That's one of the nicest things you've ever said to me.'

He tipped his head, a smile warming his eyes. 'There's more where that came from.'

She pressed her lips to his. No more talking.

CHAPTER NINETEEN

When the news broke that reality TV star and social media influencer, Connor Bright, had been brutally murdered, Lydia's first thought was that Fleet might have his case taken away. She wasn't proud of that – a human being had died, and in a most dreadful way – but it was the truth. Her second thought was for the victim and his family, but her third was to wonder why the hell Fleet hadn't told her about it before it hit the papers.

As if summoning him, her phone rang. 'I just saw,' she said to Fleet.

'It's a circus here.' Fleet's voice clear, despite the sound of traffic and people. He was outside, probably pacing around his office building. 'Higher-ups are in an emergency task meeting and then I guess I'll find out. They'll reorganise for sure, but I don't know whether I'll be kept involved. There are a few on my team who would complain if I get shunted, but I don't want them to stick their necks out.'

Fleet said a good deal more on the subject of interdepartmental politics and the idiocies perpetrated in the name of 'top-down strategical reorganisation initiatives', but Lydia wasn't entirely listening. She was wondering how Connor Bright had been killed and whether it matched the first three deaths.

'I don't know what's going to happen,' Fleet finished. 'And I'll likely be late again tonight. I'll call.'

'Is it the same guy?' Lydia managed to ask before Fleet hung up.

'I believe so.' Fleet lowered his voice. 'Multiple stab wounds.'

CONNOR BRIGHT HAD WON A SMALL BRITISH reality TV show eleven years ago. That had been followed by a successful stint on a bigger show, and then a short appearance in the quickly cancelled *Jailed For Love,* in which contestants were locked in cells for twenty hours of the day before being allowed to mingle with the other contestants and, ostensibly, try to find love. All the while, Connor was growing his Instagram presence, taking targeted sponsorship deals in the fitness and rapidly growing 'wellness' space until he was considered a voice in that industry.

Lydia learned all of this from a podcast called 'Time's Up'. The host claimed that she didn't just report and reflect on the stories of badly behaved men being called to account, but that she also broke the news on some, doing investigative journalism behind the scenes. Lydia wasn't sure which category she would put Connor

Bright, but she spoke of several allegations against him from fellow contestants, plus alluded to a recorded phone call that she would play in next week's episode.

Connor Bright charmed the nation when he appeared on our screens. And with his unbelievable blue eyes and cheeky smile, the ladies were lining up to help soothe the burn when he lost out to Joe Edge in the series finale.

Whatever the truth of his private life at this time, Connor was also playing hard at work. He parlayed his moment of fame into building his Instagram following. His content was engaging and beautifully shot. He spent hours replying to his fans and building a sense of community with his campaigns like #FittyFriday and #Protein-Power. In two thousand and eighteen, he launched his own line of supplements, but these were quietly shelved a year later after an investigation was launched into the health claims made by Bright.

This minor scandal didn't seem to dent his star power as an influencer, but he pivoted over the next twelve months into focusing on the internal work and spiritual side of self-improvement. The hashtags swapped to ones about inner peace, attitude of gratitude and recognising his own privilege. He launched a podcast and YouTube channel called 'Mr Brightside'. In one of the episodes, he spoke of his realisation that he had not always treated women with the respect that they deserved and had been 'lost in his addiction to sex'. At the time, it played like honesty and accountability and vulnerability.

With the shocking accusations that have been spilling out from several women since Mia Smith came forward with allegations of coercion, sexual and emotional abuse, it plays as rather more sinister. At best, the self-delusional ravings of an abuser-in-denial or the cynical attempt by a misogynist criminal to pre-empt and stage-manage any accusations of wrongdoing.

Lydia paused the podcast and stared out of the window for a few moments. Next, she switched to YouTube and Instagram. She scrolled through his feeds before clicking on a couple of short-form videos. She put the crime scene and postmortem images from her mind and focused on him as he was. Alive. Whole. Unbelievably phony. How had anybody fallen for his crap? The long earnest looks. The psychobabble. He spoke in convoluted sentences, peppered with three-syllable words, and it painted an illusion of intelligence and self-reflection. It was the sheer self-confidence, she supposed. It was strangely alluring, even while you thought he was a bit of a prick. And he was undeniably beautiful. She felt her tattoos burning and realised that her nose was almost pressed against her phone screen, almost touching the moving image of Connor Bright. And forty minutes had passed.

She called Fleet. 'Connor Bright was a Pearl.'

It was quiet on his end. Not just his lack of reply, but also the background. He had to be sitting in his office with the door closed.

'Sorry,' he said. 'Just woke up. I'm at home.'

Not at the office. At home. His home. Jason was right. Fleet hadn't moved into Charlie's house. And she was still calling it Charlie's house. Hell Hawk. 'Are you all right?'

'Just tired. Pulled a late shift and needed to get some shuteye before I go back in. You said Bright's a Pearl?'

'Yeah. Quite strong, judging by my reaction to his Instagram.'

'Are you still... I don't know how to phrase it...'

'Reliable?' Lydia pulled a face that she was glad he couldn't see. 'I can't be sure on the strength, I don't know if I'm feeling that in the same way as I was before. I can't measure him against the Pearl King, but if I'm sensing Pearl blood, he's definitely got some. I thought you would want to know.'

'I do.' She heard a rasping sound and knew Fleet was rubbing his jaw and that he needed to shave. 'Why didn't you come back here to sleep?' She hadn't intended to ask the question.

A pause. 'I don't know.'

She was glad he hadn't said something polite but nonsensical like 'I didn't want to disturb you', but his quiet confusion wasn't exactly a ringing endorsement in their relationship. 'Okay,' she said. 'It's okay.'

'Can we talk later? I've got to get back.'

'Of course.' She hesitated. 'Unless there's anything I can do?'

'That's okay,' he said, the words seemingly automatic.

Lydia tried not to take it as a rebuff, another widening of the gap between them, but it was difficult.

CHAPTER TWENTY

Over the next couple of days, Lydia couldn't stop herself from continuing to read the coverage of the murder. The internet was ablaze. Connor Bright had been killed so brazenly, so shockingly, it had lit a thousand theories. One poster suggested that it was a conspiracy from the left, killing one of their own to pin the blame on the right in order to... That was unclear. Stir trouble? Sow doubt in the supporters of the right? Several other posts said the opposite. That it was the right, lashing out at someone they saw as part of the leftie intellectual elite. That was followed by a few taking umbrage at the suggestion that Bright was part of the leftie intellectual elite. Someone with the handle @ActuallySmart pointed out that while Bright could string a sentence together and knew some long words, he was a working-class puppet of capitalism and as intellectually rigorous as a paper bag.

Everybody seemed to have an opinion, nobody said

anything of value to the investigation, and the whole experience left Lydia feeling in need of a long shower.

Fleet had been working long hours, but he had stayed with Lydia for the past two nights. Now he was awake. Lydia realised that a split second after she became conscious. He was sitting upright and breathing heavily. She reached for him in the dark. 'Bad dream?'

'I have to go.'

He was throwing back the covers and pulling on clothes and Lydia felt a rush of adrenaline, shaking her fully awake. 'What's wrong?'

'I saw someone getting hurt. I have to stop it.'

Lydia sat up and reached for her discarded clothes. 'Where?'

'House party.' He clicked on the bedside light and they blinked at each other in the sudden brightness. 'Camberwell. I think. I'm not sure.'

'Okay. Anything more specific? Did you see a street or just inside the house?'

Fleet gave her a grateful look, and she knew what it meant. It meant 'thank you for believing me, thank you for not wasting time'. He closed his eyes, concentrating.

Lydia swigged some flat coke and laced her DMs and waited. When he opened his eyes again, she was ready to go and so was Fleet. 'It's somewhere I know. I've been to the house. A few years back, when I was a PC. Breach of the peace. It's not far.' Fleet had an encyclopaedic memory when it came to his cases. Lydia

188

could relate. The details of every client she had ever had were etched onto her brain, too.

THEY COULD HEAR THE THUMPING BASS THE moment they opened the car doors. Lydia imagined she could see the glass of the windows pulsing in time with it and she took a deep breath before following Fleet through the unlocked front door, as if she was about to dive into water.

Fleet was in off-duty mode. He didn't flash his warrant card or introduce himself. Dressed in his gym clothes and a beanie, he probably thought he blended into the crowd. Lydia watched people glance at him and move away and knew they were thinking 'trouble'. A beanie couldn't hide his military posture and aura of authority. Fleet was a copper through and through and Londoners in this manor could spot one in the dark with their eyes closed.

She forged on through the press of bodies. The smell of skunk was thick and the smoke made her eyes prickle. Fleet had given her the name of the victim and she grabbed the shoulder of a woman with electric blue eyeshadow and an afro and shouted the name into her ear. The woman shook her head and carried on through to the adjoining room.

This was a party house or a squat or both. The walls were covered in graffiti and, underneath the skunk and body odour and clashing perfumes and booze, there was the unmistakable odour of drains and mould. She took the stairs to the first floor, squeezing past a couple who were half-naked and suctioned together, oblivious.

The upper landing was marginally quieter, but that only meant that Lydia didn't feel like her ears were about to start bleeding. Her feet stuck to the carpet and she didn't want to think about what was spilled there.

Fleet hadn't been able to say what room the victim had been in, so their plan was to search the whole house. She didn't know how much time they had, Fleet's premonitions didn't have a consistent timescale, but it was good that the party was still happening. There was still a chance the victim was alive.

The room to her left had no door. A couple were using a filthy mattress in the middle of the floor, with assorted people sitting around the perimeter, leaning against the walls. Some of them were probably enjoying the show, but most appeared catatonic. Heroin or ketamine or too much skunk.

The next room had a door, albeit one with a ragged hole in the lower half where some charmer had kicked the shit out of the cheap wood. Lydia pushed it open and knew she was in the right place.

The kid was backed against the wall, eyes round with fear. The man holding a bottle loosely by his side was skinny and had the flaking, spotty skin of either drug use or ill health. A woman, barely out of her teens by appearance, was saying 'leave him, he's all right'.

'He was laughing,' the skinny guy spat into the child's face. 'Weren't you, mate? Find something funny?'

The kid shook his head. He was trying to keep it together, but Lydia could see he was trembling.

'Can I help?' Lydia said, addressing the young woman.

The skinny guy whipped around. 'What the fuck do you want?'

Lydia kept her gaze on the woman. She was clearly on something herself, eyes darting around, leg jittering. 'You want to leave? Just nod if you want me to get you out of here.'

'We're fine. It's fine. He just gets like this.'

'What the fuck are you saying to my girlfriend?' The man had turned away from the kid, which was exactly what Lydia had wanted. Of course, now she had to defuse the situation before he started whaling on his girlfriend. Or her. 'Just checking she's all right. There's a lot of shouting.'

A frown creased the guy's face. As if he was genuinely trying to puzzle what might seem amiss in a situation in which he was yelling and physically threatening a child. It spoke volumes about his usual behaviour and Lydia knew he had learned that behaviour from someone else. Probably a father or uncle with quick fists and a mean temper. She felt a familiar wave of tiredness.

'It's none of your fucking business.' Skinny guy raised the bottle in her direction.

'I'm fine,' the young woman said. She probably meant it to be placating, but it drew her delightful boyfriend's attention.

'What the fuck are you talking to her for? Shut your face.'

The kid was sliding along the wall very slowly.

Inching his way toward the door.

Lydia stepped further into the room, away from the door. She was about to say something insulting to draw the guy's attention and give the kid a chance to slip out when the door banged open.

'Police,' Fleet said. 'Now what the hell is going on in here?'

Skinny guy and his girlfriend both shut up quick smart. You don't talk to coppers.

'We were just leaving,' Lydia said. She backed up until she was next to Fleet. The kid had frozen to the spot, but she saw his eyes flick to the open door. She hadn't noticed before, but there was a line of blood trickling down from his hairline. It had almost reached his eyebrow.

'I'm not saying nuffink,' the skinny guy said.

'Suits me,' Fleet said. 'I'm off the clock and I don't particularly want to search you. Too much paperwork. I'll have that, though.' He held his hand out for the bottle.

It was beer, half full, and the guy dropped it onto the floor, letting the liquid spill out. He smirked at Fleet.

His girlfriend, perhaps less smashed than her boyfriend, or just with more sense, crouched down to retrieve the bottle and handed it over to Fleet.

Lydia took her opportunity. She grabbed the woman's slim arm and held her close for a moment. She looked into her eyes, telegraphing as much honesty and certainty as she could. 'He won't change. You can do better. Leave him.'

CHAPTER TWENTY-ONE

Outside the house, Lydia turned toward the car, but turned back when she realised that Fleet wasn't moving. He was talking to the kid they had rescued. Lydia assumed the danger had been mortal, although she couldn't quite see skinny guy as a murderer. Not of a random kid, anyway.

'Are you coming?'

'We all are,' Fleet said.

'No. I'm not,' the kid said. Not unreasonably, Lydia thought.

'I'm not leaving you here,' Fleet argued.

'Where do you live?' Lydia asked, trying to be the voice of reason. They had saved the kid from whatever sticky situation that had been, and now they could go back to bed. She glanced at Fleet, willing him to see sense. 'We can drop you home.'

'I'm not telling you anything.'

'Charming,' Lydia said. 'I'm Lydia, by the way. And this is Fleet. We just saved your arse.'

'He's scared,' Fleet said.

'Am not.' The kid said.

'We can't just walk away.' Fleet had his hands in his pockets, and he looked immovable as a mountain.

Lydia was thinking that they absolutely could. They had saved the kid's life, prevented whatever Fleet had seen in his vision. It was almost dawn and she had a full day ahead. She didn't need to kidnap a child.

Before she could say as much, Fleet clapped a hand on the kid's shoulder and walked him to the car. As soon as they drew level with Lydia, she felt something. A tiny gleam, and then it was gone. It was as if a pinprick of sunlight had hit fast-flowing water.

Fleet put the kid in the back of the car and got into the driving seat. Sat in the passenger seat, Lydia twisted around. 'Last chance, kid. Give us your name and address or you'll have to come back to stay at ours for the night. The rest of the night.'

'He's not going to tell us,' Fleet said as he started the car. 'He thinks I'm a cop.'

'You said you were,' the kid said. 'You're not allowed to say that if you aren't. And you have to say if you are.'

It was the most she had heard him say, and it was about the legalities of police identification. Lydia squashed a smile.

'I'm a cop,' Fleet said. 'But right now I'm off duty. And I'm not going to book you. Not for nicking stuff tonight. You have my word.'

Lydia watched the kid's eyes grow bigger. He was clearly used to hiding his emotions, but he was only a child and not that skilled at it yet. She wondered how old he was. She wasn't good with kids and found it extremely difficult to pinpoint their ages. He was small and could be anything from seven to thirteen.

She turned back to address Fleet. 'He was stealing?'

'Party like that is good pickings. Time it right and everyone is off their face and not watching their stuff, or they're outright unconscious. You can have a good look through their pockets.' He raised his eyes to the rearview mirror. 'Isn't that right? And even if someone thinks it's weird that a kid is wandering about the place, you just have to say you're so-and-so's little brother and keep on moving.'

'Smart,' Lydia said.

'Not very,' Fleet said in a flat tone. 'People are off their faces and that can make them unpredictable. And it's easy to get trapped in a room with a psycho and only one exit.'

'He wasn't a psycho,' the kid said sullenly. 'He was just messing around.'

'What was he trying to do?'

Lydia didn't know what Fleet was getting at. The skinny guy had looked like he was about to hit the kid. Probably already had, judging by the head wound. Lydia wondered whether they ought to be taking the kid to A&E, although the blood seemed to have slowed and she didn't know how cooperative he would be.

Silence from the backseat.

'He was trying to get you to take something, wasn't he?' Fleet asked. 'Thought it would be funny.'

'How do you—?' The kid bit off the end of the sentence, resumed staring resentfully out of the window.

Fleet shot Lydia a glance, then put his attention back on the road. They were making good time, the roads blessedly quiet at this hour.

'He was going to force a pill into your mouth, and about ten minutes later, you were going to go into cardiac arrest.'

'All right, Grandpa,' the kid said. 'Drugs are bad. We had the talk at school.'

'You saw it happen?' Lydia asked Fleet, even though she knew the answer.

'Clear as day. His eyes rolled back in his head and he went down. Hardly had time to clutch his chest.'

Lydia looked at the kid. He had to be pretty young. Emma probably wouldn't approve of their scaring him. On the other hand, he was still staring out of the window, face blank. And he was a thief, apparently. She realised she had no idea what they were going to do with him once they got home. How would she stop him from leaving if he wanted to go? Would she wake up and find he had taken her television?

They drove for a short while in silence. Lydia was wondering how many visions Fleet was still having. Was this the latest in a long line, but just the first one he had mentioned, or had he been as untroubled as he had claimed?

'That's not what happens with E,' the kid said.

'It can,' Lydia replied absently. 'If you're unlucky. You could have an existing condition, something that makes your system susceptible.'

'Well I don't, do I? So you is talking out your—'

She twisted in her seat, trying to eyeball the kid. His

196

face was in shadow, striping with the light from the streetlights. 'You remember Christian Eriksen? Fit young footballer. Had a heart attack in the middle of a match. He would have had physical assessments as part of his training, but it wasn't picked up.'

'They fitted a device to keep his heart working normally,' Fleet said. 'Saved his life.'

'You could have something wrong and not know it. Not until you take something that stresses your heart.'

'You're just trying to scare me. Sickos.'

Lydia noticed that he hadn't said a word about his address. He really didn't want to tell them where he lived, which was good self-preservation, but it did make her think he had a plan for when they arrived at their destination.

She wasn't wrong. As soon as the car slowed, he tried the handle of the door. Luckily, the child locks were engaged.

'We're not going to hurt you,' Lydia said. She was aiming for soothing, but knew it had come out cranky. She was tired. And worried. 'We are trying to keep you safe.'

'Let me go then,' the kid said. 'I can make my own way.'

'Give me your name and address and I'll take you home right now,' Fleet said as he parked the car. 'Or you can stay with us for a few hours. Get some kip, have some breakfast, and then we'll see. Doesn't feel as bad letting you out on your own in the daytime. You're clearly used to looking after yourself.'

The boy's chest puffed up at this and Lydia was

reminded that Fleet was so much better with people than she was.

They walked up to the front door together, the boy sandwiched between her and Fleet. Inside, he whistled. 'Nice digs.'

'Don't steal anything,' Fleet said. 'I might remember I'm a cop.'

The kid nodded silently.

'You want something to eat now?' Lydia wanted to sleep, but had a feeling that she wasn't going to drop off with a tiny larcenist on the premises.

Nothing.

'Spare room is this way.' Fleet led the way to the third bedroom. It was barely big enough for the name, but there was a bed. 'I'm going to get some shuteye before my shift starts, so do me a favour and do the same. It's been a night.'

The kid didn't reply, but he shuffled obediently into the room.

'Right,' Fleet said, and walked down the hall to their bedroom.

Lydia was left standing awkwardly. She wanted to close the door, but it felt like she was keeping him prisoner. He hadn't kicked up much of a fuss, not really, but he was probably used to grownups taking control of situations, telling him what to do.

She hung in the doorway for another moment before adding, 'Don't be afraid, we really do just want to make sure you're okay.'

'I'm not scared,' the kid shot back.

'You really not going to tell me your name?'

The kid was looking around the room, and now he moved toward the bed. She realised the kid was as tired as she was and watched him sit down. His hands spread out to either side, feeling the soft duvet, his fingers curling into the fabric.

'How is your head? Do you feel sick at all?' A horrible thought had entered her mind. What if the kid had a concussion? Would Fleet have seen that too? Or had he been shown enough for them to save the kid from the angry drug-guy, only to lose him to a brain bleed they hadn't checked out? Was this what Emma felt like all the time? It was bloody exhausting.

'Ember.'

It took her a second to find her place in the conversation. 'Nice to meet you, Ember. Get some sleep.'

Lydia turned away, feeling a tiny spark of triumph. Then she realised that wasn't the only spark. The kid was closing the door, but she put a hand to stop it. Looked at the kid's face. Now that Fleet wasn't there, the constant flare of his gleam was dimmed, and she was able to see something else buried in Ember's brown eyes. The light of sunshine on a beautiful day.

CHAPTER TWENTY-TWO

As predicted, Lydia didn't sleep. She lay in the grey dawn and listened to Fleet's breath grow deep and slow. She expected to hear the door down the hallway open, Ember creep around the house, but it stayed shut.

Fleet's alarm went off at nine. He had a virtual meeting at half-past and then a face-to-face with the commissioner. Lydia had long since got used to his superhuman ability to fall asleep and then to wake up a few hours later, seemingly refreshed. She, on the other hand, felt like death warmed up.

Before his video call, she remembered to tell him about the Connor Bright podcast episode she had listened to. 'Don't know if it's worth speaking to the creators.'

He wrote down the details and said he would pass it onto the team. 'We're drowning in info for this one. Connor's life is so well documented, and people are falling over themselves to speak to us.'

'You sound as if that's a bad thing.'

'It muddies things, makes it hard to know who has real information and who just wants a chance to show they were close to a famous person. It makes them feel important, I suppose. And it all takes so much time, we're stretched as it is.'

In the kitchen, Jason was pouring a bowl of cereal. 'We have a guest,' she said. 'Is there coffee?'

Jason indicated the machine. 'I can get it.'

'Thank you.' Lydia's head was splitting.

'Who are you talking to?'

Ember had appeared in the doorway and Lydia moved to shield his view of a mug suspended in mid-air.

'Myself,' she said.

Behind her, Jason slowly replaced the mug back onto the counter. 'Who's this?'

'Do you want some cereal, Ember?' Lydia asked brightly. She was channelling Emma and her motherly competence.

'Nah,' Ember shook his head.

'What sort of name is that?' Jason said directly into her ear. Her whole body shivered from the sudden blast of cold.

'Toast?' Lydia kept her focus on Ember.

'I want to go, innit?'

It was very definitely a question.

'You got somewhere to be? Wait,' Lydia put a hand dramatically onto her forehead as if remembering something super important. 'Is it a school day?'

Ember snorted.

'Thought as much.'

'Why is there a child in the kitchen?' Jason whispered into Lydia's ear, making her shiver. 'Whose is he?'

'No idea,' Lydia said quietly, turning to get herself some bread and stick it in the toaster. She put extra in case Ember changed his mind. How anyone could resist the smell of toasting bread was beyond Lydia. It was the perfect food.

She waggled her eyebrows at Jason and then raised her voice to tell Ember they had Nutella.

'Congratulations,' he replied flatly.

'Don't be snotty,' she said. 'Fleet could've arrested you last night.'

'No he couldn't,' Ember said. 'He didn't have a warrant.'

Lydia had no idea if the kid was right. She concentrated on buttering her toast. Working on some deeply buried maternal instinct, she spread Nutella on one of the extra pieces and butter and jam on the other. She stopped short of cutting them in two, though. Ember was old enough to cut his own damn toast if he wanted.

She put the plate on the breakfast bar near to where Ember was standing, looking prickly and as if he desperately wanted to run. But she had seen the flicker in his eyes when she had mentioned Nutella. The kid was hungry.

Jason had drifted close to Ember, and Lydia watched the boy turn his head in his direction. For a second, it appeared as if he was staring directly at the ghost, but then he moved to the breakfast bar and picked up a piece of toast. Taking a big bite, he circled the room, looking at everything like he was assessing its value.

Fleet walked into the kitchen a moment later. He was showered and suited and fresh from his video call. His eyes flicked to Lydia in a silent question. She gave a small shrug.

'I'm going into work.' Fleet said. 'See you later?'

'Yep,' Lydia said.

To Ember he said, 'stop nicking stuff'. He hesitated before adding, 'get your mum to take you to the doctor' and then he left.

Lydia finished her toast and licked her fingers. 'You should, you know.'

'There's nuffink wrong with me,' Ember said around a mouthful of breakfast. 'You two are cracked.'

'If we're wrong, where's the harm?'

'Doctor isn't going to send me for some test just because I ask. Haven't you heard about the NHS crisis?'

Deciding to ignore the fact that she was being out-debated by a child, she said, 'Say you are having chest pain. Say you feel faint when you're playing football.'

'I don't play football.'

'When you're running away from someone you just pick-pocketed, then.'

Ember smiled. It was sudden and for that instant he looked very young. She could see him in one of those primary school sweatshirts, carrying a lunch box and giggling with his friends.

'You should let your parents know where you are. They'll be worried.'

His expression closed down. 'Nah they won't.'

．　．　．

When Fleet came in that evening, he didn't ask about Ember. He looked exhausted and grabbed a beer from the fridge.

'The kid left after breakfast.' Lydia had wanted to make Ember stay or to at least follow him wherever he was going, but she hadn't known what to do. Either of those options felt like kidnapping or harassment. She had asked Jason to follow the boy, just to make sure he had got home safely, but he hadn't returned. She had been trying, unsuccessfully, not to worry. She didn't know how Emma did it.

Fleet opened the bottle and took a long drink. 'Shit. I forgot about him.'

'It's okay,' Lydia said. She leaned against the cabinets and studied Fleet. 'You look knackered.'

'I feel it.' He tipped the bottle again. 'There are plenty of people with a reason to want Bright dead and even more who just want to talk about the one time they met him.'

'Do you believe it isn't Paul now?'

Fleet fixed her with an exasperated look. 'It could still be the Foxes.'

'Why would they kill Connor Bright?' Lydia amended her question. 'Messily, I mean? They are perfectly capable of taking someone out without bringing this kind of heat.'

'You would know,' Fleet said, but without malice.

Lydia shrugged, not denying it. 'You have a serial killer. It's time to stop fixating on the Foxes.'

'I haven't been fixating. I have been following several lines of enquiry.'

'Great. What have you found?'

'A serial killer could still be a Fox.' Fleet wasn't letting that go in a hurry. Then he blew out a loud breath. 'There doesn't appear to be a connection between Perry and Bright, or between Bright and Johnstone or Price. As far as we know, they never met, weren't aware of each other, and had no mutual connections.'

'Okay,' Lydia said.

'They were killed or displayed in and around Whitechapel, which is a connection. All in or close to famous Ripper murder sites.'

Lydia had been thinking about the locations herself. Whoever was doing this was going to a lot of effort to emulate the Ripper killings.

Fleet gestured with his bottle. 'If only the CCTV hadn't been bollocksed, we would be able to watch the damn thing.'

Mitre Square was a forest of cameras and the railings that held the information board about Catherine Eddowes faced multiple office buildings, each with their own security. 'If we assume they are all the same killer, then he is getting more elaborate. More daring. I would say he was choosing his victims by geographic area—'

'Like the Ripper.'

'Exactly. But he is being more selective, more targeted.'

'It looks like he lured Perry to the club. Or moved his

body after killing him elsewhere... we still haven't got an explanation for the weird blood pattern at the scene.'

'If we accept the killer is choosing his victims, rather than making opportunistic attacks, then he had to get Connor Bright to Mitre Square. The location had to be important enough for him to take the risk of committing the murder in view of a lot of security.'

'Perhaps he knew it wouldn't show on camera.'

The powerful Crows messed with CCTV. Charlie Crow and Lydia herself weren't recorded, the video just showing white snow or a blank screen. 'But how did he get Bright to Mitre Square?' Lydia pressed, not wanting to get distracted by the CCTV, or for Fleet to add the Crow Family to his suspect list. 'How did he ensure he was there at the right time?'

Fleet went still, his eyes unfocused as he thought. Then he said, 'earlier that night, he had been to a PR event at the Barbican, and then he met friends at a rooftop bar not far from the Gherkin. The friends we have interviewed have confirmed that he received a phone call and left soon after. They were all expecting him to return, but that is the last they reportedly saw him.'

'You don't believe them?'

'I am keeping an open mind.' He shrugged. 'I don't fancy any of them for it, though.' He began ticking off his fingers. 'One was in Dubai at the time of the first and second murders, one is the size of a doll and I can't imagine her shifting a body, not without help, and the third guy, Marcus Stevenage, is recorded extensively on

CCTV getting the tube home to Camden thirty minutes before the time of death.'

They had a startlingly small window for the murder, given the fuzzy CCTV, the condition of the body and the busy-ness of the area. Whoever had gutted Connor Bright had done so with nerves of steel in a vanishingly small window of opportunity. 'Is there anything useful from the postmortem?'

'Nothing new. The weapon was a blade, at least eight-inches long. Not a serrated edge and new or well-maintained, given there were no rust particles. Probably a kitchen knife, but could be a zombie knife, but only the smooth edge used.'

'Zombie knife? What on earth is that?' Jason's voice was right next to Lydia's ear. She hadn't noticed him come into the room and wondered if he had just materialised on her side of the kitchen island. She smiled at him, more relieved than she cared to admit. It was great that Jason could roam freely now, but she couldn't help worrying about him getting lost somewhere. If he needed powering up and she didn't know where he was, he might disappear forever.

'Jason's here,' she said. 'And he wants to know what a zombie knife is.'

While Fleet sketched the basics – knives inspired by zombie-apocalypse film and TV, blades over eight-inches long, with one smooth and one deeply serrated edge, and often with words etched or cut into the blade. Popular with gangs, they looked like props from The Walking Dead, but did terrifying non-fictional damage. Lydia tried to think about the attack. It was hard. She was no fan of Connor Bright and the more she discovered, the less she liked him, but the violence of the attack was shocking.

Fleet's phone rang and he took the call. He stepped out into the hallway, lowering his voice, and Lydia tried not to take it personally. They had to work out how to work around each other. They had to maintain professional boundaries.

When he walked back into the kitchen, his face was grave, but his eyes were lit up. Excitement. 'That was the station. They've found the weapon.'

'Zombie knife?' Jason asked.

It took Lydia a second to remember that Fleet couldn't hear the question. She repeated it.

'Chef's knife. Dropped into a drain not far from where Connor died.'

'How was it found?'

'There's a filter underneath the grating. We were checking them all, so it was just a matter of time. With any luck, we'll lift prints. It's a fully forged metal handle, perfect material for them.'

'Okay, then. That's good.'

He was shaking his head. 'It's so messy. So reckless. It's like they want to get caught.'

'You're always telling me that most criminals have impulse control issues. That they aren't that smart or calculated.'

'It's the essential paradox of this case. On one hand, you have someone carefully calculating and planning. They are organised and controlled enough to emulate the Ripper murders by location and timing. They have chosen their victims for what appears to be specific reasons. This requires research and resources.' Fleet shook his head. 'None of that sounds like the same person who would drop a murder weapon in a nearby drain. Or carry out such frenzied attacks.'

'That's part of emulating the Ripper, though, right? Could they be performing the frenzy?'

'I don't buy it,' Fleet said. 'It's too emotional. This level of violence.'

'Or no emotion. Sociopathy or psychopathy or one of those.'

'Up until now, I would have agreed with you, but this is beyond sloppy. We will catch him and he must know that. It makes me worry that this is a different killer. Or more than one person working together. I don't want to be too eager to wrap up all the cases in one and then find we made a mistake.'

'I get that,' Lydia said. She was going to say more, but Fleet's phone rang.

CHAPTER TWENTY-THREE

F leet walked into another room while he spoke on the phone. He left his beer on the counter and Lydia picked it up and took a swig. 'I was worried about you.'

Jason looked confused. 'What could happen to me? I'm already dead.'

Lydia decided not to voice her concerns about him getting lost. He was a grown man. And many years older than she was, if you wanted to get technical about it. It wasn't her place to baby him.

'I followed the kid home,' Jason said. 'Like you said, to make sure he had a home.'

'Thank you,' Lydia said. 'Did he get there all right?'

'Just off Rye Lane. Tenth-floor flat. Looks like he lives with his gran.'

'That's good.'

'Not really. It *looks* like he lives with his gran, but I think he's on his own.'

'What do you mean?'

'There was some unopened post addressed to a Mrs Williams and old person stuff, like a Zimmer and one of those big handles bolted to the wall by the front door, but the place is a state.'

'Things might have got too much for her. And Ember doesn't strike me as the helpful sort. I mean, he's just a kid. He might not even realise she needs help. I could pay for a cleaner.'

Jason shook his head, his whole body shimmering at the same time. He was upset, and Lydia forced herself to focus on him.

'Something's really not right there. I think you should call round. Check it out. You'll see what I mean.'

Lydia opened her mouth to say that she wasn't social services and that it wasn't her responsibility. Ember's address was barely even her rookery. It was right on the border with Peckham, but she saw Jason's expression and closed it again.

'He's in a bad way,' Jason said. He was vibrating with emotion. 'He is a child. He shouldn't be living like that.'

ONCE FLEET HAD FINISHED HIS PHONE CALL, HE heated up some leftover curry and they ate with their screens, scrolling the #RipperReturns hashtags and exchanging particularly over-the-top comments. Jason had his laptop and was doing the same, albeit without the food.

'This world,' Fleet said, putting his fork down.

'What is wrong with people? They're excited by this man. It's just going to encourage him.'

Jason twisted his laptop to show Lydia the screen. It was a page from a newspaper archive and he clicked on the image to expand it. It was a fully illustrated double-page spread with portraits of the investigating officers lining the top, an image of the street on which the body was found and, in the centre, a perfect replica of Mary Ann Nichol's mortuary photograph. The headline read 'Revolting and mysterious murder of a woman – Buck's Row Whitechapel'.

The whole page looked like something from a graphic novel, with a panel showing the body being found on the street and another with serious-looking men sitting around a table for the inquest.

'Tabloid of the day,' Jason said, registering Lydia's confusion. 'Very popular. The guy that ran the thing was hauled into court a few times on charges of "glamorising crime".'

'Did that hold up?'

'Nah. He said that the pictures helped to deter criminals. Said people were afraid of having their faces appear in the paper.'

'Is that true now?' Lydia wondered. 'Seems like everyone wants to be big on Instagram or on one of those reality TV things.'

'Not me,' Jason said. He gave a theatrical shudder. He re-angled his laptop and tapped at the keyboard.

Lydia smiled at him. 'What have you been watching?'

'What are you two talking about?' Fleet was looking

from the laptop screen to Jason's approximate location.

'Love Island,' Jason said promptly. 'Oh shit.'

'What is it?'

Jason swivelled the screen again, and Fleet echoed his words. And added a few more.

'Hell Hawk,' Lydia said.

Jason had a couple of windows open with social media sites showing the popular Ripper hashtags. Displayed several times and reposted thousands of times and counting, there was an image made to look like an old-fashioned letter. It was headed 'From Hell', emulating the letter that was supposedly sent by Jack the Ripper and fanned the flames of his notoriety.

I used to enjoy the girls but my tastes have changed. All you naughty boys had better watch out for good old Jack.

The letter appeared simultaneously on several social media accounts. The user names were strings of letters and numbers, which made them look like standard bot accounts, but the message was the same. The image posted where possible and the text added where it wasn't. And the hashtag #JackActually.

LYDIA HAD EXPECTED THE STAIRWELL TO SMELL OF piss, but she hadn't expected the human excrement that was smeared across the heavily scarred front door on the second landing. A couple of floors up and she found a pile of rubbish and used needles that resolved itself into a human being. A skinny man hunched in on himself and leaning with his back against the wall. By the time she got to the tenth floor, she knew that Ember's flat was going to have to be a goddamn palace for her not to want to scoop the kid up and take him away.

Number sixty-eight was not a palace. For starters, it didn't even have a front door.

'Hello?' Lydia called through the empty space before stepping over the threshold. The hinges were intact, and it looked as if the door had been removed, rather than kicked down.

It didn't take long to search the flat. A narrow corridor with kitchen/dining/living room off one side and a bathroom and bedroom off the other. The bedroom had clearly belonged to an elderly lady at one point, but Lydia thought that odds were good that it now belonged to Ember. Or that his gran was very chill about putting up Fortnite posters all over the walls.

Another clue was the pile of opened mail, addressed to Mrs Williams. They included letters concerning Mrs Williams's state pension.

The multi-purpose main room was neat, mainly because it was mostly empty. It looked as if it had recently been burgled by a thorough crew. Maybe the same crew that had removed the door. And then taken it with them? It struck Lydia that a sturdy front door might be one of the more valuable items in the flat. Especially if it wasn't covered in shit.

The kitchen was surprisingly clean, but Lydia wasn't getting 'gran vibes' from the selection of food. It was possible that the cupboards had been recently cleared out by the same people that took the rest of the stuff, but there were tins of spaghetti, half a loaf of value white bread and a block of cheap chocolate. The fridge revealed three cans of Red Bull and an open packet of slimy-looking ham.

Lydia's neck prickled and she felt a gleam of sunshine. She turned to find Ember standing in the doorway of the living room.

'It wasn't me,' Lydia said, and then mentally kicked herself. She sounded guilty.

'What wasn't?'

As soon as he spoke Lydia realised the kid had bigger problems than her showing up and his flat being ransacked. His voice was barely more than a whisper. Like he had a bad bout of laryngitis. Or had been strangled. She could see livid bruises on his neck, only partially hidden by his shirt collar. She forced herself to look away, to gesture to the flat. 'Someone broke in. Looks like they've taken lots...' Lydia trailed off as she registered that Ember was still. And he wasn't registering confusion or panic. The stuff from the flat had been gone for a long time.

Lydia thought she needed to triage the problems, so she asked the most pressing. 'Who hurt you?'

Ember turned away and disappeared into the corridor. She followed to find him in his bedroom. He was on the floor with his arm buried between the mattress and the divan base. He withdrew his hand, clutching some paper. He went to the chest of drawers and pulled out the bottom drawer. Stuck to the back was an envelope, and he pocketed that too.

'What are you doing? Are you leaving?'

'I'm not going into care,' Ember said matter-of-factly.

'Who said anything about care? You've got your gran...' Lydia trailed off as she realised just how stupid she was being. Ember's gran clearly hadn't lived in the flat for a while. Ember was most likely still getting her pension, or perhaps a carer's allowance for looking after her. That was how he was keeping body and soul together. That and picking pockets.

Lydia held up her hands. 'I'm not the social. I just want to know who put their hands on a kid in my rookery so that I can have a word.'

He eyed her.

'Whatcha mean?'

'Have you heard of the Crows?'

A flicker. 'Birds, like?'

Lydia gave him a look. One that said 'stop messing around'.

'I've heard of 'em,' Ember said. 'So?'

'I'm Lydia Crow. Head of the Family. And this is my manor. When something happens that I don't like, I find out about it. And then I sort it.'

Ember's expression was a mixture of hope and horror. He took a step back, as if his body was doing the thinking and its main thought was 'fly away fast'. Lydia had every sympathy, but she said. 'Don't think you can disappear. I will find you.'

He stopped moving.

'Okay.' Lydia folded her arms. 'First things first. Who choked you?'

. . .

Turned out, the wannabe strangler was a child. Which meant that Lydia couldn't do all the things she had planned and had, instead, to visit the child's parents. She took Aiden for muscle and the look of the thing. She wanted to impress upon the family that this was of grave importance.

Ember hadn't wanted to attend, which Lydia didn't understand. Why wouldn't he want to see justice done? Then Aiden pointed out that he probably didn't think that was what was going to happen. 'He's waiting to get blamed or for the older kid to get away with it or whatever. He's not seen good outcomes before, so he doesn't believe they can happen.'

Lydia took another look at Aiden. 'Speaking from experience?'

He shrugged, a shy smile playing on his lips. 'Jess is a life coach.'

Aiden had married Jess four months earlier. Lydia had given the happy couple three grand as a wedding gift and left early. Fleet had to miss it due to work.

They made their way to a marginally nicer tower block a couple of streets from Ember's. The kid who had chased Ember home from school on one of the rare days he had attended was a year older and a foot taller. His parents hadn't been thrilled to see Lydia and Aiden on their doorstep, but they had invited them in and offered tea.

'Kian is doing his homework,' the mum said.

'Get him in here,' Lydia said, her tone brooking no

argument. She had been invited to sit in on the large sectional sofa that faced a truly enormous flatscreen. There was a soundbar underneath the screen and the room was dotted with surround-sound speakers. It had been blasting when Lydia and Aiden had arrived and only been turned down to average levels now that they were sitting opposite Lydia, on their best behaviour and ready for a polite conversation with the head of the Crow Family. The neighbours had to hate them.

The dad was looming near the door, where Aiden was also standing. His hands crossed in front of his body in his standard 'quiet muscle' stance.

The dad shot a look at his wife, who nodded.

'What's he done, then?' The wife asked.

'You are Kian's mother?'

'Step-mum,' the woman answered. 'I met Neil last year. Moved in at Christmas.' She sounded defensive. The message, loud and clear, was 'this isn't my fault. I didn't raise this kid'.

'Does he have siblings?'

She shook her head. 'Neil wants to have a baby, but I'm not ready.' She flicked her chin at the doorway, where a lumpen boy had appeared next to his father. 'Got enough on my plate as it is.'

Lydia waited until the boy had been herded into the room. Physically, he looked much older than twelve. He was tall and had facial hair interspersed with purple and angry-looking acne. If you didn't look at the kid's eyes, he could have passed for sixteen. His eyes were frightened, though, and she wondered what stories he had heard about the Crows. Good, she thought savagely. Suddenly,

219

she felt the sense of what Charlie had always said. If you kept up a reputation, you didn't even need to throw a punch. If you kept up a reputation, this kid was already getting a lesson without her having to say a single word.

Still. He had wrapped his meaty hands around Ember's neck and squeezed. Hard enough and long enough to bruise his skin, to damage his larynx. He could have killed him. It would have been an accident, no doubt, but that didn't make it acceptable. And a twelve-year-old hurting a smaller kid like that? What would he do in the future if he didn't lock down that violence? Get control of his rage? Learn from his mistakes?

Lydia had taken pictures of Ember's neck and had them printed on photo paper. She knew there was something extra scary and official about glossy print outs. She took them from her bag and spread them on the coffee table. They were shocking, and she felt her anger rise all over again.

She heard Kian's step-mum make a small gasping noise. The father was silent, but he shifted uncomfortably, making a squeaking noise on the leather sofa. Lydia wasn't paying attention to them, though, she was focused on Kian.

'Let me see your hands.'

'What?'

'Your hands. Hold them out.'

The kid was shaking, she could see the tremor as he held his arms out across the photos on the table. Lydia looked him dead in the eye. 'You want to know how easy it is to kill someone smaller than you?' She glanced down at the photos. 'You nearly found out.'

'Hang on a minute,' the father said.

Lydia didn't break eye contact with his son. 'Shut up,' she said. 'I'm talking to Kian.'

The father shut up.

'I had a speech planned. I was going to tell you about learning to control yourself. To point out your cowardly weakness. I was going to threaten you that if I caught the slightest rumour that you had hurt someone smaller than yourself again, I was going to be back. And that I wouldn't be playing nice. Not like I am today.'

She paused. 'But I don't need to say any of that. I can see you already know it. You know what you did was wrong. That you were hyped up by your audience. That Ember was an easy way to show your dominance. I know the truth because I struggle with it, too.'

The kid still had his arms held stretched out, his hands were still shaking. His eyes were filled with tears and it was only a matter of time before they fell. She didn't know what his parents would do then. She leaned forward and the kid flinched. 'I know you are scared. You feel like you're in a war, danger on all sides. You feel like you have to show strength so that you don't get killed yourself.' She reached out and took his hands, lowering them to the table and squeezing very gently. 'It's not worth it. You can't do the wrong thing now just to survive, because you won't make it. Even if you keep yourself alive that way, you won't be you anymore. Trust me. You have to find another way.'

CHAPTER TWENTY-FOUR

The next day, when Aiden arrived with the day's schedule mapped out, he had a reserved, worried look on his face. It was as if he had already anticipated what Lydia was going to say. 'I can't today,' she said. 'You need to handle the meetings.'

'People want to see you,' Aiden protested.

Lydia looked around the room and realised how much she hated the furniture. It was perfectly fine, of course, and very tasteful. But it was all Charlie's. 'They'll get used to it. And you're very likeable.'

'This isn't—'

'I'm the head of the Family. I'm not doing things the same way. You're my second in command, you take the meetings and the face-to-faces. You're better with people, anyway.'

Aiden still looked unsure, but he shrugged. 'I'll try.'

'They'll adjust. You'll be great, you'll see.'

Aiden was almost out of the door when she called

him back. 'I'm sending you an address. There's a kid living there on his own. We need to look out for him.'

Aiden frowned. 'What do you mean?'

'I don't know,' Lydia said. 'No authorities, no social services. I would say drop some cash round, but that won't solve things.'

'It'll get nicked.'

'Yeah, don't want him becoming a target. He needs a family. Can I leave it with you?'

'Course, Boss.'

'He's not being trained up,' Lydia said. 'This is purely to help him. He won't owe us.'

Aiden looked even more confused, but Lydia shelved that as a problem for another day. She had to get to focus on Fleet's case. If he solved it, he would secure his position, his career. And with the increased media attention brought by the *From Hell* hoax, time was fast running out.

WITH AIDEN GONE, LYDIA MADE HERSELF A COFFEE and sat at her desk. What had she done before? She'd had clients. Cases. Now she had one case only – whoever was running around Whitechapel posing as Jack the Ripper.

As if summoned by her thoughts, Fleet called with an update.

'Only Connor's fingerprints on the knife. And we believe it was his property,' Fleet said. 'Fibres on knife match those on Connor's jacket, consistent with it having been carried in the inside pocket.'

'The fibres couldn't have been picked up during the attack?'

'Could have been, but he wasn't wearing his jacket when he was stabbed, he was carrying it, which reduces the likelihood. Plus, one of his friends has confirmed that he had taken to carrying "protection".'

'Did he say why?'

'Said that Connor was worried about his crazy fans, or that was the way he put it.'

'Did his friend believe him?'

'I think so. Why?'

'What if Connor had heard about the other deaths? Maybe he recognised them? Knew them from somewhere and had reason to believe he might be next?'

LYDIA COULDN'T SETTLE TO RESEARCH. SHE FELT antsy and unfocused, and knew that movement was the only thing that would help. An hour in the studio, working on self-defence moves and core strength, left her sweaty and sore, but calmer. Then she tried some of Charlie's old training methods, but with her coin gone, it was more frustrating than anything else. The power she had felt running through her body had been abruptly cut off and she didn't know if she would ever be able to access the source of it again. A crow, sitting on the ledge of the studio window, watched her lack of progress with a judgemental stare. By the end of her session, she was tempted to make a rude gesture. Luckily, she hadn't lost her common sense along with her power, so she headed for a shower instead.

Fleet arrived back from work while she was dressing, and she joined him in the living room for food. He had warmed up some leftover lasagne but, unlike Lydia, he took the time to plate it up with some salad.

'I've got some reading to catch up on. Sorry.' Fleet balanced his plate on his lap and reached for his work bag.

'That's okay,' Lydia said. She dug into the food and scrolled through Connor Bright's Instagram feed. It gave Lydia the opposing feelings of irritation at his nonsense-peddling wellness huckstering, and the residual pull of his Pearl magic. Even via mobile-phone video, even though the man behind those pixels was now dead, the charisma in his voice and mannerisms still contained that extra something. She still felt the tug of Pearl that made her want to buy whatever he was selling. Even though what he was selling was 'endocrine one-shots'. She wondered how much stronger it had been when he was alive. How intense it would be in person.

Thinking about the Pearl Family made her wonder when Rafferty Hill was going to return to the city.

She put her fork down. 'Have you been to Connor Bright's home?'

Fleet looked up from his work. 'You want to see my report?'

'Yes, please.'

Fleet patted the space on the sofa next to him and Lydia went to sit down. He passed across his iPad.

She scanned the report. 'There's nothing here.'

'That's because there was nothing there. Police work is ninety-nine per cent "nothing there". Besides, it wasn't the scene of the crime and it's not like we need to ID the vic.'

'But what if there is something that can tell us who will be next?'

'You really think they are all linked?'

'They were all shady.'

'True.'

'And what's the point of being police if you can't stop someone from getting offed?'

Fleet shook his head sadly. 'I've often wondered the same thing. Sometimes it feels like I'm just part of the clean-up crew.'

'But you can change that now. You can see the future.'

His expression closed down. 'Barely,' he said.

Lydia didn't like going into Whitechapel and she really didn't like going to Paul's den, but she had to make amends. The barber's with the door at the back that led to the hidden bar was just as she remembered from her first visit, complete with a surly looking barber with sharp hair and a scowl just for her. He was working, electric razor in one hand and scissors in the other. His client looked young, maybe sixteen or seventeen, but he had the Fox good looks and his expression was no less menacing.

'Truce. Remember?' Lydia said after she had closed the front door behind her.

The barber jerked his head toward the door at the

back and the teen stared at her in the mirror, his manner unchanging.

Lydia walked down the narrow stairs and pushed on the wall to open the secret door that led to the speakeasy style bar. She tried not to think about what Aiden would say about her wandering so deeply into Fox territory without backup. She wondered whether Fleet was right and her judgement was permanently clouded when it came to Paul Fox. Was it risky to wander into his den? They hadn't exactly parted on good terms. And truce or not, she had hurt a member of his Family.

The place was deserted apart from Paul, and Lydia was momentarily relieved. Until it occurred to her that there could be a whole crew hiding behind the bar. He was sitting at the back of the room, two glasses on the table, and was in the process of opening a bottle of Ardbeg as she crossed the floor to join him.

Lydia didn't want to ask how he had known she was coming. Perhaps he was expecting somebody else? Or perhaps he sat like this all the time, just waiting for her to drop in. Unlikely.

'Crow,' he said. Not raising his gaze from the bottle. 'I heard you were on your way here.'

Of course he had lookouts. That solved that mystery. And he had prepared for her arrival with whisky and not a crossbow. That was something.

'I'm sorry I went to see Aysha.' Lydia hadn't sat down yet. She held her hands palm out, showing that she came in peace. 'It was a mistake.'

Paul lifted his chin, but still didn't look at her.

She didn't know if bringing him information would

make amends, but it didn't hurt to try. And she felt genuinely bad about Aysha. 'I thought you would want an update on the Perry case. And to be reassured that the police won't be pursuing the Fox Family. Any further. I would apologise about that, too, but it wasn't my doing. I tried to convince Fleet not to question you or your Family. So,' she forced herself to finish, feeling the words becoming a torrent, 'you should really be thanking me for that.'

Paul met her eyes. 'Are you sitting down sometime today?'

Lydia took the invitation. She didn't want to sit opposite him, it left her back open to the room, but she wasn't going to slide in next to him either. That would be presumptuous. And pretty much fatal for her thought processes. Having Paul Fox pressed up against the side of her body, close enough to smell his skin...

Instead, she moved the chair to the side of the table. A compromise between line of sight on the rest of the room and not combusting from Fox-induced lust. She quickly outlined what the police knew about Perry's murder and the suspected link to Johnstone. 'There isn't a direct link to Price or Connor Bright, but the dominant theory is that Johnstone is linked to Price and Perry is linked to Johnstone. Connor is the real wild card, but they are combing through his life, his thousands of contacts. They'll find something. The common denominator.'

Paul was holding himself very still, but she could feel the tension rolling from him. 'You said the police weren't looking at me anymore?'

'No. They were interested in your Family, just because of the locations, but they haven't found anything else that points your way.'

'Aysha?'

Lydia shook her head. She had been avoiding using Fleet's name, but now she couldn't avoid it. 'I told Fleet that Perry was a scumbag, but I didn't name names. I've kept Aysha out of it. I don't want him jumping to the wrong idea. Or interviewing Aysha. I told you, I'm sorry.' She picked up her whisky. 'I want to make amends.'

Paul picked up his own drink and regarded her over the rim of the glass. His gaze was searching, and Lydia felt it to her toes. Her stomach was liquid and she wasn't sure if it was fear or arousal. After what felt like an inordinate amount of time, Paul nodded slightly and drank.

Lydia did the same.

'They think it's the same killer? For all four?'

'The method is the same,' Lydia said. 'Pretty distinctive, too. The attacks are frenzied. Multiple stab wounds.'

Paul nodded, looking grimly satisfied. 'That's something.'

Lydia knew she definitely shouldn't share any more details. But she wanted Paul to know, to feel involved. He had wanted to kill the man himself. He needed to feel connected to the investigation. 'Whoever did this took half of Perry's kidney.'

'A trophy? That's some proper serial killer shit.' Paul shook his head. 'What are the chances?'

'How do you mean?'

'Perry was always going to die, that's not a surprise. But that it would be a serial killer looking for kicks? Not because of the things he has done.'

'Perhaps it's both?'

Paul nodded, acknowledging the point. 'Either way, I wish they had invited me along.'

Lydia had seen the pain in his eyes before, knew how deeply he meant that statement. 'How is she?'

His whole body tensed and she had the feeling he wasn't going to answer her. After a moment, his shoulders shifted and he took a sip of whisky. Then he said, 'Bit better.'

'That's good.'

'She's finally agreed to start seeing a counsellor. Found one she really likes. Trusts. Don't know if it's going to make any difference, but it's something.'

'What about you?'

A lopsided smile. 'I'm not going to therapy.'

Before Lydia could rephrase her question, he continued: 'Nice that you care, Little Bird.'

The flash of red fur filled her mind. It was probably a result of not getting enough personal time with Fleet, but the pull of desire, the promise of carnal delight, ran through her whole body like an electric shock, temporarily short-circuiting her brain. 'Shut up.' Not her wittiest repartee, but all she could manage in that moment.

His smile widened.

'Shut up,' she said, again, and finished her whisky. When Paul poured another measure, she should have stopped him. She had drunk wine with meals, had the occasional single measure here and there, but hadn't tested her tolerance. And getting buzzed while in the presence of Paul Fox, especially while she was feeling so guilty about visiting Aysha, was a terrible idea.

'Does Fleet know you're here?'

The smart play was to say 'yes'. Indicate back-up even if it's not visible. 'No.'

'Everything good at home?' He managed to make the question sound filthy, holding eye contact and curling his lip just the barest amount.

'I'm not here to talk about Fleet.'

He knocked back his whisky, poured another, splashing more into her glass at the same time. 'Fair enough.'

Lydia took a bigger mouthful than she had intended and then another. She felt some of the knots of tension in her body loosen.

'Do you know the worst thing?' Paul had finished his glass and poured another.

'About Perry?' It was like he was drinking with purpose, and she commanded herself not to care. It was none of her concern if he was distressed. She had apologised, made peace. Done the right thing for the truce. It was all just business.

'He ground her down. She is a thousand times the person he would ever be, even at sixteen, and he made her believe she was nothing. He broke her bones and for that I am glad he is dead, but he broke her spirit and there is no retribution big enough for that. There's no restitution. No justice. No revenge that can give satisfaction—' He stopped speaking abruptly, looking faintly surprised and embarrassed. He hadn't meant to say so much, to reveal the depth of his feelings.

Well, Lydia knew she could be a dick, but she wasn't that big of an arsehole. She wasn't going to use this moment to her advantage, so she just nodded her agreement and looked away, giving Paul a moment to compose himself.

It didn't take long. Lydia concentrated on finishing her drink and thinking about how she was going to politely leave. She had little practice of that with Paul. They usually insulted each other before walking away.

'I will ask Aysha about Johnstone, Price and Bright. See if she ever met them or heard Perry talk about them at all.'

'Thank you,' Lydia said.

'If he had just done Perry, I wouldn't help the police find him. Not even if I had the guy's address. But this feels bigger. And it's my den.' He bared his teeth. 'If someone's on a killing spree in Whitechapel, it ought to be me.'

CHAPTER TWENTY-FIVE

Lydia was looking at Connor Bright's social media profiles. She followed the #RipperReturns hashtag and found several others including #NewRipper, #From-Hell and #Ripped, often used alongside images of a shirtless Connor Bright. The world seemed to be following the case like it was a Netflix drama. She wondered whether Mary had been aware of the press around Jack the Ripper, how that must have felt as the victim of a violent man herself. As Jason had pointed out, there were some theories that George Chapman was Jack the Ripper, so she might even have been seeing press attention for the man who killed her.

And what about the other Ripper victims? Had any of those women become ghosts? If Martha Tabram, Mary Ann Nichols, Annie Chapman, Elizabeth Stride, Catherine Eddowes or Mary Jane Kelly had become restless spirits, they might have seen the sensationalist newspaper coverage that followed their deaths. All that grubby and voyeuristic coverage, over years and years.

It wasn't exactly respectful. And all the speculation and fear, the nickname Jack the Ripper, like he was the important one. The interesting one. Those women were just the corpses. Remembered for their possible sex work and violated bodies. Objects, not human beings.

Her dark thoughts were interrupted by her mobile ringing. It was a withheld number, but she saw a flash of red fur as she answered.

'Paul doesn't want me talking to you,' Aysha said.

Lydia waited. Her fingers were gripping the phone and she didn't know whether she ought to say something to let Aysha know she was listening. Or whether that would scare her off. She could hear her breathing and the sounds of traffic in the background.

'The police are going to pin it on us. Because of me.'

'They don't know about you. And I won't tell them.'

Another silence. 'I would like to believe that. But we all think my cousin has a blind spot when it comes to you.'

'Can you believe that I wouldn't do anything to jeopardise the truce?'

'I'm not willing to risk my Family's freedom, but...'

Lydia waited, staying quiet. She could sense Aysha wrestling with something.

'There's this thing. I've been thinking about it a lot. I'm feeling better now he's dead. The shock was bad, thinking about him again and how much he's still in my head. But I've got a kind of justice. He's dead.'

Aysha sounded strong when she said this. And satisfied.

'But you know Bright? I saw him at a party. And Chris was there, too.'

'Chris Perry was at a party in London?' That made no sense. The man had run from London, the Foxes on his heels, and changed his name.

'About five years back. I saw him, yeah. He didn't see me. I left straight away, I couldn't...' Her voice trailed away, but then came back. Strong. Determined. 'So, you can tell your copper about me. I'll speak to him if I have to. Give a statement. Not anybody else, though.'

Lydia was still caught on Chris Perry. She supposed he had felt safe after five years. Anonymous with his new name. 'Can you tell me about—'

'Tell him to look up the name Cherish.'

'Who is that?'

'I didn't really know her, but she was at this party.'

'Okay—'

'She was working there,' Aysha said, putting emphasis on the word 'working'.

Lydia had the impression she wasn't referring to waitressing or bar tending.

'And no one saw her after. I heard the rumours, though. Through friends of friends, you know that kind of thing? The story goes that she was in a private room with some clients, but that nobody saw her after. She went missing that night. Just disappeared.'

Lydia was cold.

'Do you know what happened?'

Aysha went quiet again. There was the sound of a siren. Then she said, 'I know what I suspect. And I know that no one is looking for her.'

. . .

THAT EVENING, LYDIA WAS WAITING IMPATIENTLY for Fleet to return from work. 'Did you look it up?'

'I did.' Fleet dropped his bag onto the floor and sank onto the sofa. He looked exhausted, and Lydia felt a stab of concern.

'Your source is telling the truth. A young woman went missing after a party in Spitalfields on the sixteenth of October, five years ago. She is named as Cherish, but there are no other details, not even a surname.'

She paced the room to let out some of her energy. 'Hell Hawk. My source said nobody was looking for her.'

'That might be true,' Fleet said. He told her what he had found out. The party had been a bacchanalian affair, put on for the movers and shakers in the London club scene. DJs, promoters, club owners, PR people, and agents, plus models, minor celebs, and musicians. The kind of people that brought kudos to clubs, ensuring their reputation grew, they were the place to be seen, and the lines outside their doors stayed long.

At this party, there were layers of access. The party itself was secret and exclusive, with invitations that were seemingly blank, black cards. You used a UV light to reveal the details, presumably making people who already thought of themselves as cool feel like spies. Maybe it had been cool enough to entice Chris Perry out of hiding for one night.

'There was an investigation of sorts. There's a case number and a few witness statements, taken from people that attended the party, but not much else. And with no body and no further evidence coming to light, it was dropped pretty quickly and filed as a missing person.'

'Does that happen? Something going from suspicious to missing person?'

'It can,' Fleet said. 'But in this case, there was more to it. I got called into the Guv's office after I pulled the records. She said I had better have an extremely good reason to be searching for that particular incident, as it was flagged as diplomatically sensitive. And parts of the file are redacted.'

Lydia stopped pacing. 'What does that mean?'

Fleet shrugged. 'Guv didn't know or wasn't saying. But if I had to guess, someone important or politically sensitive, or pertinent to a larger investigation, attended that party.'

'Feathers.'

'It's not helped that there were no identifying details for Cherish. The report has a memo addendum which suggests the original tip, which was anonymous, was a hoax. That Cherish doesn't even exist.'

'Or she's a trafficked sex worker who was drafted into this party by her handler. I'm guessing there are women like that who don't officially exist in the system?'

'Yeah.' Fleet sighed loudly. He tipped his head back against the sofa cushions, rolling his eyes to stare at the ceiling as if it was the whole of the Metropolitan police and had severely disappointed him. 'I hate this.'

'I know.' Lydia was going to sit next to him on the sofa, but decided to just get onto his lap instead. His arms wrapped around her and she tucked her head into the gap between his neck and shoulder. It felt good. Safe.

She closed her eyes and wished she could just stay like that. But there was work to do.

He mumbled something. She pulled back. 'What?'

'I feel like I'm losing the moral high ground. A bit more every day.'

'You like having the moral high ground?'

A small smile. 'It's where I live.'

'And you've just found another piece of corruption in the organisation you pledged your life to?' Lydia pulled a face. 'Yeah, no. Can't relate. Like, at all.'

CHAPTER TWENTY-SIX

The next day, Fleet had a rare day off, and he was encouraging Lydia to take time off with him. So far, she was resisting. 'Too many women dead.' Lydia rubbed her eyes as she looked away from her laptop screen. The area around Dorset Street had been infamous for deprivation, poverty, violence and misery, but it was still shocking to read the stark timeline. There were five murders officially attributed to the serial killer known as Jack the Ripper, but the 'autumn of terror' included many more. Lydia had been reading their names and their stories, trying to remember the human beings whose difficult lives had been cut short, but she found her mind skating over the details. She could face horror in the course of an investigation. Focus on the information, knowing that it might be key to gaining justice or, at least, solving the puzzle. But these murders were long past. There was nothing to be done for the women who had died. No justice could be offered, no comfort for their loved ones. Just another bleak reminder that where there is hardship, women usually bore the brunt of it.

Fleet was stretched out on the sofa. Lydia assumed he had fallen asleep, but then he spoke. 'I think you're right.'

It took Lydia a beat. 'About the murders?'

'He is emulating the Ripper. Which tells us he is going to kill again.' He opened his eyes. 'Unless the Mitre Square killing was the last one?'

'Second to last. Of the ones that are still considered to be Jack the Ripper. There's been a lot of debate over the years.'

'I hate that.' Fleet closed his eyes again. 'The murderer shouldn't be famous. Shouldn't be talked about.'

'It's human nature,' Lydia said. She had read too many of the Victorian Penny Dreadfuls and the newspapers that looked like graphic novels to believe it was a modern sickness. 'And maybe it makes people feel safe in a weird way. Like if they are informed with every detail they can stay out of trouble?' She crossed to the sofa, carrying her laptop to show Fleet. He swung his legs around and sat up, making room for her to sit next to him.

'Connor Bright in Mitre Square is out of order, Ripper-wise.' She pointed at her research notes. 'He killed Catherine Eddowes in Mitre Square at about quarter to two in the morning on the thirtieth of September, but Elizabeth Stride's body was found that same night an hour earlier.'

'Two murders within hours of each other. I think I

remember hearing that,' Fleet said. 'Bit of an embarrass-
ment for the police that he wasn't caught.'

'Apparently, there were detectives patrolling in plain
clothes and they didn't see a thing. Theory is that the
Ripper lived in the East End, because we know he
headed back that way.'

'To his bolthole?'

Lydia nodded. 'That's the theory.'

'How wasn't he seen? He had to be covered in
blood.'

'Like our guy,' Lydia said. 'Same issue. But the
Ripper was targeting sex workers. Idea is that he was
wearing a big coat, and he took this off before getting
close to his victims. They wouldn't have thought this was
strange.'

'Because they'd be expecting intimate activity.'

'Exactly. Then he could put it on after to hide his
blood-stained clothes.'

'That doesn't help us with our vics. They would
have been suspicious if some geezer approached them
and took off his coat.'

'So, we don't have an exact match on the locations,'
Lydia counted off the differences on her fingers. 'And
the Ripper killed women, while our guy is targeting men
who have a history of abusing women.'

'And men with connections to sex work.'

'Some of them, sure. Johnstone and Price.'

'What did you say you found out about Bright?'

Lydia gave him a precis of the #MeToo and
#TimesUp coverage of Bright. 'There's a lot of "was he
so bad" and counter-arguments about him now that he

has died this way. It's ironic that killing him so messily might actually rehabilitate his reputation.'

'Probably not what they were hoping for.'

'No. But that's the great British public for you.'

Fleet muttered a very rude word.

'And our guy didn't strangle his victims before killing them.'

'No,' Fleet frowned. 'I didn't know the Ripper had done that.'

'Mostly, yeah. It's another reason it wasn't quite as messy as it could have been. Less arterial spurt.'

Jason had appeared during their conversation and now he said. 'Arterial spurt sounds like a goth band name.'

'Not helpful,' Lydia said, but she smiled at him. Glad he was making jokes again.

'Jason's here?' Fleet asked.

'At your service.' Jason made a deep bow.

'Does he have any theories?' Fleet rubbed a hand across his head. 'I'll take any help at this point.'

'Charming,' Jason said and made a rude gesture.

'No theories,' Lydia said diplomatically.

LYDIA DIDN'T KNOW IF FLEET WAS FRUSTRATED BY her inability to switch off or whether he was having the same difficulty. After lunch, he changed into his sports clothes and headed out for a run. 'You're welcome to join?'

'That's all right.' She was going to pace the house and think.

'You're allowed to take a break, you know,' Fleet said. He dipped his head to look into her eyes.

She knew he was right, but if he said anything about applying her own oxygen mask first, she was going to scream. Instead, she reviewed the scant details of Cherish's case, grateful that Fleet had shared the notes.

It turned out that the minimal checking included a statement about the VIP room at the party. According to a woman who had been working as a server, the party itself was very small, with only about thirty people in attendance. The VIP room was even more exclusive, but there was no way of knowing if the list from the file was complete. It listed only four people, but there were lots of redacted details. Those named included Tyler Baxter, AKA Chris Perry, and Connor Bright. Lydia stared at the other two names. One was unknown to her, but the other leapt from the page like a jump scare. Brad Carter. She felt like the past was rushing up from behind and was about to cosh her over the back of the head. What had Brad Carter been doing in London five years ago? And why had he merited an invitation to this exclusive party? He was rich, of course. Maybe richer than she had realised. Perhaps his money was enough.

The server's statement also confirmed Lydia's suspicion that there had been at least one sex worker, although the statement didn't use that term. She was recorded as saying: 'There was a hooker in the VIP room. When I took champagne in, it was basically an orgy. I would have refused to go in again, but I wasn't told to.' Lydia did a basic search on the unknown name from the VIP list. Kevin Cartwright had died three years ago in a jet ski accident while on holiday in Florida.

She looked at the news item and thought about the people who slipped through the cracks in society, their deaths never reported, mysteries never solved. Trafficked sex workers could disappear and nobody would ever know to look for them. Their families, back in their own countries, would be powerless to do anything, even if they suspected that something bad had happened. She wondered if that was what had happened to Cherish.

If so, did that link Craig Johnstone and Raymond Price to this party? Their names hadn't appeared on the VIP list, but they might have been at the party as ordinary guests. They weren't movers and shakers, beautiful people or minor celebs, so it seemed unlikely. They could be linked by Cherish, though. If Cherish was a sex worker, somebody had procured her. Craig Johnstone, the pimp, and Raymond Price, the trafficker. It made an awful sense.

She picked up her phone and called Fleet. 'What if our killer knew about Cherish's death? What if that's the link?'

Fleet was breathing hard and she imagined him standing in the park, sweaty from running. 'Killing the people involved? Retribution?' She had wondered if he would be annoyed with her for interrupting his exercise time, but he sounded alert. Interested.

'Just because they didn't care about Cherish, doesn't mean that nobody did.'

'Maybe,' Fleet said. His tone turned cautious. 'It

doesn't give us any more details about her, though. No new leads—'

'If Johnstone and Price died because they were the reason Cherish was in that line of work, and Perry and Bright were targeted because they were in that VIP room when she died, that's a lead. It means the names from the VIP room is a kill list.'

IF LYDIA HAD THOUGHT ABOUT SUCH A THING, SHE would have supposed that when you were providing sex for a luxury party, there were certain standards that were expected. She had imagined top shelf workers, the kind who ran their own businesses and didn't look out of place in fancy hotel bars. Knowing she was out of her depth, she made a couple of calls and arranged a friendly conversation with someone in the business.

Lydia pulled on her jacket and drove to the other side of Burgess Park. She met her contact as he left his gym, sports bag in one hand and wet hair slicked back off his craggy face. He shook her hand. 'Mick says I need to speak to you. No names, though, yeah?'

'Sure,' Lydia said, getting straight down to business. 'I was told you knew Craig Johnstone. In a professional capacity.'

'Yeah,' the man said. 'Johnstone provided talent. Men like pretty girls to drink with them, laugh at their jokes, make them feel big.'

'I'm talking about more than that.'

He held up his hands. 'I don't trade in anything illegal.'

'Of course not.' She couldn't keep the sarcasm out of her voice. To be fair, she wasn't trying all that hard.

He grinned at her. 'Everyone gets paid, and everyone consents.'

'To the laughing?'

'Exactly.'

'And if something goes wrong?'

'That's what I'm there for. Well, my security staff these days. I'm not hands on in the business anymore.' He rolled his shoulders back, unable to conceal his pride. 'I'm the CE-fucking-O.'

'I guess not a lot of fuss gets made? If one of your workers goes missing?'

He gave her an odd look. 'Now why would you be asking me that?'

'Cherish.'

He looked genuinely blank. 'Not one of mine.'

'I know that. That's why this chat is so friendly.'

'Now hang on—'

'I'm not asking you to give information on one of your rivals. I know you're a man of honour and would never do anything like that.'

'Well—'

'But a woman called Cherish went missing five years ago. She had been working a VIP room at a very fancy event. And I think she's dead.'

'Bad business,' he said, shaking his head.

Lydia wasn't sure if he was expressing sympathy for the dead woman or making a statement about how it would affect a profit and loss statement. 'I want to know whether that's possible? With one of your workers?'

'What do you mean? I told you she's not—'

'One of yours, you said. What I mean is, if Johnstone was providing women for a luxury event, wouldn't he use one of his top-shelf workers?'

'High-class hooker? Sort that can speak Japanese to the businessmen?' The man smiled indulgently. 'You've been watching too much TV, love.'

Lydia put her hands in her pockets to hide the fact that they had curled into fists.

'Depends on the tastes of the client,' the man continued. 'Top-shelf clients don't always want top-shelf girls. Sometimes they're in the market for steak, sometimes they want a kebab, know what I'm saying?'

Lydia squeezed her fists tighter. 'Cherish must have had colleagues, but they didn't go to the police. And neither did her handler.'

He looked at her in a way that reminded her of Aiden. Slightly incredulous that she could be in her position and still not fully get it. 'No one goes to the police, darling.'

CHAPTER TWENTY-SEVEN

Lydia was on her way back to the house when her phone buzzed with a text. It was Fleet, asking if she was free to join him in an interview. He had added the word 'unofficial', which wasn't really necessary given the location was a pub in Battersea.

Lydia had missed working with Fleet, and she felt a flutter of excitement as she made her way to the waterfront address on the edge of Battersea. The pub had a garden with a view of the Thames and the traffic thundering across Wandsworth Bridge.

Fleet was already sitting at a table in the corner. It had a parasol to protect them from the midday sun and being outside would make it extremely difficult for anybody to listen in unobtrusively. Lydia approved.

Fleet stood up and greeted her with a quick kiss. 'I've ordered drinks.'

'Is it all right that I'm here? It won't put him off?'

Fleet gestured for her to take the seat next to him. 'It

was part of the deal. Gary really wants to meet you.' Then he flashed her a smile. 'And I want you here.'

Before Lydia could respond, a powerful-looking man wearing jeans and a polo shirt walked into the garden and immediately made a beeline for their table. He had neatly cut short grey hair and the kind of posture that suggested a military background before joining the police.

'Fleet,' Gary said, shaking Fleet's hand. 'And you must be Lydia. Pleased to meet you.'

'Likewise,' Lydia said, shaking his hand. Fleet's text had described Gary Higgs as ex-CID, now retired. He looked like he had kept up with a strict exercise routine and had lightly tanned skin, like he spent a lot of time outdoors.

The server arrived with a tray and proceeded to transfer glasses to the table. Two pints of ale, a glass of red wine, and a pint of orange juice and lemonade. 'Take your pick,' Fleet said and Gary selected an ale.

Lydia took the orange juice.

'I really appreciate you talking to me about this,' Fleet said. 'And I promise to keep your name well out of it.'

Gary raised his glass. 'Cheers to that.'

Lydia and Fleet followed suit.

'I'll get straight to it,' Gary said, leaning his elbows on the table. 'It never sat right with me.'

'Gary worked the Cherish case,' Fleet explained to Lydia. 'He was listed in the redacted report. I reached out on the off-chance.'

'And I have nothing better to do now that I'm a man

of leisure. Only so much golf a man can take.' Gary flashed a disarming smile at Lydia and she found herself smiling back. 'Cherish was one of my last cases. I retired the month after and, just between us, it made me glad to be leaving. Being warned off—' He stopped speaking abruptly and shook his head. 'I was ready to be finished with the job, don't get me wrong, but it left a bad taste.'

'You were warned off a suspect?' Lydia asked.

'The whole bloody lot. And told not to discuss the matter. Not if I wanted my pension.'

There was nobody sitting at any of the nearby tables, but they all looked around anyway, instinctively checking they wouldn't be overheard.

'You know it was a small party? Very exclusive.' Gary was speaking quietly, and Lydia and Fleet leaned in closer. 'We had an anonymous tip that a girl called Cherish had been booked to work and that she hadn't been seen since.'

'The case was changed to missing person later, wasn't it?' Lydia confirmed.

Gary nodded. 'I didn't believe that. Or the bollocks about the tip being a hoax. Cherish was killed at that party.'

'You know that for a fact?' Fleet asked, his expression serious.

Gary pulled a rueful face. 'I believe that's the truth, but I couldn't prove it.'

'What made you so sure?' Lydia asked.

'One of the slimy bastards admitted it.' Gary sat back.

Fleet was shaking his head. He didn't say anything,

but Gary was watching him, and his blue eyes were kind. 'I know, mate. I know. Hard to believe.'

Fleet was struggling. 'If you had a confession...'

'Case was going well. Lack of progress was not the issue.' Gary took a long drink, almost draining his glass.

Lydia pushed the full pint toward him. 'Who confessed?'

'Kevin Cartright.'

Lydia looked at Fleet. The guy who had died in a jet ski accident.

'You know about the VIP room?' Gary asked.

'That bit wasn't redacted,' Fleet said, his voice bitter.

'Well, the others weren't saying a thing. Not even admitting they had met a woman called Cherish, much less partied with her in a private room.'

Lydia wondered how much say in her work Cherish had been given. Whether she had any choice at all. Her orange juice was turning to acid in her stomach.

Fleet hadn't touched his drink. 'But Kevin broke?'

Gary finished his pint and moved onto the next. He had the air of a man who had come to do a job and he was going to get it over with. 'Kevin Cartright told us everything. How they had been partaking of some illegal substances and necking champagne. How Cherish was excellent at her job and that they had all appreciated her skills. Individually and as a group. Kevin was very keen to emphasise that. Group activity, where everything got blurred as to who was doing what. Seemed to think that was going to be a key part of his defence.'

'Always the sign of an innocent man,' Lydia said drily.

Gary lifted the corner of his mouth, but then his voice lowered. 'He said it was an accident. That they didn't realise she wasn't breathing.'

'It was a sexual game that got rough?' Fleet asked.

'According to Kevin, Cherish was an enthusiastic participant, but she had also been drinking and taking drugs. He said things had got a bit out of hand and it took a few minutes before they realised she had gone quiet.'

Lydia felt sick. She looked at her glass of orange juice and wished it was whisky. Actually, she wished she could upend the table and smash it all. 'Did they try first aid?'

'Kevin said that he did, but that the others told him there was no point. They also convinced him not to call an ambulance.' Gary shrugged. 'I didn't believe he took much persuading, but I played along. Being sympathetic to keep him talking.'

'Why did he confess?' Fleet was frowning.

'Because I was really good at my job,' Gary said sharply. 'Despite this,' he added, looking at Lydia. 'I don't want you to think I dropped cases like this all through my career. This was the first and last and I've felt sick about it ever since.'

'Why did you want to meet me?' Lydia asked. 'Just curiosity?'

'You're Crow Family,' Gary said, holding her gaze. 'I grew up in Camberwell. I know that if the Crows want something, you had better stump up.'

That explained that. Sometimes infamy had its uses.

'Lydia's not like that—' Fleet began.

'Depends on the day,' Lydia broke in, flashing her shark smile. She wished she could produce her coin, but her expression seemed pretty effective on its own.

Gary finished the last dregs of his pint. He nodded to Fleet. 'If you can use what I've told you to make this right, I'll sleep easier.'

To Lydia, he raised both palms. 'Are we good?'

'The Crows appreciate your assistance,' Lydia said. 'And we shouldn't need to call on you again.'

That night, lying in bed next to Fleet, Lydia was staring into the darkness and trying not to think about the party. She remembered being in the hotel room with Brad Carter and how powerless she had felt for a second. Five men. One woman. Had they been careless? Or had they known that Cherish was trafficked, unknown, and they could do whatever dark things they wanted?

She blinked. She needed to go to sleep. It had been a long day, and the next was likely to be just as busy. Fleet shifted and she realised that he was awake, too.

'I can't stop thinking about that party,' Lydia said quietly.

'I know.' Fleet took her hand in the dark.

'It's so much easier to kill someone than people realise. They probably didn't even mean to do it.' Lydia didn't know why that felt even worse.

He squeezed her hand.

'If they had just called an ambulance, maybe she would have survived. Why wasn't she worth saving?'

'I'm sorry,' Fleet said.

Lydia didn't know why he was apologising, but she curled into him and let the tears fall.

CHAPTER TWENTY-EIGHT

F leet's horror, mirroring her own, had forged a bond between them. His arms wrapped around Lydia as they slept and, when they woke up, they spent some quality time remembering all the ways in which they fitted together.

While Fleet was in the shower and Lydia was enjoying a celebratory mug of coffee, a crow landed outside the French windows and gave her a silent and knowing look. 'I'm allowed to have some fun,' she told the bird.

A moment later, the single crow was joined by several others. They were lined up outside the glass and one by one they tapped on the surface.

'Okay, okay. I'm getting back to work,' Lydia said, throwing her hands up. She didn't know if the crows disagreed with her having a lie-in or whether they weren't sure about Fleet or whether they were just messing with her for fun. She reached for her coin and felt the blow of its absence all over again.

'I'm sorry,' she said over the sound of insistent tapping. 'I don't know what you want from me.'

LATER THAT DAY, AIDEN HAD ARRIVED. LYDIA WAS glad she had got out of bed and put clothes on.

'I've got news.' Aiden inclined his head toward the office, and Lydia followed, trying to switch gears. She wouldn't think about poor dead Cherish. Wouldn't think about Paul Fox and his cousin. Or any of them.

Once she was seated behind her desk, she grabbed her new Sherlock Holmes mug. It was a replacement for the one destroyed in The Fork, and a reminder that she owed Emma a visit. Her head felt like it was filled with buzzing insects and her eyes were gritty with exhaustion.

Aiden was carrying an energy drink in a can and he took a swig before explaining exactly what was so urgent.

'It was Jade.'

It was a mark of just how tired Lydia was that it took her a beat to place the name. Jade was Jez's girlfriend. 'What was Jade?'

'Jez. She killed him.'

Lydia glanced into her empty mug, wishing it would magically refill. She slid open the bottom drawer of the desk and took out a fresh bottle of whisky. The bottle made a muffled thunking sound when she put it in between them. She had been doing really well at cutting down on alcohol, but that had been before The River Man had drained her and she had stepped into Charlie's role. She was still drinking nowhere near what she used to, not wanting to risk dulling her senses when she was already weak from the loss of her power, but she thought about it a great deal. The unopened bottle in her desk drawer seemed like a joke, a nod to Sam Spade and all the gumshoes, but it was actually a test. She wanted to prove to herself that she could keep it on hand and not crack the lid.

'I'm all right with this,' Aiden said, lifting his can.

Lydia stared at the bottle for a beat. 'I'm going to need some more coffee.'

'Shall I?' Aiden began to stand, but Lydia waved him back down.

'Tell me about Jade first. What makes you think she killed him?'

'He was banging her sister.'

'Didn't she have an alibi?'

'She said she was shopping with a mate. The mate lied for her, but when I pressed, she got hazy on the timing. I told her we had checked the CCTV and she crumbled.'

'Had we?'

'Course not,' Aiden said.

'There were shopping bags in the flat,' Lydia said, remembering. She opened her desk drawer and plucked out the receipt she had taken from Jez's flat. 'I should have given you this,' she said. She scanned the piece of paper. The time looked right, just after three o'clock, but the date was the day before Jez was murdered. She passed it across the desk.

'So she did go shopping,' Aiden said, 'just not on the right day?'

'Either she was thinking the clothes would act as proof, forgetting that receipts are dated, or she just reached for a lie that was close to truth in the panic of the moment. Said the first thing that came to her mind.'

'And then got her mates to back her up,' Aiden said.

'Maybe they did more than provide an alibi. I can't believe she killed him on her own.'

'That's what she claims.'

'You're telling me she stabbed him in the back and then got him onto the bed? She was half his size.'

'Sleeping tablets dissolved in whisky. He would have been fast asleep on the bed. Possibly on his front or curled on his side, which will be why she went in from the back. She may have had advice on where to aim for or she was just lucky. She went straight through his liver. A killing spot.'

'There's probably advice online,' Lydia said, thinking out loud. 'We could check her browsing history for proof.'

'Don't need proof. Once she confessed, she seemed almost proud. Told me that the knife slid in much easier than she expected.'

Lydia was still trying to imagine it. 'You think he was that heavily drugged? Wouldn't the pain have brought him out of it?'

'It was a very narrow blade. Nerves are in the skin, not the flesh and organs. It's conceivable that he didn't wake up.'

Lydia put the whisky bottle back in the drawer and

closed it. 'You know more than I am comfortable with about stabbing people.'

Aiden gave her a grim smile, but didn't say anything.

'Hell Hawk.' Lydia leaned back, feeling suddenly heavy. 'She planned it, lied about it. Killed him in cold blood.'

'Icy,' Aiden agreed. 'We could use that.'

Lydia was thinking about the police. The missing person case that was open on Jez. There was no clean way to tell the truth. No way to do it without endangering her Family. Then her brain caught up with Aiden's words. 'What do you mean?'

'Put her to work,' Aiden said. 'And she can't refuse a job now. It's us or prison.'

'That's blackmail. Coercion.'

Aiden looked like he wanted to say 'duh'. Instead, he said 'yes, Boss.'

It was a solution. And Lydia had the tiniest bit of admiration for Jade's ingenuity. 'She killed a man. There have to be consequences.'

'There are,' Aiden said. 'Ours.'

Lydia thought for a few moments. It was wrong, of course, but on the other hand they would be handing out their own kind of justice. She would have to work for them, which was arguably better than being in prison, but was still having her freedom taken away. Which was what prison did. Maybe she was spending too much time with her Family but it made a kind of sense. And Jade was clearly a cool head. Resourceful. 'Shame to waste a resource like that.'

Aiden looked relieved. 'There's a shop near Broome

Way. Lot of hassle. I think a female energy there would settle things down.' He caught Lydia's expression. 'The men tend to behave a bit better with a good-looking woman around.'

'Really?' Lydia frowned. 'Not my experience.'

CHAPTER TWENTY-NINE

Lydia opened her eyes to darkness. As her eyes adjusted, she could see a sliver of light along the edge of the blackout blinds. It was cold. She touched her face and found it chilled, the tip of her nose icy. Fleet was next to her, snoring very lightly. He must have crept in from work without waking her.

Her phone told her it was three o'clock. And the light from her screen showed her that Fleet had wound the duvet around himself in his sleep, so that only the top of his head was visible. Now that Lydia was properly awake, she could tell that it was really cold. And, by holding her phone up to illuminate the bed, she could see the cause.

Mary was standing on Fleet's side, gazing down. She wasn't actually on his side of the bed as much as inside the bed. Her torso rising above the lumpy form of a duvet-wrapped Fleet.

'Mary,' Lydia whispered. 'What are you doing?'

Mary didn't move. Lydia wondered if she only

responded to Jason, either because she could only really hear him or because she wasn't interested in making friends with the living.

'Mary,' she tried again.

The ghost reached out a hand and touched Fleet's hair. He shuddered and sat up abruptly. Mary disappeared in the same moment and the room instantly rose a couple of degrees in temperature.

'Shit,' Fleet said, rubbing his face. 'Sorry. Did I wake you up?'

'No,' Lydia, reached for the beside light, wanting to be able to see his face properly. 'Are you okay?'

'I think so. I was dreaming.'

His eyes were unfocused, like he was watching something else, something she couldn't see. It was the expression she knew meant he was having a vision. So why wasn't he telling her?

Once his eyes refocused and he looked at her, Lydia asked, 'what did you see?'

'Nothing bad. Just the garden. You're standing in the garden with your back to me. I couldn't see your face. And there are about a million crows on the grass.'

'That sounds like an exaggeration,' Lydia said, hoping it was. Even a hundred crows would mean big trouble.

'Maybe.' Fleet's voice was getting clearer as he woke up fully.

He sounded bemused, but not alarmed, and she began to think that he was right. It was a benign vision. She wondered if he had lots of them, wondered just how many things went unsaid.

'It's fine, though. It doesn't feel like you're in any danger.' He reached for her. 'You're safe here.'

'I hate it here.' Lydia hadn't known she was going to say that.

Fleet propped himself on one elbow and looked into her eyes. 'Me, too.'

LYDIA LACED UP HER TRAINERS AND LEFT THE house. A run would clear her head. She had been running a lot over the last year and it didn't take a psychologist to work out why. Luckily, she hadn't bothered to visit one, so she could enjoy the activity in peace.

Except that Aysha Fox was walking down the street with her phone in hand, as if she was consulting a map app.

Lydia got to within a couple of paces of the woman before she noticed. 'Looking for me?'

Aysha looked better than the last time Lydia had seen her. Her eyes weren't bloodshot, and she was standing straighter. She sounded clearer and more focused when she spoke, too. Maybe off the heavy-duty narcotics or the weed or both. 'Can we talk?'

'Technically, no,' Lydia said. 'What's this about?'

'Can we go somewhere?'

'I was heading to the park,' Lydia said. 'I don't mind if you walk with me.' She began moving in the direction of Ruskin Park, uncertain as to whether Aysha would keep her nerve or hightail it back to Whitechapel.

Aiden loved a face-to-face meeting, but Lydia had always found that people often opened up more when you weren't eyeballing them. Walking side-by-side, even as they dodged other pavement-users, gave them a chance to speak without looking directly at each other. 'How are you doing?'

'I was hoping you had news,' Aysha said, ignoring Lydia's question. 'About Cherish.'

A woman with a pushchair broke them apart for a moment.

'You can't tell Paul about this,' Aysha said as they entered the park, near to the labyrinth garden. 'He'll kill me.'

'I highly doubt that.'

She shook her head. 'Promise.'

'I promise.'

Aysha still looked doubtful. 'Swear on your Family. As head of your Family.'

Lydia did not want to be reminded of her role right at that moment. The head of the Crow Family shouldn't be anywhere near Aysha Fox. She was risking a diplomatic incident. But the woman had asked for help. And she had been through enough. Lydia nodded. 'I swear on my Family. I swear it as the head of the Crows.' She wished she could produce her coin, nudge Aysha with a little Crow whammy to move things along, but, as usual, there was nothing there. An absence. A gap where it felt like a limb was missing, leaving her off-balance and vulnerable.

Aysha stared ahead, to the pond surrounded by trees and shrubs. 'You asked your copper about Cherish?'

'We should sit down,' Lydia said. She could feel the

urge to stretch her wings. To avoid the sadness and fragility she could sense in Aysha.

Aysha stopped walking and kept her gaze on the pond. 'Just tell me.'

'You were right about your friend, I'm sorry. She was filed as a missing person by the police. No leads.'

'She wasn't my friend. Not really. I just knew her from—' Aysha stopped speaking.

Lydia kept quiet, leaving space for Aysha to gather her thoughts.

'I hoped you would have found her,' Aysha said eventually. 'Paul says you're a decent investigator and I hoped...'

'I'm sorry,' Lydia said. It would be nice to tell Aysha that she had found Cherish alive and well, sipping margaritas on a beach somewhere. But the truth was important. 'She's dead.'

Aysha nodded in grim acknowledgement. She seemed to make a decision. 'A few years back, I had been doing some stuff that wasn't very good for me. And I had a bit of money trouble.' She glanced at Lydia. 'My family don't know. I don't want them to know. I'm fine, now. I'm sober.'

Lydia didn't think Aysha was just talking about booze. 'Who told you about the party?'

'Cherish. When I couldn't pay, Rob suggested I chat to her about ways to make fast cash. He introduced us, told her to tell me how it was easy money. I wasn't interested, but we got on. I liked her.'

Lydia thought there might be some half-truths in there, but she wasn't interested in forcing Aysha to reveal personal things she didn't wish to. Addiction made people do all kinds of things out of desperation, and Aysha had every reason to be vulnerable to addiction and substance abuse.

'Rob?'

'The guy I went to for stuff.'

Her dealer. 'Okay. So you went to the party?'

'It wasn't like I'd told Cherish about him, so she wasn't to know.' Aysha took a deep breath, as if gearing herself up to say the name. 'Perry. He was there.'

'That must have been a shock.'

A nod.

'What happened?'

'I left before he saw me. I couldn't be there. I couldn't do it. I was panicking, all sweaty and like I was having a heart attack. And I never told anyone. Not Paul or any of my cousins.'

'They were still looking for him?'

'You can't tell Paul.' Aysha shook her head. 'If he finds out, he'll be so mad.'

'I won't tell him. You have my word.'

'Everyone wanted to kill Perry, see? They would tell me that he was going to pay. I told them I didn't want them to, but they wouldn't listen. I just thought about them getting banged up for it. He wasn't worth that. And it would be all my fault.'

'For your family,' Lydia said, nodding. 'I understand. You would feel the burden of their actions.'

'It's all my fault.' The words were a whisper.

'Sorry,' Lydia tilted her head toward Aysha. 'I didn't catch what you said—'

Aysha looked into Lydia's eyes, her own filled with a deep horror. 'I should have warned her. But I just left. I should have gone and found her, told her what kind of man... It's my fault.'

'It is not your fault,' Lydia said firmly. If she had her coin, it would work better, but she tried anyway. She wasn't a touchy-feely person, but she took Aysha's hand and squeezed, looked into her eyes as she spoke. 'Perry and four other men were in that room. They are the ones who killed her. They are the ones who didn't call an ambulance. Walked away like it was nothing.'

Aysha blinked. 'She would have known to be careful...'

'It wouldn't have made a difference,' Lydia said firmly. 'She already knew to be careful. This wasn't her first job. Even if you had warned her about Perry, she might not have listened. Or she would have gone ahead with the job, but requested Perry be removed. But he wasn't the only one in that room, the sex game or whatever it was, would have still happened. The drugs would have still been taken.'

Aysha looked down, as if realising a Crow was holding her hand. She snatched it back, scrubbed at her face. 'We've all got regrets, right?'

Lydia thought about Carter and his wife. She had left Aberdeen and barely thought about the man again. She had known he was bad, but when his wife had changed her mind about leaving, it had caused Lydia personal trouble. She hadn't thought too much about what she was going through, let alone checked in on her since. Now she was in hospital. It didn't make her responsible for his actions, but it was weight nonetheless. Another stone on her shoulder, pushing her down to the earth.

Back at Charlie's house, Lydia found Jason in the kitchen scrolling on his iPad. The From Hell letter had been widely discredited as a hoax, with the social media sites being forced to add 'misinformation' pop-ups to any post circulating it. 'The hashtags #RipperReturns and #NewRipper are still trending,' Jason said. 'And there's a new podcast called The Feminist Ripper. Bit of a stretch. I don't think that's going to help the cause for equality.'

Lydia was listening to Jason but was distracted by the line of crows that were standing sentry outside the French doors. She could hear cawing and feel the ink on her skin tingling, as if it wanted to move. She didn't like to think that fate existed and part of her wanted to resist the urge to go into the garden, to spite Fleet's vision and refuse to make it true, but the cawing was getting louder. One crow was making a sound like a car alarm and another was calling with such a scratchy, angry sound, that she didn't dare disobey for another moment.

'What's wrong?' Jason asked as she opened the doors. The cacophony was deafening now that it wasn't muted by the double-glazing.

'I'm just—' Lydia stepped into the garden. The long grass was damp and there were black feathered bodies all around. Sitting on the roofline, on wires, on the unkempt lawn and in the hornbeam tree at the bottom of the garden.

At the base of the tree was something that Fleet wouldn't have seen in his vision, presumably because he wouldn't see it if he was standing with her at this moment. Mary.

The ghost was almost translucent in the afternoon sun, the dappled shade from the tree branches casting little leafy shadows across her long skirts and cloth bonnet. She had her back to Lydia and seemed to be doing something with her hands. It looked like a washing movement and Lydia remembered Jason's theory that there had been some kind of outhouse or laundry room at the back of the garden, back in her time. Looking at the old gnarled tree with its spreading branches and the dense foliage, it was strange to think that it had been planted after Mary's time. That all those years had passed between her life and theirs. She wondered whether the tree bothered Mary or whether she didn't really see it at all.

'Mary,' Jason said quietly. He had joined Lydia and was watching Mary with such gentle compassion that Lydia felt her own heart squeeze.

Mary turned at the sound of his voice. Her small features were hard to make out, but Lydia thought she looked surprised. Maybe a little guilty.

'I was doing the washing, sir.'

Jason's face creased in sympathy. 'It's all right, Mary. It's me. Jason. You're not in any trouble.' To Lydia, without turning his head, he whispered. 'She gets confused. Especially out here. She's repeated the same thing so many times it takes her a moment to remember the present.'

Lydia took a few paces closer, the wet grass clinging to her boots and a crow moving out of her way with a disgruntled croak. 'Hello, Mary. I'm Lydia. We've met before, but it's all right if you don't remember me.'

The crows were still making a racket. Lydia looked up and saw several in the tree. There was a nest high up in the branches, and she wondered if there were nestlings. That would account for their agitation. Perhaps they didn't like a ghost so close to their nest. 'It's okay,' Lydia said to the crows. 'She won't hurt you. Mary's a friend.'

The birds went silent. All at once. Small black eyes fixed on Lydia with an intensity that was unnerving, even to her.

'What's that?' Jason was saying to Mary.

'I hide things here. Treasures.' Mary's hands were in her apron, twisting the material.

'That's okay,' Jason said. 'This is your home. You can do what you like. You won't get into any trouble. There's nothing to be afraid of.'

Mary's form was vibrating. She shook her head, the edges of her bonnet quivering. 'I mustn't be late,' she said.

The crows closest to Lydia were staring at the tree trunk, and Lydia had the strangest impression that they were trying to show her something. Something that they were extremely displeased about. She took a few steps closer and saw something wedged into a hollow in the bark.

'No!' Mary screamed as Lydia reached for it.

In an instant, the ghost was in front of Lydia. The tree trunk was visible through her body, but all Lydia could see was Mary's rage. Her face had twisted into a mask of fury. 'You mustn't.' She sprang at Lydia as if intending to rake her nails down her face.

Jason was there, wrapping his arms around her ghostly body and gripping her. Lydia appreciated the gesture, even though Mary's hands looked so translucent she imagined they would have simply passed through Lydia's head.

'Mary, what's wrong?' Jason wasn't loosening his hold, but his voice was gentle and concerned.

Lydia had the urge to ask 'what the feathers?' and she knew it wouldn't have sounded gentle in the slightest.

Then Mary disappeared, and Jason was left holding thin air.

'What did you do?' Jason asked. 'You frightened her.'

'Nothing. I was just looking at this—' Lydia stopped speaking. The thing wedged in the tree. It was a lump of organic matter. About six centimetres long. Black and dried-up around the edges and with a distinctive odour. Lydia was no expert in human organs, but she couldn't shake her certainty of what she was looking at. Half a human kidney.

CHAPTER THIRTY

'Crows eat anything. It's a miracle they left it intact.' Fleet was looking at the kidney that was now sitting in one of the plastic boxes Angel used to leave portions of food in the fridge.

Lydia didn't say anything. Privately, she thought that the crows had known it was evidence, known it was important to Lydia somehow. They had been trying to get her out into the garden for weeks.

'I can't believe that's been there for days,' Jason said. 'I need to find Mary.' He had already been through the house, calling for her in a coaxing manner, and he headed off into the garden, presumably to do the same out there. 'Be careful,' Lydia called after him. She didn't think Mary could hurt Jason, even if she wanted to do so, but the discovery of grisly treasures put a different perspective on the Victorian ghost.

She had thoroughly checked the tree after retrieving the kidney and dug up a piece of material buried at its base. She had worn gloves and put the scrap into a plastic ziplock bag. It was stained black with what, Lydia assumed, was Price's blood.

'I'll get it to the lab. And check that the kidney is Perry's.'

'It's half a human kidney,' Lydia said. 'Whose else would it be? It's the right size for the missing half, right?'

'Yep.' Fleet caught her eye and grimaced.

'Well, I guess we've found our killer.' Mary's furious face flashed into her mind. She wondered how she had managed to miss the ghost's anger before. It was like someone had flipped a switch.

'This is not going to help,' Fleet said.

'It's not ideal. Unless you think the Met is ready to accept a ghost as a suspect?'

'That's not the biggest problem.'

At once Lydia realised what he meant. He could hardly turn up to work with a piece of one of the victims and tell them he had found it at his girlfriend's house. Charlie Crow's house. 'You could find it somewhere else, maybe?'

'Plant it?'

'I don't know.' Lydia was trying to think where Fleet could 'find' the kidney that wouldn't send the Met off on a wild goose chase.

'Are we sure Mary is our killer?'

'Well I don't think she just stumbled across half a kidney and decided to keep it for a lark.'

'Did you say she was a Victorian?' Fleet asked. 'Times were different, maybe organ collecting was a thing. They didn't have Netflix.'

There was no amount of joking about that was going

to make this okay, but Lydia attempted a smile for Fleet's benefit. He was trying. And he was thinking about protecting her and her Family.

'What are you going to do?'

'I need to talk to Jason,' Lydia said. 'He's not going to like this.'

LYDIA WENT TO FIND JASON. HE WASN'T IN THE garden and neither was Mary. She found him upstairs.

'I can't find Mary,' he said.

'When did you last see her?'

Jason was hovering above the carpet in his room, looking unhappy. He wanted to help Mary and it had given him a sense of purpose, something to focus on after he had endured loss after loss. She hated that this was the outcome. 'We need to speak to her.'

He shook his head. 'She can't have done it. She wouldn't hurt anyone. I know she wouldn't. And why would she be killing those men? How would she even know about them? She's tied to this area. It doesn't make any sense.'

'It's unusual, I know,' Lydia said. 'But maybe she is drawn to the unsolved murder of Cherish? The crime could have left some kind of psychic signature. Something that has drawn Mary because of her own unsolved death.'

'But we're anchored.' Jason was getting increasingly upset. 'I know Mary's been out and about, looking for her Georgie, but she follows her old patterns. She can't have been slipping out to

Whitechapel to kill scummy men. It makes no sense. It's not the Mary I know.'

'It's not something we've seen before, but that doesn't make it impossible. I think she's a victim,' Lydia said. 'And I think she wanted to be found. To be stopped.'

He was shaking his head, his whole body vibrating in distress. 'She has never seemed violent. Not for a moment. Not ever.'

'Do you know why I went into the garden today?'

Jason stopped shaking. 'No. Why?'

'Mary visited Fleet in the night. She was standing in the bed, touching him, and he had a vision of me in the garden. I think she was trying to get me to see. I think she was trying to guide us to her.'

Jason looked down, clearly conflicted.

'Please. I just want to talk to her.'

He looked up. 'Come on, then.'

Jason was up and leading the way. Once they were outside, he stood for a moment as if listening. Then walked down the hill briskly towards Camberwell Green. 'Where are we going?'

'Park,' he said. 'She likes to watch the children.'

Lydia was thinking that sounded a bit creepy, when Jason said something that stabbed her. 'She always wanted to be a mother.'

It was a grey afternoon, threatening rain, but the play area was packed. Parents stood around the perimeter, phones and takeaway coffees in hand, interspersed with buggies and dogs on leads. The few available benches were all taken, one by a whole family who were in the middle of a picnic. The play equipment was almost fully obscured by bodies. Small children in brightly coloured coats were climbing and dangling, screaming and laughing.

There was a lone tree just outside the fence that enclosed the play area. And underneath the spreading branches, Lydia saw a tiny female figure in long skirts. The sunlight that was fighting its way from behind the clouds shot a shaft of light that illuminated the ground, passing through the ghost's body and showing its other-worldly translucency. It was beautiful. But not as beautiful as Mary's face. Upturned and pointed in the direction of the children playing, her expression rapt and eyes shining.

Lydia approached cautiously, not wanting to spook the spook.

'Mary?' Jason got to the ghost first and raised his hand in greeting.

For a moment, Lydia wasn't sure she was going to acknowledge him, her attention was still fixed on the children, but then she turned and smiled. 'This is my favourite place.'

'I remember,' Jason said.

She turned her attention to Lydia. 'Have you come to see the little ones?'

Lydia was struggling to keep calm. The last time she had seen Mary, she had been trying to launch herself at Lydia with violence in her eyes. She had seen her bucking and twisting in Jason's arms, her face contorted in thwarted fury. Lydia had no doubt whatsoever that if Jason hadn't grabbed her, she would have tried to rip

Lydia apart with her bare hands. 'We've come to see you.'

The white-hot rage was nowhere to be seen. Mary now appeared just as she had before. Her expression mild and open. Lydia remembered her crying and asking where her 'dear Georgie' had gone. It was like two different ghosts existed. If it wasn't ridiculous, Lydia would think Mary had an evil twin.

'Do you remember going to Mitre Square?'

Mary looked at Jason with that same mild expression. 'I don't know where that is.'

'Whitechapel,' Jason said.

'Do you remember Connor Bright?'

She shook her head.

'Chris Perry? You met him at a nightclub called Cerberus.'

A flicker of recognition. 'That's a bad place.' Mary pursed her lips in distaste. 'Not safe for young ladies.'

'You took his kidney and hid it in your treasure spot. The old laundry. Do you remember I saw it?'

Mary didn't respond.

Lydia tried a different tack. 'You were in Mitre Square. You met Connor Bright and you took his knife.' Lydia didn't quite manage to say 'and you plunged it repeatedly into his body', but she thought it pretty loudly.

Mary was watching the children, but Lydia had the distinct impression that she was listening. 'Did you know Connor was going to be there? Did you choose that place for a particular reason?'

Mary shuddered. She became more solid and Lydia

took a step back, glancing around at the parents and kids. It struck her that this wasn't the safest place to rile up a homicidal ghost.

'It's all right,' Jason was saying softly. 'Nobody is going to hurt you. You're safe.'

He must have had the same thought as Lydia as he added. 'Shall we go for a walk? To the duck pond?'

Mary's face brightened and she nodded once. Jason offered her his arm and she placed her small hand on top, smiling up at him prettily.

Lydia trailed them out of the play area and along the wide main path that led to the pond. The height difference wasn't the only startling thing about Jason and Mary, of course. They looked like they were heading to a fancy-dress night.

'I lived on Denmark Hill. Not far from here,' Mary said conversationally. 'The Gibbs family. Very nice people. Very clean.' She nodded in approval. 'Cleanliness is next to godliness.'

'Quite,' Jason said. 'What about George? He lived in Whitechapel, I think?'

'I don't know about that,' Mary said, pursing her lips. 'He visited me. We were courting. He brought me lilacs. Ever so pretty.'

They had reached the pond by this point. It was grey and flat with scrubby grass and a crisp packet floating near the edge. Lydia couldn't see any ducks.

'Do you know the names Craig Johnstone, Raymond Price, Chris Perry, Connor Bright?' As she listed the names again, Lydia watched Mary carefully and her eyes didn't so much as twitch. Her expression remained open and guileless as she looked between Lydia and Jason.

'I don't believe so. Should I?'

'How about Brad Carter?'

'You do ask peculiar questions,' Mary said. And disappeared.

CHAPTER THIRTY-ONE

Lydia called Karen. She wanted to hear that Brad Carter was safely locked up waiting his trial and far away from Whitechapel. Something that would make the man not her problem. Unfortunately, he had been granted bail and, as far as Karen was aware, he wasn't in Aberdeen. 'He's got an address here and according to the terms of his bail, he's supposed to be there, but the place is quiet.'

'You're keeping an eye on him?'

'I am,' Karen confirmed. 'Or, I was. He's the kind that thinks he's above the rules. He might have gone on holiday for all we know. Let me know if you hear anything?'

'Of course.'

Jason was hovering by Lydia's desk. 'That didn't sound like good news?'

'Brad Carter isn't in Aberdeen. What's Mary's routine? After her walk to the park?'

He looked dubious. 'You really think she's a killer?'

'I don't think Mary just stumbled across half a kidney, no.' Lydia was struggling to keep her tone gentle. 'If we're right and she was murdered, and it was never solved, never even acknowledged as a crime, she might be drawn to the death of Cherish. Another terrible injustice. An unsolved murder, just like her death. Maybe it gives out, I don't know, energy? Something that a restless spirit would tune into?'

Jason checked the time. 'She hangs out in her old room until six. Then she likes to be in the kitchen, in case she's needed by the cook.'

'Show me.'

Mary wasn't in the exercise studio on the top floor of the house. Jason assured Lydia that this was converted attic space and used to house Mary and the scullery maid. She wasn't downstairs, either.

Lydia put her hand on Jason's cold arm. 'What if she's going after Brad?'

'She might just be hiding from us,' Jason said, but his voice lacked conviction. 'And what are you going to do if you find her? You can't hurt her. She's like me.'

'We have to stop her from killing. I think part of her wanted me to know. I believe she wants to be stopped.'

Jason's face closed down. 'You're going to tell her about George Chapman and hope it makes her move on.'

'If we're right about Chapman being her Georgie, then it might be enough to release her from this.' Lydia waved her hand. 'We thought that she's looking for him out of love, but maybe she wants justice. Or to solve the puzzle of her own death. If we do that for her, she can move on. Be at peace.'

'Be properly dead,' Jason said.

'Everyone dies,' Lydia said. 'Or they should.'

For a moment, Jason stared at her. Lydia wasn't sure if he was going to help or walk away. Then he shoved his suit sleeves up to his elbows. 'We know she's been following the Ripper locations, or close to them. Where was the next Ripper murder?'

Mary Jane Kelly had been killed at her home. The twenty-five-year-old lived in a rented room on Dorset Street in Spitalfields. Dorset Street was the heart of a poverty-stricken and lawless area, and described as the 'worst street in London'. It had since been renamed Duval Street and the lane itself bulldozed to make way for warehousing for the nearby Spitalfields Market. In 2012, it became part of a shiny new redevelopment. The London Fruit and Wool Exchange was demolished, all apart from its Georgian frontage, and a multi-million-pound glass and metal compound erected on the site. Now it housed restaurants and shops at street level and luxury offices above. An international law firm, business consultancy and a bank moved in, and the project was declared a success.

Standing outside the building, Lydia tried to imagine the Victorian slum. There had been a warren of dark lanes, pickpockets and gangs, ordinary people struggling to survive through hunger and illness and the ever-present threat of violence and death. A young woman, probably the same age as poor Mary Jane Kelly, walked past them carrying an over-sized pink insulated water bottle and a Pret sandwich. A moment later, Jason hopped sideways to avoid a couple walking right through him.

'Anything?' Lydia asked after a few minutes of watching Jason look around, an expression of intense concentration on his face.

Jason shrugged. His form was translucent, and the motion shimmered slightly. Lydia avoided focusing on him too hard so that she didn't give herself a headache. 'Nothing solid. I keep thinking I can hear voices, but I can't tell what they are saying. I get it a lot when I'm exploring. It's a kind of humming background noise.'

'I don't know how close to Mary Jane Kelly's room we are. I'm guessing it's somewhere in there.'

'Hang on,' Jason walked toward the wall of glass and disappeared through it.

Lydia waited. She took a few photos, more for something to do than because she thought they would be useful, and scrutinised the air around her in case Mary suddenly materialised.

When Jason appeared again, his form moved through the brickwork of the building as easily as a clear doorway. He shook his head. 'I don't think she's there. Where now?'

'We need to find Brad Carter.'

Brad Carter was co-owner of a hotel near to Aldgate. 'It's almost Whitechapel,' Jason reported. 'But it bills itself as "straddling the beguiling City and the creative melting pot of London's vibrant East End".'

Lydia mimed sticking her fingers down her throat.

'He is listed as managing director of the company that part-owns a bar and club, this place, and an "art consultancy". Whatever that is.'

'Let me see the hotel,' Lydia leaned across to look at Jason's screen. He clicked on the tab for the hotel website. 'Boutique aparthotel,' she read out loud. 'Residents' lounge, yoga studio, high-tech gym, modern art, rooftop terrace.'

'It's listed as his address,' Jason explained. 'I guess he decided that he may as well make money from his need for a residence in London.'

'We thought the killings were linked by the Ripper locations, but now we know they are linked by the death of Cherish. All of the victims were connected to that party where she died.'

'Some of the locations have been close. Connor's was spot-on.'

'But the locations aren't the most important link, and we know Mary is okay with close enough.'

'What are you thinking?'

'Mary Jane Kelly was killed in her lodging house. Her home.'

Understanding dawned on Jason's face. 'You think she will go for Carter at his hotel? We have to stop her.'

Lydia didn't have any fond feelings for Brad Carter, but she wanted to stop Mary from adding another body to her conscience. Unfortunately, she couldn't just hand the information to Fleet and let him close his case with it. He could hardly go to his team and tell them that it was a homicidal ghost and they wouldn't be able to stop her, either. 'She won't talk to us about him, I think we need to assume she's going ahead.'

'I don't think she remembers anything about the murders,' Jason said. 'It's like she's doing them in her sleep.'

Lydia watched the horror cross his face, and she knew exactly what he was thinking. 'You are not like Mary,' she said.

'What if I go on a murder spree every time I disappear? How would I know?'

Lydia wrapped her arms around Jason's shoulder and hugged him tightly, ignoring the freezing cold of his body and the tingling in her skin.

THE RECEPTION DESK HAD ONE PERSON BEHIND IT. He was dressed entirely in black, had a neat black beard, and was unfeasibly handsome. If he had said he was a reality TV star, she would have believed him, and almost expected to see cameras in the lobby. Lydia had sent Jason in ahead of her to scope out the layout, so she was able to walk confidently past the desk and to the stairwell next to the lifts. Going into places you didn't belong was ninety per cent brass neck.

It was the middle of the day. At this time, cleaning staff would be turning over the rooms, so Lydia just cruised a couple of floors until she found an open door. A woman was stripping the bed and she turned a questioning face when Lydia stepped into the room.

'I would like to borrow your key card,' Lydia said,

deciding just to be direct. She held out five twenty-pound notes, fanned out like a hand of cards.

The cleaner's gaze flicked to the money and then back up. She didn't look to the corners of the room, so Lydia assumed that meant there weren't cameras in the room. At least, not that the cleaner knew about.

'I need it,' the cleaner said. Which wasn't a no.

'I'm going to open one door,' Lydia said. 'You can have it back in half an hour, or you can come with me, open the door for me and it never leaves your sight. Are there cameras in the halls?'

She shook her head.

'Your choice, then,' Lydia said. She pulled another couple of twenties from her pocket and added them to the five.

The woman passed over a white key card. It had the letter J scribbled on it in Sharpie.

'Thanks, J,' Lydia said, handing over the cash.

'I'm filling in for Jared,' the woman said. 'It's his card.'

SHE AND JASON GOT INTO THE LIFT AND TRAVELLED to the tenth floor in silence. Lydia was thinking about being in that mirrored lift with Brad Carter. Ten years ago, when she had been so much greener.

She wasn't green, now, knew exactly what she was getting herself into. But she didn't know exactly what she was going to do. Part of her didn't want to stop Mary. The woman had been badly treated in her life and now she was going to be banished. However they dressed it up, they were going to give her information that would likely send her on to whatever came next.

'She's not really here,' Jason said. He had clearly been thinking along the same lines. 'She didn't remember hurting those men. She isn't evolving or living. She's just stuck.'

'I know,' Lydia said. She had no idea if she could help, but she knew she had to try.

There were only two doors on the tenth floor. Presumably they were both apartments, rather than standard hotel rooms. Lydia nodded at Jason, who stuck his head through the door.

When he pulled back, he whispered that the coast was clear. 'It opens into a small hall, which leads into a living room with a kitchen area. There's a door immediately to the right. No sign of Carter, but the television is on.'

Lydia swiped the key card and walked in, closing the door behind them as quietly as possible. The living room was decorated in shades of brown, grey, and mustard and was probably very tasteful in a 1950s retro kind of way. The large windows on the far wall showed the grey London skyline. Jason floated through the wall to the right and then returned, pointing through a closed door. He mouthed 'bathroom'. A moment later, a toilet flushed.

The door opened and Brad Carter stepped into the room. In the same instant, Mary materialised in the middle of the yellow velvet sofa. She moved quickly out of it, her body becoming more solid by the second.

Brad's mouth had opened to yell. Presumably at

Lydia, as she doubted he could see the ghost that was looking at him with murderous intent.

Lydia used both hands and all of her body weight to shove Brad back into the bathroom. She slammed the door shut and shouted through the wood. 'Stay in there if you want to live.'

CHAPTER THIRTY-TWO

Mary's expression shifted from murderous to confused. Like a switch had been flicked. She looked around, as if confused by her location.

Lydia took the opportunity. 'Hello, Mary. It's Lydia. Do you remember me? And Jason's here too.'

'Hi Mary,' Jason said.

Mary turned to look at him. Her face was blank now, and Lydia didn't know if she was trying to process their unexpected presence or whether she had shut down.

Jason was reaching for Mary, patting her on the arm. Even though she still looked fairly translucent, his hand seemed to connect. 'It's all right,' he was saying, 'we're here to help'.

Mary's eyes flicked to the closed bathroom door. Brad Carter hadn't done anything yet, he was probably listening, trying to work out what was going on. The door handle turned and she braced herself. It shuddered as he tried to push it open. Lydia was about half the man's bulk and wasn't going to be able to stop him if he really put his weight into it. 'Seriously,' she said to the door. 'I'm trying to save your stupid life.'

There was a muffled response, but Lydia didn't have time to spare.

'Jason. I need you to distract Brad. Keep him in there.'

He didn't look happy to leave Mary, but passed through the wall and into the bathroom. If he couldn't get corporeal enough to hold Brad, Lydia was hoping he could make the man cold enough to distract him or write on the mirror or something. Ideally, without giving him a heart attack.

She focused on Mary. 'Do you know where you are?'

Mary looked around slowly. 'Is this London?'

'It is. My London. Not yours.'

A frown.

'You lived a long time ago. Near to Camberwell Green.'

Mary nodded, the movement making Lydia want to throw up. Her outline was vibrating in the way that Jason's did when he was upset. She really didn't want to see what Mary would do if she got distressed. She knew it would be stabby.

'Why am I here?' Mary asked. 'This ain't...' She trailed off, looking around the room.

Lydia's fingers curled, automatically looking for her coin. She wanted its reassurance. She wanted to feel like Lydia Crow. 'We're in Whitechapel. Near Aldgate.'

Mary looked shocked. 'Whitechapel ain't safe. Not for nice girls.' She examined Lydia. 'You don't look like a nice girl. Your clothes,' she swept a disparaging look at Lydia's attire, 'are proper peculiar.'

'This is my London. Years and years after your time. You died a long time ago, do you remember?'

Mary shook. 'I've got something... something I need to...'

'No. There's nothing you need to do. You can rest now, Mary. There's nothing here for you.'

Mary was looking around the room, but her voice took on a sudden intensity. 'I need to find my Georgie. Have you seen him?'

Lydia could taste feathers, and she welcomed it. 'George is dead,' she said. Like ripping off a plaster.

Mary's head whipped in her direction. Mary's eyes were furious, burning with an otherworldly light. She hissed.

'It's been years,' Lydia said, trying to stay calm. She could feel the ink of her tattoos, the skin tingling as they tried to move. The feathers in her throat choking. 'So many years that he must have died of old age by now. I don't know if that's what happened, not for sure. I'm sorry I can't tell you exactly.' If Mary's Georgie was indeed George Chapman, then he had been hanged. But like the identity of the Ripper, Lydia wasn't certain that they had solved the mystery, and she didn't want to lie. She was hoping that she could make Mary remember for herself.

Lydia didn't see Mary move. One moment she was in the middle of the room and the next she was pressed against Lydia, her small hands wrapped around her throat.

'I don't have a knife,' Lydia said, trying to stay calm as the terrible cold seeped into her bones. She wasn't a tall woman, but she was looking onto the top of Mary's head. This close, she could see the rough cotton of her bonnet. 'You always cut them, don't you? The men you killed. Why is that?'

Mary's grip loosened and she peered into Lydia's face. Lydia took the opportunity to break away. She took a punt. 'You use a blade because it's how you died.'

Mary shook her head. 'Not dead.' She gestured at her semi-translucent body with a cheeky expression that made Lydia's heart squeeze. 'See.'

'Prove it,' Lydia said. 'Show me you're not dead. Show me you didn't die.'

'I don't—'

'I think you were cut.' She mimed a finger across her throat. 'Or maybe stabbed.' She pointed at Mary's midriff. She was being deliberately blunt. Hurtful. She had to provoke Mary into unlocking her memories.

There was a muffled sound from the bathroom. A thump like someone very large had fallen over. Feathers. Lydia was running out of time. If Carter was having a heart attack, she had to get an ambo. But if she opened that door, Mary would stab him. While she couldn't see Carter, she seemed to have forgotten he was there.

'You were killed. I'm very sorry.' She put every ounce of Crow into her voice as she could. She knew that her presence would be powering up Mary and that she would soon be too strong for Lydia to fight physically. And the moment Mary realised that Carter was in the bathroom, she was likely to go mindless and ragey, just as she had been in the garden by the tree. She had to get Mary to listen to her, to understand that she had been murdered. Lydia's theory was that it would make her move on. Break whatever hellish loop she was reliving over and over again.

Mary shook her head. Her body was far more solid now, and Lydia could no longer see through it. Quicker than a human should move, Mary darted across the room and picked up a bottle of wine from the dinky retro drinks-cart. With one movement, she smashed it against the coffee table, spilling red wine all over the mustard rug. Her gaze was moving around the room, searching. Another noise from the bathroom.

'When was the last time you saw Georgie?' Lydia spoke loudly, trying to cover up the sounds of Carter and Jason. Now that Mary was powered up enough to pick up solid objects, she would be at killing force. If she caught sight of Carter, it would likely trigger the mind-less rage Lydia had seen before.

Mary blinked. Distracted.

'Did he have a temper? I think he did.'

Mary held up the broken bottle. She took a step toward Lydia, her feet not quite touching the carpet. Her outline was vibrating, but she was definitely more solid.

She wasn't listening. Wasn't believing what she was hearing. Lydia was trying to put authority into her voice, the calm tone of certainty of a leader. Without her Crow power, she couldn't compel Mary, couldn't make her understand.

She squeezed her hand, willing her coin to appear. It

didn't. 'Georgie had a knife. He cut you.' If Lydia was wrong, then she was getting these details all wrong. She thought about switching to another scenario, but her gut told her she was right.

Mary stopped moving. She raised the bottle, the jagged edge barely inches from Lydia's face. 'He killed lots of other women later, but I think you were his first. He lost control. Or maybe he planned to do it. Maybe he was excited. It must have been so scary for you. I'm so sorry it happened. You loved him and he stabbed you.'

Mary looked completely solid now. Lydia could see every detail of her cloth skirts, the apron that almost reached the floor. Brown leather boots peeked out below the hem. They were as dainty as the rest of her, and looked soft and well worn. Lydia was used to seeing Jason, of course, but this was something else. The woman was so clearly from another time, but so human and alive-looking. Lydia could see the pockmarks on her forehead, the pretty rose-tint of her cheeks and the sweet light in her hazel eyes. She was pretty. And very young. 'I'm sorry,' Lydia said, her own heart breaking a little. Her tattoos were painful now, tugging at her skin, and she felt a pressure through her body. Something wanted to be let out. Her arms wanted to stretch into wings, the urge to fly was almost overpowering.

There was a red flower blooming on Mary's white apron. Mary looked down in surprise. 'I—'

'I'm sorry,' Lydia said again.

The flower was spreading, a crimson blood stain that covered Mary's midriff from above the waistband of her apron to her knees. Mary buckled as she viewed the blood saturating the material, she reached out a hand to steady herself and it connected with the furniture. Mary's head was bowed, but Lydia could feel the wave of desolation and fear that was rolling from the ghost. She felt her throat close-up in sympathy.

The pain in her arms had reached a crescendo. It felt like her skin was on fire and she had to push the sleeves of her jacket and look. Abruptly, as if waiting for her to do just that, the pain was doused. The black ink was moving, wings beating on her skin, just as they had used to do.

Lydia's face was wet and she realised she was crying. She wasn't a crier, but she was powerless to stop the tears from falling. Everything was sharper, clearer, as if she was seeing it with new eyes. Sympathy for Mary warred with euphoria. Now that her tattoos were moving, she realised just how constant and unpleasant the feeling of them being stuck had been. Her wings were stretching out and she was soaring high in a vast blue sky.

'Georgie?' Mary said, looking at Lydia in a pleading way. Her palms turned outward in supplication, and she dropped the broken bottle.

Lydia reached for the ghost, ignoring the broken glass on the floor between them, and clasped her hand. It was like holding a glove filled with ice, but she squeezed gently, trying to offer comfort.

The blood was spreading across Mary's clothes. There was more pouring down her front. A line of red had appeared across her neck and was now opening into a grotesque wound. The poor woman had been cut multiple times. Her throat slashed. Although it had happened long ago and this was a spirit, there was the smell of iron in the air, and Mary was keening like a wounded animal.

Lydia couldn't stop crying, and she wiped her eyes with her free hand. She had done this, she had told Mary the truth, and now she had to bear witness to the suffering she had caused. She might not have killed poor Mary all those years ago, but she was forcing her to relive it. She squeezed Mary's cold hand, trying to convey some comfort, but her mind was becoming blank with fear. A terrible curtain was being drawn across her rational thought.

The fear was battling her sense of flying, pulling her back to earth. Lydia was feeling what Mary had experienced in her last seconds. The disbelief and confusion almost as strong as the terror, all of it flowing through her like she was reliving the moment with Mary. The terror and the pain. The fight to survive. The desperate fluttering of her heart as the lifeblood drained away.

Lydia's hand was numb from the cold, but she didn't let go. Her vision had gone jittery with the adrenaline. She was seeing staccato images that weren't joined up the way they ought to be. But she wasn't going to leave Mary alone. A flash of something looming above her. A man's face. Hooded black eyes, thick whiskers, the smell of sour beer and pipe smoke. The betrayal of it took her breath. Her Georgie. The man she had loved turned monstrous before her eyes. How could this be? How could he do this? He would—

The thought cut off. It had been a surge of anger.

302

The desire for revenge. Lydia struggled to separate her own thoughts from Mary's. She focused on her tattoos, on the feeling of her wings. A thousand hearts fluttering with life, a thousand wings beating, the sky beckoning, wide open and free. She wasn't a maid called Mary. She was Lydia Crow. She remembered. Her power surged through her body, making her nerves sing.

Lydia blinked. She was back in the hotel room, looking into Mary's knowing eyes. Her anger was there, a banked fire. 'He's long dead,' Lydia said. Her lips and tongue felt awkward, as if they still weren't quite her own. 'Georgie is dead and buried.'

The ghost looked furious. Like she might still pick up the bottle and start slashing. She had been so badly hurt, Lydia didn't know what she could say to make that right. 'There's no justice,' she said. 'I'm sorry. He murdered you. You died in pain and fear, utterly betrayed, and there is no retribution for that, no way to make it right. I know it, though. I know what happened.' Lydia wanted to say something about documenting Mary's death so that others would know, or that she would dedicate her life to stopping it happening to other women, but wasn't going to make promises she couldn't keep. Mary had been lied to enough in her life.

Mary nodded once, then she pulled her hand back. She wasn't moving quickly or with any strength, but Lydia's grip slipped. Her fingers closed around nothing, the cold hand was there but not there. She could feel the chill, but it was passing through her own flesh, no longer resisting. Mary's body was fading. Was that it? Enough closure?

The ghost was staring into Lydia's eyes. Her expression was patient now. Calm. It was as if she was waiting for something.

'I will try,' Lydia said in a rush. 'I will try to stop this happening to other women. Wherever I can.'

Mary sighed. Her lips turned up at the corners and she looked, for a brief moment, like she had while she had watched the children playing in the park. And then she disappeared. There was no final fading. It was as if she had blinked out of existence and Lydia had the strong feeling that she truly had. She had moved on and wasn't about to pop back and frighten the life out of her. There was the lingering smell of lilac blossom in the air.

And something else. In the place that Mary had been standing, her terrible wounds bleeding freshly down white cotton, there was something catching the sunlight flooding through the windows.

A single gold coin suspended in mid-air.

CHAPTER THIRTY-THREE

The bathroom door burst open and Brad Carter thundered into the room. He stopped short of Lydia, gaping at her in confusion. 'What the hell are you doing in my room?'

'Nothing,' Lydia said. She reached out and plucked her coin from the air, hardly daring to believe it was real. But it was truly there. Solid. And the familiar weight settled into her palm as if it had never left.

'I know you.' Carter had gone still, staring at her as if he was seeing a ghost. 'You're that investigator. The one...' He trailed off, but Lydia could see him silently filling the blanks. He remembered her as the woman he had threatened to kill after his wife had confessed to booking the services of Karen's PI firm. She didn't know if he remembered assaulting her in a hotel room, didn't know if a man like him would even consider it assault.

The exhilaration of the power running through Lydia's body was distracting. She needed to focus. She needed to stop staring at her coin like a woman in love. 'I'm just leaving.'

She took a step toward the door and Carter landed a meaty hand on her arm, gripping her painfully above the elbow.

'Not until you've given me an explanation, young lady.'

Jason strolled through Carter, making the man convulse and drop Lydia's arm. He looked around with sudden panic, trying to make sense of the wave of cold that had just passed through his body. 'What the hell?'

Lydia planted her feet and faced Carter. She focused on his chest, still a little bit frightened to see his eyes. To remember the way he had made her feel all those years ago, for that brief and unpleasant moment in the hotel room in Aberdeen. She had been rubbing the surface of her coin with her thumb and it felt more than pure comfort, it felt like an invocation. She could feel her tattoos moving freely, the unpleasant electric tingling was entirely gone. 'I just saved your life,' she said, finally looking at Brad Carter's red and sweaty face.

He stopped blustering for a second and looked uncertain. 'What are you talking about?'

Lydia flicked her coin into the air and slowed its spin. Brad was looking at it and she felt a surge of relief. It was her coin. She could still suspend it in mid-air. It still obeyed her like it was part of her body. The rush was euphoric.

'Where's Mary?' Jason asked, his voice small.

'Cherish,' Lydia said, still focused on Carter.

'Who?'

She didn't need to be a Crow to see the flicker in his eyes as he lied. 'You invested in a nightclub a few years back. There was a party and you were there.'

'I've been to a lot of parties, you can't expect me to remember—'

'She died. Cherish. You might not remember her name, I don't know if you ever knew it, but I think you met her that night.'

'I don't—' The coin was still revolving in the air between them. Carter was staring at it, eyes wide. He swallowed. 'I didn't know. I swear I didn't know anything about it.'

'Anything about what?' Lydia pushed. 'Your name was on the VIP list. You were in the room that night, weren't you? With Cherish.'

Carter visibly sagged. His gaze didn't leave the slowly revolving coin, the image of the crow appearing to flap its wings as the metal disc turned. 'It wasn't meant to... No one meant for her to...'

Lydia waited.

'There was some rough stuff.' Carter swallowed. 'Too rough, maybe. It didn't seem too bad at the time. She seemed... I don't know. But then we realised she'd gone quiet. Been quiet for a while.' He didn't stop staring at the coin, his eyes wide. 'It wasn't meant to happen.'

'But nobody called an ambulance.' A statement. Lydia knew they hadn't.

'It was too late. I'm sure it was. It was the best of everything. A special night. Champagne, girls, sweeties.

There were important people...' His face hardened. 'The bill was massive for that night. You have no idea.'

'I think Cherish has some idea.'

'What?'

Lydia thought about saying more, but she didn't think Carter was worth her breath. 'Well, you're safe now.' Lydia plucked her coin from the air and pocketed it, satisfied that Carter was telling her the truth. Not that it mattered. She turned to Jason, who was standing in the middle of the room, waiting. 'She's gone.'

'Who's gone?' Carter said. He followed her eyeline, frowning. 'Who was here? I heard you talking.'

Lydia touched Jason's arm, not caring how it would look to Carter. 'I'm sorry,' she said quietly. 'But she's at peace now.' She hoped that was true.

Jason nodded sadly and then disappeared.

'What the hell are you talking about,' Carter's voice was increasing in volume. Now that the coin was no longer holding his attention and he was getting used to the situation, his bombastic nature was surging back. 'Who was here? I demand answers.'

Lydia spared him a single glance as she walked out of the expensive room. 'Just another dead girl.'

In the lobby of the hotel, Lydia nodded to Fleet. He lifted his walkie talkie and four uniformed police passed through the main entrance and headed for the lift. Lydia had saved Brad Carter's life long enough for him to be arrested for breaking the terms of his bail and the domestic abuse of his wife. He wouldn't be convicted for Cherish's death, but at least he would suffer some consequences.

Lydia took a seat in one of the armchairs and called Karen. 'He's being arrested right now,' she told her old mentor. 'Met will hand him over to the Scottish police later today.'

'Thank you, hen,' Karen said.

The doors to the lift opened, revealing a small crowd of blue uniforms with a cuffed Brad Carter in their midst. He was blustering at full volume, promising to sue the officers, the Met police and the whole of England.

Lydia held up her phone camera so that Karen could watch. And she just hoped that the case held and that she wouldn't live to regret taking the legal option and not just letting Mary finish the guy off.

CHAPTER THIRTY-FOUR

Back at Charlie's house, Lydia went out to the garden to thank the crows. She had bought a bag of unsalted peanuts on the way and she shook them out on the grass and stepped back. Within seconds, the lawn was covered with black-feathered bodies and sharp beaks. She waited, politely, until the feeding frenzy was over, before speaking. 'Thank you.'

Most of the crows flew off, but a couple retreated to the hornbeam. A couple of harsh caws let her know that they were still aware of her presence. 'I'm sorry about your tree.'

Lydia had already removed the trophies from the bark, but she checked over the trunk and the surrounding grass to make sure there was nothing else. She felt as if she hadn't done enough to show her gratitude and wondered whether she should gather nesting materials or get some more peanuts.

Then she felt her tattoos moving and her coin materialised at the tips of her fingers. It was as if she was being reminded all over again. She was Lydia Crow. Head of the Crow Family. She stepped back from the tree so that she had a clear line of sight to the crows on the branches and bowed her head in a formal gesture.

Back in the house, Jason was listlessly beating eggs. 'You need to eat,' he said when she crossed to the sink to wash the peanut residue from her hands.

He was trying to sound chirpy, she could tell, but there was a shroud of sadness hung around his shoulders.

'I've got my coin back,' Lydia said, drying her hands on a dish towel.

He stopped whisking. 'Let me see.'

She uncurled her fingers and held out her palm, willing the coin to appear. It did. She marvelled all over again at its return. The rightness of feeling it sitting in her hand. The part of her that had been missing all year was back, and she couldn't stop herself smiling.

'That's great,' Jason said. 'Really good. You must be feeling more... I don't know.'

'Myself?' Lydia supplied. 'Yes.' She took a deep breath and released the tension in her shoulders. 'It's a relief. Are you making scrambled eggs?'

'Omelette,' Jason said. 'Unless you want scrambled?'

'Whatever you feel like making, I will gratefully eat.'

'Is that so?' A small spark of Jason's usual humour broke through. 'Sounds like a challenge.'

Lydia smiled at Jason, but was then distracted by her

coin again. 'I don't know what brought it back.' She flipped it over her knuckles, watching the gold flash as it caught the light. 'When Mary left, it was just there.'

'She had it?' Jason put some butter in a pan and turned on the burner.

'I don't think so.' Lydia had been thinking about it. 'I wondered if there was an energy surge or, maybe, exchange, when Mary left. She was there, powered up and solid and able to interact with the world, and then she disappeared. Moved on, or whatever. Maybe that moment left her energy here? Or maybe my Crow power was just increasing all the time and it just happened to reach critical mass at that exact moment. I don't know...'

Jason had dumped the eggs into the pan and was wielding his spatula like a professional chef. He sprinkled some grated cheese across the surface and added freshly ground black pepper. His hand hovered over the bottle of honey. 'You said "whatever I felt like making", right?'

Lydia grabbed the honey from his cold hand. 'Funny guy.'

Jason smiled as he expertly folded the omelette and slid it onto a plate.

'You shouldn't mess with me,' Lydia said, gesturing with her fork before diving into the omelette. 'I'm a very important and powerful woman.'

Jason leaned against the counter and gave her a fond look. 'Shut up and eat your eggs.'

.   .   .

FLEET WAS AT WORK, AND LYDIA KNEW HE WOULD be having a bad time. He might have known that the culprit had been caught and banished, but it wasn't something he could put in a report to tie up the case. He was trying to rehabilitate his reputation as a rational and capable copper, and chatting about ghost killers wouldn't exactly help. Lydia thought of him going through the motions with his team and waiting for his boss to pull him off the case. She wished she could have helped Fleet to have a professional success, but she couldn't see how. Unless Fleet was willing to frame someone for them, the murders would remain officially unsolved.

The phone call she had been expecting occurred in the middle of the afternoon. 'That arsehole Dominic,' Fleet said when she answered, 'is having a field day.'

'What's happened?' Lydia gripped the phone tightly.

'Guv has announced that I'm no longer leading the New Ripper investigation. The team are being really supportive, actually, saying nice things, but that's that. Don't know where I'll be assigned next.'

'Feathers. I'm sorry.'

'Ah, it's all right.' His voice held a smile and she could picture him rolling his shoulders, shrugging off the latest barbs from DCI Moss. 'I've had worse. Did I ever tell you about my training?'

'You solved the case,' Lydia said. 'I wish you could get the credit.'

'First off,' Fleet said, 'you solved it. And secondly, it's not important. Nobody else is going to get hurt. We know the truth. And Mary's at peace.' He lowered his voice for the last bit.

'You did say you didn't do the job for the glory.' Lydia lightened her tone, trying to match his energy. If Fleet was determined to make the best of things, then she was going to fall in line.

'Exactly.' Fleet was sounding more cheerful by the second. Lydia wondered how much of it was an act for her benefit. 'Besides, the Guv has given the case to DCI Moss.'

It took Lydia a second to realise why Fleet was so gleeful.

'Good luck to him,' he said happily. 'It's going to royally fuck with his arrest record.'

Aiden arrived at the house not long after. 'No meetings.' He held up his hands in defence before Lydia could say anything. 'I just wanted to update you on that job.'

'Job?'

'The kid you told me to look out for.'

'Ember.' Lydia hated that all thoughts of the boy had been shoved from her mind with the race to stop Mary. She would tell Emma that it was excellent evidence that she wasn't cut out for motherhood.

'Yeah. I've called round a couple of times. Took some food, checked the electricity meter was paid up. Dunno if that's what you were thinking?'

'That's really good.' Lydia admired Aiden's practicality. He really was a decent human. Maybe the Crow Family could change its ways.

Aiden looked uncomfortable at the praise. 'I didn't see the kid, though. He might have moved on.'

Feathers. 'Thank you,' she said absently, as her mind whirled. She would have preferred to include Fleet, but she wasn't expecting him back until much later and this seemed pressing.

Finding Ember wasn't as difficult as she had imagined. She drove to the flats and parked where she could see the entrance. Then, armed with her surveillance kit of crisps, coffee and a scope, she waited. It was like old times. A lot of investigation work involved patience. Waiting and watching. Waiting and hoping. Waiting and—Ember popped up from the subway that led under the main road outside the flats. He was wearing a backpack that looked comically big on his small frame and a hunted expression that wasn't funny in the slightest.

Lydia got out of the car and caught up with him in the stairwell. He whirled around, his teeth bared with a fierce expression. It relaxed the moment he realised it was her, which made her chest warm up in a strange way. 'Hi, kid,' she said.

The golden light she remembered as a gleam was spilling from him, lighting up the dingy surroundings. Now that her power had returned, her senses were back to full volume. It was a little overwhelming.

'You need somefink?'

'It's not about what I need.' Lydia put an arm around Ember's shoulders and steered him back down the stairs.

316

'I assume you're carrying everything important in that dinky little bag.'

Ember shot her a mutinous glance. 'What's it to you?'

'I promised you no social services.'

The kid stopped moving. Feet planted.

'You know who I am,' Lydia said, keeping her tone gentle, but dipping her head to look directly into Ember's frightened eyes. 'When I give my word, you can trust it.'

'Where are we going then?' Ember asked as they left the flats.

'A safe nest.'

AUNTIE'S FLAT WASN'T LARGE OR LUXURIOUS, BUT IT was clean and warm and homely. Ember's eyes as he looked around were wide with longing. He saw Lydia watching him and his expression shuttered, his mouth twisting into a sneer.

Auntie, or one of her many relatives, had been busy in the kitchen when they arrived and the flat smelled of cooking. Lydia identified garlic, ginger, and cumin, and her mouth watered.

'Go on,' Lydia pushed Ember's back, gently, until he stepped forward.

Auntie was shaking her head. 'Too skinny, child. You need to eat.'

She moved, revealing a plate of spiced rice and chicken thighs, sitting on one of the many side tables.

There was a cloth napkin on one side and cutlery. They had evidently interrupted her meal.

Ember's eyes got wide and he inhaled. It smelled good, but Lydia wasn't going to get distracted. She was watching Auntie carefully. The woman picked up the plate and motioned to the kitchen. 'Wash your hands, child.'

Ember obeyed, much to Lydia's annoyance. She wasn't surprised, though. Auntie had that effect on people.

'You too, if you want to eat,' Auntie said, and Lydia followed Ember and dutifully rinsed her hands in the kitchen sink.

Auntie had put out two full plates on the small table. Lydia thought one of them might be her own meal. She gestured at Lydia and Ember to sit and eat.

'What about you?' Lydia asked. 'We're interrupting—'

Auntie shook her head. 'Don't you go worrying about me, child. Not with your hands already full.' She filled glasses of water and put them on the table, before sitting down.

'I'm okay,' Lydia said. Her hands were automatically picking up cutlery, digging into the food. Her head bowed low to catch more of the rich aroma. 'Just been busy.'

'No,' Auntie said.

'You don't know what I was going to say.' She took a forkful of rice and closed her eyes for a moment in appreciation. Smoky, rich, tomatoey and with a sweet heat from the chili.

'I cannot take the boy,' Auntie said. She smiled at Ember, who was wolfing down the food like he hadn't eaten since Lydia had fed him toast and Nutella. 'You are a person, are you not? You are not to be taken or given.'

He nodded, chewing frantically and sawing at the chicken. It was like watching someone who thought the food was going to be whipped away at any second, and Lydia felt that strange squeezing sensation again. It was annoying.

Auntie looked at Lydia. 'He will have to make his own choice.'

Ember spluttered, rice falling from his mouth in his desire to speak. 'I'm not going to social—'

'Hush,' Auntie said. 'Eat your meal.'

'Besides,' Auntie was nodding now, looking at Lydia with great satisfaction. 'It will be good for you and Ignatius.'

'We are...' Lydia stopped speaking when she realised she didn't know how to finish that sentence.

'Ignatius is empty. He always does his best and that is very good, but anyone can see he needs to be refilled.'

Ember's plate was empty, save for the chicken bones. He picked them up and gnawed on them.

Lydia expected Auntie to correct his table manners, but she just smiled. When he had sucked them clean, she reached out and slid his plate over to her place.

'What are you looking for?' Ember was watching, wide-eyed, as Auntie stared at his plate.

Auntie drew her gaze back to the boy. 'Who are your people? Your parents?'

He shrugged.

'Don't even think about lying, child.'

'My gran was Aminata Williams. She's gone now.'

Auntie nodded her understanding. 'And your mother?'

Ember looked away.

Auntie looked at Lydia. 'This seals it.'

'What seals what?'

'He belongs with us.'

CHAPTER THIRTY-FIVE

Claridge's Bar was a long way from Camberwell. The beautiful art déco interior boasted leather chairs, staff in jackets and bow ties, and the unmistakable scent of wealth. Lydia appreciated the low lighting and 'no photography' rules, though.

Maria had already arrived and ordered champagne. A waiter darted forward and poured Lydia a glass, placing a silver dish of olives onto the table. Lydia had hardly time to think of something suitably irritating to say to Maria when she realised that the woman's attention had been taken. She turned to see what Maria was staring at.

Paul Fox was wearing a suit. She didn't think she had seen him in one before, and it was disconcerting. He was also standing with a woman that Lydia didn't know. A very beautiful woman who would have been deliciously attractive even without the seductive pull of Pearl. She had smooth brown skin and braids that reached to the middle of her back.

'This is Scarlett,' Paul said, pulling out a chair for her. 'She is going to speak for the Pearl Family.'

'On what authority?' Maria said, glaring at Paul. 'There are thousands of Pearls running around the city. The Family is no longer a functional unit.'

'It will be,' Scarlett said, her voice smooth and low-pitched. 'And I'm their representative.'

'This makes no sense,' Lydia said. She knew that the woman wasn't giving off as strong a Pearl vibe as Rafferty Hill, the man who she believed had absorbed the Pearl King's essence when she had destroyed the ancient Family beneath London. But, of course, she couldn't say that. It was an old habit not to reveal her powers, and she had no desire to give information to Maria. 'What about Rafferty? He represented the Pearl Family when we restated the truce. Shouldn't he have a say in who replaces him?'

'Scarlett is a Pearl,' Paul said calmly. 'Lydia can confirm that. I am satisfied that she speaks for her Family.'

Maria looked at Lydia, an eyebrow raised.

Lydia shot an irritated glance in Paul's direction. So much for discretion. 'Yes. She's Pearl. Not as strong as Rafferty, but more than most.'

'Rumour has it, you're not what you were,' Paul said. 'Maybe your radar doesn't work as well as it used to.'

'Rumours aren't to be trusted,' Lydia said. 'Especially in the mouth of a Fox.'

Maria was watching the exchange with interest. 'What's going on with you two? Lovers' tiff?'

Paul glanced briefly at Scarlett before replying. 'Nothing of the kind.'

'I am here in good faith as the representative and leader of the Pearl Family,' Scarlett said. Her beautiful voice floated across the table like music. 'Is my request to join the truce being denied?'

Maria and Lydia looked at each other. Lydia didn't like the feeling of being on the same page as the Silver, but they had both been blindsided.

'Of course not,' Maria said smoothly. 'Welcome. Would you like a glass of champagne?' She glanced up and within seconds a waiter had brought another stem glass. Paul took the bottle from the ice bucket before the waiter could reach for it and poured. He topped off the other glasses, emptying the bottle.

'To the truce,' he said, raising his glass. He looked at Lydia. 'Long may it hold.'

They all raised their glasses in salute and drank.

LYDIA HAD JUST OPENED THE GATE ON THE GARDEN and greeted the line of crows sitting sentinel by the front door.

She saw the flash of red fur a millisecond before she heard Paul's voice. She knew she had been distracted, but there was no excuse for letting a Fox sneak up behind her like that. Not for the first time, she wondered if she had permanently lost her edge. The instincts that had kept her safe for all this time appeared to be muffled, and it was terrifying.

'Hello, Little Bird.'

Lydia realised that she had missed him calling her Little Bird. That was also terrifying. Turning, she caught his stricken expression before it smoothed out and she realised something: he hadn't intended to use the nickname.

'Hello, Fox,' she said. 'That was an interesting surprise. Where did you find her?'

He flashed white teeth. 'I decided it was time to play the game.'

'Accepting your place. I know how that feels.' She held up a hand. 'The Foxes don't have a leader, I know.'

His Fox sneer disappeared, and he glanced away. 'You were right. I'm Tristan's heir.'

'And you were right about me, too.' Maybe it was the darkness, the presence of the crows, or just the crushing exhaustion from the last few days, but Lydia couldn't find the strength to spar. Paul Fox had known her since she was nineteen years old, and that suddenly felt important. He had known her before. Before any of it. 'I'm Charlie's replacement. In every sense.'

His smile was sad this time. His eyes full of sympathy. It made her want to cry.

'I'm sorry, Lydia.'

She nodded. Pressed her tongue against the roof of her mouth to stop the tears.

Paul put his hands into his pockets, suddenly looking nervous.

She didn't have Fleet's gift, but she knew without a doubt that something bad was about to happen. 'What? What did you come here to say?'

'I'm going to marry Scarlett.'

'What?' Lydia didn't want to feel anything, but her gut wasn't playing ball. Her stomach swooped, and she had the urge to put out her wings to stop the free fall. 'How long have you known each other?'

'It's a smart move,' Paul said. 'For my Family.'

Lydia pressed her lips together. She already regretted her first question. She wished she could reel the words back. She had shown him that she cared. She shouldn't care.

He looked her in the eye. 'I asked you first.'

That was true. A long time ago, he had proposed. Made it sound like a business deal. She forced a single word out. 'Congratulations.'

'It's not too late,' Paul said. 'But soon it will be.'

Did he mean it wasn't too late for Lydia to take Scarlett's place? That he would cast the Pearl aside and marry Lydia instead? When he had picked her up off the street after the River Man had drained her power, he had taken her to a safe house and nursed her back to health. They had shared a moment. A split second when Lydia had known he would kiss her, given the slightest encouragement. It was something she had tried very hard not to think about in the intervening time.

The hard thing was, she could see it. More clearly than ever before. She and Paul made a good team. And their marriage would solidify the truce between the Foxes and the Crows. Two united Families against the Silvers and the Pearls. Even if the latter coalesced into a powerful unit, they would still be one against two. It was a safe option. Lydia hesitated, more tempted than she would ever admit.

Paul tilted his head. 'Things won't stand still forever. Change is coming.'

'It always is,' Lydia replied.

A smile. Sharp white teeth. 'I am not your problem, Little Bird.'

LYDIA WAITED UNTIL PAUL HAD SAUNTERED AWAY, watching him until he got halfway down the street and into a waiting car. Once the vehicle was out of sight, Lydia turned back to Charlie's house and let herself in through the front door.

She found Fleet in the kitchen, getting mugs down from the cupboard. 'Coffee?'

'Please.'

'Are you all right?' Fleet's forehead was creased with concern and his eyes were soft. 'Are you thinking about Mary?'

'I feel sad for her, but I hope I did the right thing.'

'You gave her peace, right?' Fleet said. 'That's the best she could hope for.'

'I suppose,' Lydia leaned against the kitchen counter. She still wasn't sure how Mary had known about Cherish. Her best guess was that the unsolved crime had given off an energetic signature, something that had drawn Mary's attention as she searched London for her Georgie, but it was certainly new ghost behaviour. And it bothered Lydia that Mary had seemed largely unaware of her own actions. The uncertainty itched her mind and she changed the subject to a problem she had a chance of solving. 'I was actually thinking about Ember. I took him to Auntie.'

'I know,' Fleet said, smiling. 'My cousin rang to fill me in. Family gossip.'

'She won't keep him for long.'

He nodded. 'She's done her time looking after kids.'

'We need to work out a permanent arrangement and I don't know what to do—'

'We'll work it out,' Fleet said. 'It's a good thing, what you're doing.'

Hell Hawk. Lydia didn't know about that. She changed the subject. 'Are you really okay about your case? I wish there was a way we could tell your work—'

'I'm really okay,' Fleet said. 'The media attention will wane soon, too. With no new developments, no new murders. People will move on. They always do.'

Lydia had checked social media before Fleet had got home and seen different trending topics creeping in, #NewRipper had already slipped down the rankings.

'And if it proves stubborn, my boss will call in a favour. Before you know it, a juicy story will get leaked. Something controversial that will go viral and cause a good old-fashioned flame war.'

Lydia knew he was right. 'There'll be conspiracy theorists on Reddit and a few blogs and podcasts will keep a few candles burning, but the bonfire will be out.' Jason had showed her places online where every possible opinion could be found, and they could act as a barometer for wider social change, but not always. Sometimes, they were just a small virtual box in which a tiny group of hateful people were shouting at each other, signifying nothing.

'You think distraction will work?'

Fleet nodded soberly. 'I think it's scary how well it will work.'

Lydia let that sink in. 'And to think how many times that move has been pulled for important news.'

She busied herself with making some toast to go with their drinks. She wasn't especially hungry, but craved the soothing weight of carbohydrate.

'The Jez McAllister missing person case has been closed. Thought you'd want to know.'

'Oh?' Lydia kept her gaze on the toaster.

'His dad called the station and said that he'd spoken to him. Apparently he's island-hopping in Greece.'

'All right for some.' Lydia risked a glance at Fleet. He was staring at her with his copper-face. The one that told her that he knew something was off about the situation and that he intended to find out what.

'Apparently he had an email from Jez.'

'Well, that's a relief,' Lydia said. 'I've still got to replace a manager, though, so it's not all good news.'

'That all you want to say?'

It was. Jade must have convinced Jez's dad, or perhaps Aiden had set up the email account to put off Jez's dad. She knew that the Crows had been working in the shadows for many years and they weren't about to stop just because Lydia was the current leader. She squeezed her coin in her hand, keeping her fist closed.

Fleet was still studying her with a questioning look,

but she didn't have anything she wanted to share. Years and years of history and tradition had a momentum. Changing things in the Crow Family was going to be like turning a supertanker. And she wasn't entirely sure how much she wanted to change. Not anymore. Mary had been murderous and murder was wrong, but the world was down a few abusive scumbags. They had abused and hurt and murdered women, and the legal system had failed to do anything remotely proportional. Mary herself had been killed and had been buried without justice. Now, maybe, she had retribution. Maybe the scales had been balanced.

'Lydia?'

She stepped close to Fleet, letting go of her coin and returning it to wherever it went while it waited for her summons. She could feel her Crow power flowing, her tattoos moving on her skin, and could hear hundreds of wings beating. 'How do you feel about gutting this place and starting again?'

'The house?' Fleet asked, placing his hands onto her waist.

She ran a hand over his chest and neck, and then cupped his cheek. He leaned down to kiss her.

'Everything,' she answered.

JASON CLEARED HIS THROAT, AND THEY BROKE apart.

He was holding his iPad out. 'There's something you need to see.'

Lydia took it, seeing that the screen was showing

search results for #RipperReturns, #ActuallyRipper and #FromHell.

'That account is a hoax,' Fleet said.

'I'm not so sure,' Jason said. 'How else would they know?'

'Know what?' Lydia said, a split second before her mind caught up with the words on the screen. A message, posted on a couple of social media sites simultaneously. Plain text, no graphic, no emojis.

I've finished playing with sweet Mary, but I ain't finished with you.

THE END

THANK YOU FOR READING!

I hope you enjoyed reading about Lydia Crow and her family as much as I enjoyed writing about them!

I am busy working on my next book. If you would like to be notified when it's published (as well as take part in giveaways and receive exclusive free content), you can sign up for my FREE readers' club online:

geni.us/Thanks

If you could spare the time, I would really appreciate a review on the retailer of your choice.

Reviews make a huge difference to the visibility of the book, which make it more likely that I will reach more readers and be able to keep on writing. Thank you!

ACKNOWLEDGMENTS

Thank you for reading! I am so grateful for the enthusiastic support for the Crow Investigations series. I thoroughly enjoyed spending time with these characters again. Writing is my dream, and I still have to pinch myself that this is my actual real life.

To my writing coven, Hannah Ellis and Clodagh Murphy, and all my author pals – thank you for everything!

Thank you to Matthew and Fay for the anecdote that inspired one of the scenes, and to my dad, Michael, for regular tea, cake and encouragement.

Thank you to Stuart Bache for another brilliant cover, and to the team at Siskin Press. Many thanks to my wonderful ARC readers for their early feedback:

Desiree Arnold, Sue Bruce, Elizabeth Butcher, Ronnie Calderwood-Duncan, Sherrill Cormany, Cathy Evans, Bryan Francis, Erin Gately, Jenni Gudgeon, Mel Horne, Michelle Hunter-Gray, Kathryn Jamieson-Sinclair, Sandra Keller, Christina Lindholm, Caroline Nicklin, Lizzie Noblett, Andrew Peachey, Becky Reed, Karan Sebert, Patrice Smith, Faith Stevens, Jacquie

Thornber, Amba Wade, Walt Wallmark, Sara Wolfe, David Wood

Thank you to my friends and family for their love and support. I am very lucky indeed. And, as always, my deepest love and gratitude to Holly and James, and my wonderful husband, Dave.

ABOUT THE AUTHOR

Sarah Painter is a bestselling author of magical fiction, including the Crow Investigations urban fantasy mystery series. She also writes non-fiction for introvert authors.

Having always been a reader and a daydreamer, she now puts those skills to good use with a strict daily schedule of faffing, thinking, reading, napping and writing. She also spends a portion of every day thanking her lucky stars for her good fortune. Sarah lives in rural Scotland, drinks too much tea, and is the proud owner of a writing shed.

Head to the website below to sign-up to the Sarah Painter readers' club. It's absolutely free and you'll get book release news, giveaways and exclusive FREE stuff!

www.sarah-painter.com

facebook.com/SarahPainterBooks
twitter.com/SarahRPainter
instagram.com/SarahPainterBooks

Set in the same world as 'Crow Investigations', The Ward Witch is the first book in the 'Unholy Island' series by Sarah Painter.

**Mysterious, magical, and a little bit deadly...
Welcome to Unholy Island.**

Esme Gray runs the guest house and tends to the ethereal wards that protect the island.

Luke Taylor has been searching for his missing twin for months, but a tip off leads him to a remote tidal island in the North Sea.

Esme is drawn to Luke, but she doesn't trust her own instincts. That's not ideal for a witch — especially when there is a killer on the loose and a storm is rolling in...

Made in United States
Troutdale, OR
05/23/2025

31616556R00204